TIME TRAVELERS

Space glittered and flared with a million stars, thronging against the tremendous dark, the Milky Way foamed around the sky in a rush of cold silver, and it was shattering to a human in its utter immensity. Saunders felt the loneliness of it as he had never felt it on the trip to Venus – for Sol was dwindling behind them, they were rushing out into the void between the stars.

*Also by Poul Anderson
in Sphere Books:*

THREE WORLDS TO CONQUER
THE PEOPLE OF THE WIND
THE AVATAR
MIRKHEIM
A CIRCUS OF HELLS
THERE WILL BE TIME
A KNIGHT OF GHOSTS AND SHADOWS
DANCER FROM ATLANTIS
ORION SHALL RISE
TWILIGHT WORLD
THE LONG NIGHT
TIME PATROLMAN
THE MERMAN'S CHILDREN
THE BROKEN SWORD

Past Times

Poul Anderson

Sphere Books Limited

First published in Great Britain by Sphere Books Ltd 1987
27 Wrights Lane, London w8 5tz
Copyright © 1984 by Poul Anderson
First published in the United States of America by Tom Doherty Associates, 1984

Acknowledgements: The stories contained herein were previously
published and are copyrighted as follows:

'Wildcat', *Magazine of Fantasy and Science Fiction*, © 1958 by Mercury Press
Inc.

'Welcome', *Magazine of Fantasy and Science Fiction*, © 1960 by Mercury
Press Inc.

'The Nest', *Science Fiction Adventures*, © 1953 Future Publications.

'Eutopia', *Dangerous Visions*, edited by Harlan Ellison, © 1967 by Harlan
Ellison.

'The Little Monster', *Way Out*, edited by Roger Elwood, © 1974 by Roger
Elwood.

'The Light', *Galaxy*, © 1957 by Galaxy Publishing Corporation.

'The Discovery of the Past', © 1984 by Poul Anderson. A small part of this
essay was published in *Profanity* magazine, © 1977 by Bruce Pelz.

'Flight to Forever', *Super Science Stories*, © 1950 Popular Publications.

TRADE
MARK

Printed and bound in Great Britain by
Cox & Wyman Ltd, Reading

Contents

Wildcat

It was raining again, hot and heavy out of a hidden sky, and the air stank with swamp. Herries could just see the tall derricks a mile away, under a floodlight glare, and hear their engines mutter. Further away, a bull brontosaur cried and thunder went through the night.

Herries' boots resounded hollowly on the dock. Beneath the slicker, his clothes lay sweat-soggy, the rain spilled off his hat and down his collar. He swore in a tired voice and stepped onto his gangplank.

Light from the shack on the barge glimmered off drenched wood. He saw the snaky neck just in time, as it reared over the gangplank rail and struck at him. He sprang back, grabbing for the Magnum carbine slung over one shoulder. The plesiosaur hissed monstrously and flipper-slapped the water. It was like a cannon going off.

Herries threw the gun to his shoulder and fired. The long sleek form took the bullet – somewhere – and screamed. The raw noise hurt the man's eardrums.

Feet thudded over the wharf. Two guards reached Herries and began to shoot into the dark water. The door of the shack opened and a figure stood back against its yellow oblong, a tommy gun stammering idiotically in his hands.

'Cut it out!' bawled Herries. 'That's enough! Hold your fire!'

Silence fell. For a moment, only the ponderous rainfall had voice. Then the brontosaur bellowed again, remotely, and there were seethings and croakings in the water.

'He got away,' said Herries. 'Or more likely his pals are now scraping him clean. Blood smell.' A dull anger lifted in him, he turned and grabbed the lapel of the nearest guard. 'How often do I have to tell you characters, every gangway has to have a man near it with grenades?'

'Yes, sir. Sorry, sir.' Herries was a large man, and the other face looked up at him, white and scared in the wan electric radiance. 'I just went off to the head—'

'You'll stay there,' said Herries. 'I don't care if you explode. Our presence draws these critters, and you ought to know that by now. They've already snatched two men off this dock. They nearly got a third tonight – me. At the first suspicion of anything out there, you're to pull the pin on a grenade and drop it into the water, understand? One more dereliction like this, and you're fired – No.' He stopped, grinning humorlessly. 'That's not much of a punishment is it? A week in hack on bread.'

The other guard bristled. 'Look here, Mr Herries, we got our rights. The union—'

'Your precious union is a hundred million years in the future,' snapped the engineer. 'It was understood that this is a dangerous job, that we're subject to martial law, and that I can discipline anyone who steps out of line. Okay – remember it.'

He turned his back and tramped across the gangplank to the barge deck. It boomed underfoot. The shack had been closed again, with the excitement over. He opened the door and stepped through, peeling off his slicker.

Four men were playing pool beneath an unshaded bulb. The room was small and cluttered, hazy with tobacco smoke and the Jurassic mist. A fifth man lay on one of the bunks, reading. The walls were gaudy with pinups.

Olson riffled the cards and looked up, 'Close call, boss,' he remarked, almost casually. 'Want to sit in?'

'Not now,' said Herries. He felt his big square face sagging with weariness. 'I'm bushed.' He nodded at Carver, who had just returned from a prospecting trip further north. 'We lost one more derrick today.'

'Huh?' said Carver. 'What happened this time?'

'It turns out this is the mating season.' Herries found a chair, sat down, and began to pull off his boots. 'How they tell one season from another, I don't know – length of day, maybe – but anyhow the brontosaurs aren't shy of us any more – they're going nuts. Now they go gallyhooting around and trample down charged fences or anything else that happens to be in the way. They've smashed three rigs to date, and one man.'

Carver raised an eyebrow in his chocolate-coloured face. It was a rather sour standing joke here, how much better the Negroes looked than anyone else. A white man could be outdoors all his life in this clouded age and remain pasty. 'Haven't you tried shooting them?' he asked.

'Ever tried to kill a brontosaur with a rifle?' snorted Herries. 'We can mess 'em up a little with .50-caliber machine-guns or a bazooka – just enough so they decide to get out of the neighborhood – but being less intelligent than a chicken, they take off in any old direction. Makes as much havoc as the original rampage.' His left boot hit the floor with a sullen thud. 'I've been begging for a couple of atomic howitzers, but it has to go through channels . . . Channels!' Fury spurted in him. 'Five hundred human beings stuck in this nightmare world, and our requisitions have to go through channels!'

Olson began to deal the cards. Polansky gave the man in the bunk a chill glance. 'You're the wheel, Symonds,' he said. 'Why the devil don't you goose the great Transtemporal Oil Company?'

'Nuts,' said Carver. 'The great benevolent all-wise United States Government is what counts. How about it, Symonds?'

You never got a rise out of Symonds, the human tape recorder: just a playback of the latest official line. Now he laid his book aside and sat up in his bunk. Herries noticed that the volume was Marcus Aurelius, in Latin yet.

3

Symonds looked at Carver through steel-rimmed glasses and said in a dusty tone: 'I am only the comptroller and supply supervisor. In effect, a chief clerk. Mr Herries is in charge of operations.'

He was a small shrivelled man, with thin gray hair above a thin gray face. Even here, he wore a stiff-collared shirt and sober tie. One of the hardest things to take about him was the way his long nose waggled when he talked.

'In charge!' Herries spat expertly into a gobboon. 'Sure, I direct the prospectors and the drillers and everybody else on down through the bull cook. But who handles the paperwork – all our reports and receipts and requests? You.' He tossed his right boot on the floor. 'I don't want the name of boss if I can't get the stuff to defend my own men.'

Something bumped against the supervisors' barge; it quivered and the chips on the table rattled. Since there was no outcry from the dock guards, Herries ignored the matter. Some swimming giant. And except for the plesiosaurs and the non-malicious bumbling bronties, all the big dinosaurs encountered so far were fairly safe. They might step on you in an absent-minded way, but most of them were peaceful and you could outrun those which weren't. It was the smaller carnivores, about the size of a man, leaping out of brush or muck with a skullful of teeth, which had taken most of the personnel lost. Their reptile life was too diffuse: even mortally wounded by elephant gun or grenade launcher, they could rave about for hours. They were the reason for sleeping on barges tied up by this sodden coast, along the gulf which would some day be Oklahoma.

Symonds spoke in his tight little voice: 'I'd send your recommendations in, of course. The project office passes on them.'

'I'll say it does,' muttered young Greenstein irreverently.

'Please do not blame me,' insisted Symonds.

I wonder. Herries glowered at him. Symonds had an in of some kind. That was obvious. A man who was simply a

4

glorified clerk would not be called to Washington, for un-specified conferences with unspecified people, as often as this one was. But what was he, then?

A favorite relative? No ... in spite of high pay, this operation was no political plum. FBI? Scarcely ... the security checks were all run in the future. A hack in the bureaucracy? That was more probable. Symonds was here to see that oil was pumped and dinosaurs chased away and the hideously fecund jungle kept beyond the fence according to the least comma in the latest directive from headquarters.

The small man continued: 'It has been explained to you officially that the heavier weapons are all needed at home. The international situation is critical. You ought to be thankful you are safely back in the past.'

'Heat, large economy-size alligators, and not a woman for a hundred million years,' grunted Olson. 'I'd rather be blown up. Who dealt this mess?'

'You did,' said Polansky. 'Gimme two, and make 'em good.'

Herries stripped the clothes off his thick hairy body, went to the rear of the cabin, and entered the shower cubby. He left the door open, to listen in. A boss was always lonely. Maybe he should have married when he had the chance. But then he wouldn't be here. Except for Symonds, who was a widower and in any case more a government than com-pany man, Transoco had been hiring only young bachelors for operations in the field.

'It seems kinda funny to talk about the international situation,' remarked Carver. 'Hell, there won't be any inter-national situation for several geological periods.'

'The inertial effect makes simultaneity a valid approximational concept,' declared Symonds pedantically. His habit of lecturing scientists and engineers on their professions had not endeared him to them. 'If we spend a year in the past, we must necessarily return to our own era

5

to find a year gone, since the main projector operates only at the point of its own existence which—'

'Oh, stow it,' said Greenstein. 'I read the orientation manual too.' He waited until everyone had cards, then shoved a few chips forward and added: 'Druther spend my time a little nearer home. Say with Cleopatra.'

'Impossible,' Symonds told him. 'Inertial effect again. In order to send a body into the past at all, the projector must energize it so much that the minimal time-distance we can cover becomes precisely the one we have covered to arrive here, one hundred and one million, three hundred twenty-seven thousand, et cetera, years.'

'But why not time-hop into the future? You don't buck entropy in that direction. I mean, I suppose there is an inertial effect there, too, but it would be much smaller, so you could go into the future—'

'—about a hundred years at a hop, according to the handbook,' supplied Polansky.

'So why don't they look at the twenty-first century?' asked Greenstein.

'I understand that that is classified information,' Symonds said. His tone implied that Greenstein had skirted some unimaginable gross obscenity.

Herries put his head out of the shower. 'Sure it's classified,' he said. 'They'd classify the wheel if they could. But use your reason and you'll see why travel into the future isn't practical. Suppose you jump a hundred years ahead. How do you get home to report what you've seen? The projector will yank you a hundred million years back, less the distance you went forward.'

Symonds dove back into his book. Somehow, he gave an impression of lying there rigid with shock that men dared think after he had spoken the phrase of taboo.

'Uh . . . yes, I get it.' Greenstein nodded. He had only been recruited a month ago, to replace a man drowned in a grass-veiled bog. Before then, like nearly all the world, he had had

6

no idea time travel existed. So far he had been too busy to examine its implications.

To Herries it was an old, worn-thin story.

'I daresay they did send an expedition a hundred million years up, so it could come back to the same week as it left,' he said. 'Don't ask me what was found. Classified: Tip-top Secret, Burn Before Reading.'

'You know, though,' said Polansky in a thoughtful tone, 'I been thinking some myself. Why are we here at all? I mean, oil is necessary to defense and all that, but it seems to me it'd make more sense for the U.S. Army to come through, cross the ocean, and establish itself where all the enemy nations are going to be. Then we'd have a gun pointed at their heads!'

'Nice theory,' said Herries. 'I've day-dreamed myself. But there's only one main projector, to energize all the subsidiary ones. Building it took almost the whole world supply of certain rare earths. Its capacity is limited. If we started sending military units into the past, it'd be a slow and cumbersome operation – and not being a Security officer, I'm not required to kid myself that Moscow doesn't know we've got time travel. They've probably even given Washington a secret ultimatum: "Start sending back war material in any quantity, and we'll hit you with everything we've got." But evidently they don't feel strongly enough about our pumping oil on our own territory – or what will one day be our own territory – to make it a, uh, *casus belli.*'

'Just as we don't feel their satellite base in the twentieth century is dangerous enough for us to fight about,' said Greenstein, 'but I suspect we're the reason they agreed to make the Moon a neutral zone. Same old standoff.'

'I wonder how long it can last?' murmured Polansky.

'Not much longer,' said Olson. 'Read your history. I'll see you, Greenstein, boy, and raise you two.'

Herries let the shower run about him. At least there was no shortage of hot water. Transoco had sent back a complete atomic pile. But civilization and war still ran on oil, he thought, and oil was desperately short up there.

7

Time, he reflected, was a paradoxical thing. The scientists had told him it was utterly rigid. Perhaps, though of course it would be a graveyard secret, the cloak-and-dagger boys had tested that theory the hard way, going back into the historical past (it could be done after all, Herries suspected, though by a roundabout route which consumed fabulous amounts of energy) in an attempt to head off the Bolshevik Revolution. It would have failed. Neither past nor future could be changed – they could only be discovered. Some of Transoco's men had discovered death, an eon before they were born . . . But there would not be such a shortage of oil up in the future if Transoco had not gone back and drained it in the past. A self-causing future—

Primordial stuff, petroleum. Hoyle's idea seemed to be right, it had not been formed by rotting dinosaurs but was present from the beginning. It was the stuff which had stuck the planets together.

And, Herries thought, was sticking to him now. He reached for the soap.

Earth spun gloomily through hours, and morning crept over wide brown waters. There was no real day as men understood day – the heavens were a leaden sheet with dirty black rainclouds scudding below the permanent fog layers.

Herries was up early, for there was a shipment scheduled. He came out of the bosses' messhall and stood for a moment looking over the mud beach and the few square miles of cleared land, sleazy buildings and gaunt derricks inside an electric mesh fence. Automation replaced thousands of workers, so that five hundred men were enough to handle everything, but still the compound was the merest scratch, and the jungle remained a terrifying black wall. Not that the trees were so utterly alien – besides the archaic grotesqueries, like ferns and mosses of gruesome size, there were cycad, redwood and gingko, scattered prototypes of oak and willow and birch. But Herries missed wild flowers.

A working party with its machines was repairing the fence the brontosaur had smashed through yesterday, the well it had wrecked, the viciously persistent inroads of grass and vine. A caterpillar tractor hauled a string of loaded wagons across raw red earth. A helicopter buzzed overhead, on watch for dinosaurs. It was the only flying thing. There had been a nearby pterodactyl rookery, but the men had cleaned that out months ago. When you got right down to facts, the most sinister animal of all was man.

Greenstein joined Herries. The new assistant was tall, slender, with curly brown hair and the defenseless face of youth. Above boots and dungarees he wore a blue sports shirt; it offered a kind of defiance to this sullen world. 'Smoke?' he invited.

'Thanks.' Herries accepted the cigarette. His eyes still dwelt on the derricks. Their walking beams went up and down, up and down, like a joyless copulation. Perhaps a man could get used to the Jurassic rain forest and eventually see some dark beauty there, for it was at least life; but this field would always remain hideous, being dead and pumping up the death of men.

'How's it going, Sam?' he asked when the tobacco had soothed his palate.

'All right,' said Greenstein. 'I'm shaking down. But God, it's good to know today is mail call!'

They stepped off the porch and walked toward the transceiving station. Mud squelched under their feet. A tuft of something, too pale and fleshy to be grass, stood near Herries' path. The yard crew had better uproot that soon, or in a week it might claim the entire compound.

'Girl friend, I suppose,' said the chief. 'That does make a month into a hell of a long drought between letters.'

Greenstein flushed and nodded earnestly.

'We're going to get married when my two years here are up,' he said.

'That's what most of 'em plan on. A lot of saved-up pay

9

and valuable experience – sure, you're fixed for life.' It was on Herries' tongue to add that the life might be a short one, but he suppressed the impulse.

Loneliness dragged at his nerves. There was no one waiting in the future for him. It was just as well, he told himself during the endless nights. Hard enough to sleep without worrying about some woman in the same age as the cobalt bomb.

'I've got her picture here, if you'd like to see it,' offered Greenstein shyly.

His hand was already on his wallet. A tired grin slid up Herries' mouth. 'Right next to your . . . er . . . heart, eh?' he murmured.

Greenstein blinked, threw back his head, and laughed. The field had not heard so merry a laugh in a long while. Nevertheless, he showed the other man a pleasant-faced, unspectacular girl.

Out in the swamp, something hooted and threshed about.

Impulsively, Herries asked: 'How do you feel about this operation, Sam?'

'Huh? Why, it's . . . interesting work. And a good bunch of guys.'

'Even Symonds?'

'Oh, he means well.'

'We could have more fun if he didn't bunk with us.'

'He can't help being . . . old,' said Greenstein.

Herries glanced at the boy. 'You know,' he said, 'you're the first man in the Jurassic Period who's had a good word for Ephraim Symonds. I appreciate that. I'd better not say whether or not I share the sentiment but I appreciate it.'

His boots sludged ahead, growing heavier with each step. 'You still haven't answered my first question,' he resumed after a while. 'I didn't ask if you enjoyed the work, I asked how you feel about it. Its purpose. We have the answers here to questions which science has been asking – will be asking – for centuries. And yet, except for a couple of under-equipped paleobiologists, who aren't allowed to publish their findings, we're doing nothing but rape the earth in an age before it has even conceived us.'

Greenstein hesitated. Then, with a surprising dryness: 'You're getting too psychoanalytic for me, I'm afreud.'

Herries chuckled. The day seemed a little more alive, all at once. *'Touché!* Well, I'll rephrase Joe Polansky's questions of last night. Do you think the atomic standoff in our home era – to which this operation is potentially rather important – is stable?'

Greenstein considered for a moment. 'No,' he admitted. 'Deterrence is a stopgap till something better can be worked out.'

'They've said as much since it first began. Nothing has been done. It's improbable that anything will be. Ole Olson describes the internal situation as a case of the irresistibly evil force colliding with the immovably stupid object.'

'Ole likes to use extreme language,' said Greenstein. 'So tell me, what else could our side do?'

'I wish to God I had an answer.' Herries sighed. 'Pardon me. We avoid politics here, as much as possible; we're escapists in several senses of the word. But frankly, I sound out new men. I was doing it to you. Because in spite of what Washington thinks, a Q clearance isn't all that a man needs to work here.'

'Did I pass?' asked Greenstein, a bit too lightly.

'Sure. So far. You may wish you hadn't. The burning issue today is not whether to tolerate "privileged neutralism," or whatever the latest catchword is up there. It's: Did I get the armament I've been asking for?'

The transceiving station bulked ahead. It was a long corrugated-iron shed, but dwarfed by the tanks which gleamed behind it. Every one of those was filled, Herries knew. Today they would pump their crude oil into the future. Or rather, if you wanted to be exact, their small temporal unit would establish a contact and the gigantic

11

main projector in the twentieth century would then 'suck' the liquid toward itself. And in return the compound would get – food, tools, weapons, supplies, and mail. Herries prayed there would be at least one howitzer . . . and no VIP's. That Senator a few months ago!

For a moment, contemplating the naked ugliness of tanks and pumps and shed, Herries had a vision of this one place stretching through time. It would be abandoned some day, when the wells were exhausted, and the rain jungle would rapidly eat the last thin traces of man. Later would come the sea, and then it would be dry land again, a cold prairie scoured by glacial winds, and then it would grow warm and . . . on and on, a waste of years until the time projector was invented and the great machine stood on this spot. And afterward? Herries didn't like to think what might be here after that.

Symonds was already present. He popped rabbit-like out of the building, a coded manifest in one hand, a pencil behind his ear: 'Good morning, Mr Herries,' he said. his tone gave its usual impression of stiff self-importance.

'Morning. All set in there?' Herries went in to see for himself. A spatter of rain begain to fall, noisy on the metal roof. The technicians were at their posts and reported clear. Outside, one by one, the rest of the men were drifting up. This was mail day, and little work would be done for the remainder of it.

Herries laid the sack of letters to the future inside the shed in its proper spot. His chronometer said one minute to go. 'Stand by!' At the precise time, there was a dim whistle in the air and an obscure pulsing glow. Meters came to life. The pumps began to throb, driving crude oil through a pipe which faced open-ended into the shed. Nothing emerged that Herries could see. Good. Everything in order. The other end of the pipe was a hundred million years in the future. The mail sack vanished with a small puff, as air rushed in where it had waited. Herries went back outside.

'Ah . . . excuse me.'

He turned around, with a jerkiness that told him his nerves were half unraveled. 'Yes?' he snapped.

'May I see you a moment?' asked Symonds. 'Alone?' And the pale eyes behind the glasses said it was not a request but an order.

Herries nodded curtly, swore at the men for hanging around idle when the return shipment wasn't due for hours, and led the way to a porch tacked onto one side of the transceiving station. There were some camp stools beneath it. Symonds hitched up his khakis as if they were a business suit and sat primly down, his thin hands flat on his knees.

'A special shipment is due today,' Symonds said. 'I was not permitted to discuss it until the last moment.'

Herries curled his mouth. 'Go tell Security that the Kremlin won't be built for a hundred million years. Maybe they haven't heard.'

'What no one knew, no one could put into a letter home.'

'The mail is censored anyway. Our friends and relatives think we're working somewhere in Asia.' Herries spat into the mud and said: 'And in another year the first lot of recruits are due home. Plan to shoot them as they emerge, so they can't possibly talk in their sleep.'

Symonds seemed too humorless even to recognize sarcasm. He pursed his lips and declared: 'Some secrets need be kept for a few months only; but within that period, they *must* be kept.'

'Okay, okay. Let's hear what's coming today.'

'I am not allowed to tell you that. But about half the total tonnage will be crates marked Top Secret. These are to remain in the shed, guarded night and day by armed men.' Symonds pulled a slip of paper from his jacket. 'These men will be assigned to that duty, each one taking eight hours a week.'

Herries glanced at the names. He did not know everyone here by sight, though he came close, but he recognized

13

several of these. 'Brave, discreet, and charter subscribers to National Review,' he murmured. 'Teacher's pets. All right. Though I'll have to curtail exploration correspondingly – either that, or else cut down on their guards and sacrifice a few extra lives.'

'I think not. Let me continue. You will get these orders in the mail today, but I will prepare you for them now. A special house must be built for the crates, as rapidly as possible, and they must be moved there immediately upon its completion. I have the specifications in my office safe: essentially, it must be air-conditioned, burglar-proof, and strong enough to withstand all natural hazards.'

'Whoa there!' Herries stepped forward. 'That's going to take reinforced concrete and—'

'Materials will be made available,' said Symonds. He did not look at the other man but stared straight ahead of him, across the rain-smoky compound to the jungle. He had no expression on his pinched face, and the reflection of light off his glasses gave him a strangely blind look.

'But – Judas priest!' Herries threw his cigarette to the ground; it was swallowed in mud and running water. He felt the heat enfold him like a blanket. 'There's the labor too, the machinery, and – How the devil am I expected to expand this operation if—'

'Expansion will be temporarily halted,' cut in Symonds. 'You will simply maintain current operations with skeleton crews. The majority of the labor force is to be reassigned to construction.'

'*What?*'

'The compound fence must be extended and reinforced. A number of new storehouses are to be erected, to hold certain supplies which will presently be sent to us. Bunkhouse barges for an additional five hundred are required. This, of course, entails more sickbay, recreational, mess, laundry, and other facilities.'

Herries stood dumbly, staring at him. Pale lightning flickered in the sky.

The worst of it was, Symonds didn't even bother to be arrogant. He spoke like a schoolmaster.

'Oh, no!' whispered Herries after a long while. 'They're not going to try to establish that Jurassic military base after all!'

'The purpose is classified.'

'Yeah. Sure. Classified. Arise, ye duly cleared citizens of democracy, and cast your ballot on issues whose nature is classified, that your leaders whose names and duties are classified may – Great. Hopping. Balls. Of. Much.' Herries swallowed. Vaguely, through his pulse, he felt his fingers tighten into fists.

'I'm going up,' he said. 'I'm going to protest personally in Washington.'

'That is not permitted,' Symonds said in a dry, clipped tone. 'Read your contract. You are under martial law. Of course,' and his tone was neither softer nor harder, 'you may file a written recommendation.'

Herries stood for a while. Out beyond the fence stood a bulldozer wrecked and abandoned. The vines had almost buried it and a few scuttering little marsupials lived there. Perhaps they were his own remote ancestors. He could take a .22 and go potshooting at them some day.

'I'm not permitted to know anything,' he said at last. 'But is curiosity allowed? An extra five hundred men aren't much. I suppose, given a few airplanes and so on, a thousand of us could plant atomic bombs where enemy cities will be. Or could we? Can't locate them without astronomical studies first, and it's always clouded here. So it would be practical to boobytrap only with mass-action weapons. A few husky cobalt bombs, say. But there are missiles available to deliver those in the twentieth century. So . . . what *is* the purpose?'

'You will learn the facts in due course,' answered Symonds. 'At present, the government has certain military necessities.'

'Haw!' said Herries. He folded his arms and leaned against the roofpost. It sagged a bit . . . shoddy work, shoddy world, shoddy destiny. 'Military horses' necks! I'd like to get one of those prawn-eyed brass hats down here, just for a week, to run his precious security check on a lovesick brontosaur. But I'll probably get another visit from Senator Lardhead, the one who took up two days of my time walking around asking about the possibilities of farming. *Farming!*'

'Senator Wien is from an agricultural state. Naturally he would be interested—'

'—in making sure that nobody here starts raising food and shipping it back home to bring grocery prices down to where people can afford an occasional steak. Sure. I'll bet it cost us a thousand man-hours to make his soil tests and tell him, yes, given the proper machinery this land could be farmed. Of course, maybe I do him an injustice. Senator Wien is also on the Military Affairs Committee, isn't he? He may have visited us in that capacity, and soon we'll all get a directive to start our own little Victory gardens.'

'Your language is close to being subversive,' declared Symonds out of prune-wrinkled lips. 'Senator Wien is a famous statesman.'

For a moment the legislator's face rose in Herries' memory; and it had been the oldest and most weary face he had ever known. Something had burned out in the man who had fought a decade for honorable peace; the knowledge that there was no peace and could be none became a kind of death, and Senator Wien dropped out of his Free World Union organization to arm his land for Ragnarok. Briefly, his anger fading, Herries pitied Senator Wien. And the President, and the Chief of Staff, and the Secretary of State, for their work must be like a nightmare where you strangled your mother and could not stop your hands. It was easier to fight dinosaurs.

He even pitied Symonds, until he asked if his request for an atomic weapon had finally been okayed, and Symonds replied, 'Certainly not.' Then he spat at the clerk's feet and walked out into the rain.

After the shipment and guards were seen to, Herries dismissed his men. There was an uneasy buzz among them at the abnormality of what had arrived; but today was mail day, after all, and they did not ponder it long. He would not make the announcement about the new orders until tomorrow. He got the magazines and newspapers to which he subscribed (no one up there 'now' cared enough to write to him, though his parents had existed in a section of space-time which ended only a year before he took this job) and wandered off to the boss barge to read a little.

The twentieth century looked still uglier than it had last month. The nations felt their pride and saw no way of retreat. The Middle Eastern war was taking a decisive turn which none of the great powers could afford. Herries wondered if he might not be cut off in the Jurassic. A single explosion could destroy the main projector. Five hundred womanless men in a world of reptiles – he'd take the future, cobalt bomb and all.

After lunch there was a quiet, Sunday kind of atmosphere, men lay on their bunks reading their letters over and over. Herries made his rounds, machines and kitchen and sickbay, inspecting.

'I guess we'll discharge O'Connor tomorrow,' said Dr Yamaguchi. 'He can do light work with that Stader on his arm. Next time tell him to duck when a power shovel comes down.'

'What kind of sick calls have you been getting?' asked the chief.

Yamaguchi shrugged. 'Usual things, very minor. I'd never have thought this swamp country would be so healthful. I guess disease germs which can live on placental mammals haven't evolved yet.'

Father Gonzales, one of the camp's three chaplains, buttonholed Herries as he came out. 'Can you spare me a minute?' he said.

'Sure, padre. What is it?'

'About organizing some baseball teams. We need more recreation. This is not a good place for men to live.'

'Sawbones was just telling me—'

'I know. No flu, no malaria, oh, yes. But man is more than a body.'

'Sometimes I wonder,' said Herries. 'I've seen the latest headlines. The dinosaurs have more sense than we do.'

'We have the capacity to do nearly all things,' said Father Gonzales. 'At present, I mean in the twentieth century, we seem to do evil very well. We can do as much good, given the chance.'

'Who's denying us the chance?' asked Herries. 'Just ourselves, H. Sapiens. Therefore I wonder if we really are able to do good.'

'Don't confuse sinfulness with damnation,' said the priest. 'We have perhaps been unfortunate in our successes. And yet even our most menacing accomplishments have a kind of sublimity. The time projector, for example. If the minds able to shape such a thing in metal were only turned toward human problems, what could we not hope to do?'

'But that's my point,' said Herries. 'We don't do the high things. We do what's trivial and evil so consistently that I wonder if it isn't in our nature. Even this time travel business . . . more and more I'm coming to think there's something fundamentally unhealthy about it. As if it's an invention which only an ingrown mind would have made first.'

'First?'

Herries looked up into the steaming sky. A foul wind met his face. 'There are stars above these clouds,' he said, 'and most stars must have planets. I've not been told how the time projector works, but elementary differential calculus will show that travel into the past is equivalent to attaining, momentarily, an infinite velocity. In other words, the basic natural law which the projector uses is one which somehow goes beyond relativity theory. If a time projector is possible, so is a spaceship which can reach the stars in a matter of days, maybe of minutes or seconds. If we were sane, padre, we wouldn't have been so anxious for a little organic grease and the little military advantage involved, that the first thing we did was go back into the dead past after it. No, we'd have invented that spaceship first, and gone out to the stars where there's room to be free and to grow. The time projector would have come afterward, as a scientific research tool.'

He stopped, embarrassed at himself and trying awkwardly to grin. 'Excuse me. Sermons are more your province than mine.'

'It was interesting,' said Father Gonzales. 'But you brood too much. So do a number of the men. Even if they have no close ties at home – it was wise to pick them for that – they are all of above-average intelligence, and aware of what the future is becoming. I'd like to shake them out of their oppression. If we could get some more sports equipment—'

'Sure. I'll see what I can do.'

'Of course,' said the priest, 'the problem is basically philosophical. Don't laugh. You too were indulging in philosophy, and doubtless you think of yourself as an ordinary, unimaginative man. Your wildcatters may not have heard of Aristotle, but they are also thinking men in their way. My personal belief is that this heresy of a fixed, rigid time line lies at the root of their growing sorrowfulness, whether they know it or not.'

'Heresy?' The engineer lifted thick sandy brows. 'It's been proved. It's the basis of the theory which showed how to build a projector: that much I do know. How could we be here at all, if the Mesozoic were not just as real as the Cenozoic? But if all time is coexistent, then all time must be fixed – unalterable – because every instant is the unchanging past of some other instant.'

'Perhaps so, from God's viewpoint,' said Father Gonzales. 'But we are mortal men. And we have free will. The fixed-time concept need not, logically, produce fatalism; after all, Herries, man's will is itself one of the links in the causal chain. I suspect that this irrational fatalism is an important reason why twentieth-century civilization is approaching suicide. If we think we know our future is unchangeable, if our every action is foreordained, if we are doomed already, what's the use of trying? Why go through all the pain of thought, of seeking an answer and struggling to make others accept it? But if we really believed in ourselves, we would look for a solution, and find one.'

'Maybe,' said Herries uncomfortably. 'Well, give me a list of the equipment you want, and I'll put in an order for it the next time the mail goes out.'

As he walked off, he wondered if the mail would ever go out again.

Passing the rec hall, he noticed a small crowd before it and veered to see what was going on. He could not let men gather to trade doubts and terrors, or the entire operation was threatened. *In plain English*, he told himself with a growing bitter honesty, *I can't permit them to think*.

But the sounds which met him, under the subtly alien rustle of forest leaves and the distant bawl of a thunder lizard, was only a guitar. Chords danced forth beneath expert fingers, and a young voice lilted:

'. . . I traveled this wide world over,
A hundred miles or more,
But a saddle on a milk cow,
I never seen before! . . .'

Looking over shoulders, Herries made out Greenstein, sprawled on a bench and singing. There were chuckles from the listeners. Well-deserved: the kid was good; Herries wished he could relax and simply enjoy the performance. Instead, he must note that they were finding it pleasant, and that swamp and war were alike forgotten for a valuable few minutes.

The song ended. Greenstein stood up and stretched. 'Hi, boss,' he said.

Hard, wind-beaten faces turned to Herries and a mumble of greeting went around the circle. He was well enough liked, he knew, insofar as a chief can be liked. But that is not much. A leader can inspire trust, loyalty, what have you, but he cannot be humanly liked, or he is no leader.

'That was good', said Herries. 'I didn't know you played.'

'I didn't bring this whangbox with me, since I had no idea where I was going till I got here,' answered Greenstein. 'Wrote home for it and it arrived today.'

A heavy-muscled crewcut man said, 'You ought to be on the entertainment committee.' Herries recognized Worth, one of the professional patriots who would be standing guard on Symonds' crates; but not a bad sort, really, after you learned to ignore his rather tedious opinions.

Greenstein said an indelicate word. 'I'm sick of committees,' he went on. 'We've gotten so much into the habit of being herded around – everybody in the twentieth century has – that we can't even have a little fun without first setting up a committee.'

Worth looked offended but made no answer. It began to rain again, just a little.

'Go on now, anyway,' said Joe Eagle Wing. 'Let's not take ourselves so goddam serious. How about another song?'

'Not in the wet.' Greenstein returned his guitar to its case. The group began to break up, some to the hall and some back toward their barges.

Herries lingered, unwilling to be left alone with himself. 'About that committee,' he said. 'You might reconsider. It's probably true what you claim, but we're stuck with a situation. We've simply got to tell most of the boys, "Now it is time to be happy," or they never will be.'

Greenstein frowned. 'Maybe so. But hasn't anyone ever thought of making a fresh start? Of unlearning all those bad habits?'

'You can't do that within the context of an entire society's vices,' said Herries. 'And how're you going to get away?'

Greenstein gave him a long look. 'How the devil did you ever get this job?' he asked. 'You don't sound like a man who'd be cleared for a dishwashing assistantship.'

Herries shrugged. 'All my life, I've liked totalitarianism even less than what passes for democracy. I served in a couple of the minor wars and – No matter. Possibly I might not be given the post if I applied now. I've been here more than a year, and it's changed me some.'

'It must,' said Greenstein, flickering a glance at the jungle.

'How's things at home?' asked Herries, anxious for another subject.

The boy kindled. 'Oh, terrific!' he said eagerly. 'Miriam, my girl, you know, she's an artist, and she's gotten a commission to—'

The loudspeaker coughed and blared across the compound, into the strengthening rain: 'Attention! Copter to ground, attention! Large biped dinosaur, about two miles away north-northeast, coming fast.'

Herries cursed and broke into a run.

Greenstein paced him. Water sheeted where their boots struck. 'What is it?' he called.

'I don't know . . . yet . . . but it might be . . . a really big . . . carnivore.' Herries reached the headquarters shack and flung the door open. A panel of levers was set near his personal desk. He slapped one down and the 'combat stations' siren skirted above the field. Herries went on, 'I don't know why anything biped should make a beeline for us unless the smell of blood from the critter we drove off yesterday attracts it. The smaller carnivores are sure as hell drawn. The charged fence keeps them away – but I doubt if it would do much more than enrage a dinosaur – Follow me!'

Jeeps were already leaving their garage when Herries and Greenstein came out. Mud leaped up from their wheels and dripped back off the fenders. The rain fell harder, until the forest beyond the fence blurred; and the earth smoked with vapors. The helicopter hung above the derricks, like a skeleton vulture watching a skeleton army, and the alarm sirens filled the brown air with screaming.

'Can you drive one of these buggies?' asked Herries.

'I did in the Army,' said Greenstein.

'Okay, we'll take the lead one. The main thing is to stop that beast before it gets in among the wells.' Herries vaulted the right-hand door and planted himself on sopping plastic cushions. There was a 50-caliber machine-gun mounted on the hood before him, and the microphone of a police car radio hung at the dash. Five jeeps followed as Greenstein swung into motion. The rest of the crew, ludicrous ants across these wide wet distances, went scurrying with their arms to defend the most vital installations.

The north gate opened and the cars splashed out beyond the fence. There was a strip several yards across, also kept cleared; then the jungle wall rose, black, brown, dull red and green and yellow. Here and there along the fence an occasional bone gleamed up out of the muck, some animal shot by a guard or killed by the voltage. Oddly enough, Herries irrelevantly remembered, such a corpse drew enough scavenging insects to clean it in a day, but it was usually ignored by the nasty man-sized hunter dinosaurs which still slunk and hopped and slithered in this neighborhood. Reptiles just did not go in for carrion. However, they followed the odor of blood. . . .

'Further east,' said the helicopter pilot's radio voice. 'There. Stop. Face the woods. He's coming out in a minute. Good luck, boss. Next time gimme some bombs and I'll handle the bugger myself.'

'We haven't been granted any heavy weapons.' Herries licked lips which seemed rough. His pulse was thick. No one had ever faced a tyrannosaur before.

The jeeps drew into line, and for a moment only their

windshield wipers had motion. Then undergrowth crashed, and the monster was upon them.

It was indeed a tyrannosaur, thought Herries in a blurred way. A close relative, at least. It blundered ahead with the overweighted, underwitted stiffness which paleontologists had predicted, and which had led some of them to believe that it must have been a gigantic, carrion-eating hyena! They forgot that, like the Cenozoic snake or crocodile, it was too dull to recognize dead meat as food, that the brontosaurs it preyed on were even more clumsy; and that sheer length of stride would carry it over the scarred earth at a respectable rate.

Herries saw a blunt head three man-heights above ground, and a tail ending fifteen yards away. Scales of an unfairly beautiful steel gray shimmered in the rain, which made small waterfalls off flanks and wrinkled neck and tiny useless fore-paws. Teeth clashed in a mindless reflex, the ponderous belly wagged with each step, and Herries felt the vibration of tons coming down claw-footed. The beast paid no attention to the jeeps, but moved jerkily toward the fence. Sheer weight would drive it through the mesh.

'Get in front of him, Sam!' yelled the engineer.

He gripped the machine-gun. It snarled on his behalf, and he saw how a sleet of bullets stitched a bloody seam across the white stomach. The tyrannosaur halted, weaving its head about. It made a hollow, coughing roar. Greenstein edged the jeep closer.

The others attacked from the sides. Tracer streams hosed across alligator tail and bird legs. A launched grenade burst with a little puff on the right thigh. It opened a red ulcer-like crater. The tyrannosaur swung slowly about toward one of the cars.

That jeep dodged aside. 'Get in on him!' shouted Herries. Greenstein shifted gears and darted through a fountain of mud. Herries stole a glance. The boy was grinning. Well, it would be something to tell the grandchildren, all right!

His jeep fled past the tyrannosaur, whipped about on two

wheels, and crouched under a hammer of rain. The reptile halted. Herries cut loose with his machine-gun. The monster standing there, swaying a little, roaring and bleeding, was not entirely real. This had happened a hundred million years ago. Rain struck the hot gun barrel and sizzled off.

'From the sides again,' rapped Herries into his microphone. 'Two and Three on his right, Four and Five on his left. Six, go behind him and lob a grenade at the base of his tail.'

The tyrannosaur began another awkward about-face. The water in which it stood was tinged red.

'Aim for his eyes!' yelled Greenstein, and dashed recklessly toward the profile now presented him.

The grenade from behind exploded. With a sudden incredible speed, the tyrannosaur turned clear around. Herries had an instant's glimpse of the tail like a snake before him, then it struck.

He threw up an arm and felt glass bounce off it as the windshield shattered. The noise when metal gave way did not seem loud, but it went through his entire body. The jeep reeled on ahead. Instinct sent Herries to the floorboards. He felt a brutal impact as his car struck the dinosaur's left leg. It hooted far above him. He looked up and saw a foot with talons, raised and filling the sky. It came down. The hood crumpled at his back and the engine was ripped from the frame.

Then the tyrannosaur had gone on. Herries crawled up into the bucket seat. It was canted at a lunatic angle. 'Sam,' he croaked. 'Sam, Sam.'

Greenstein's head was brains and splinters, with half the lower jaw on his lap and a burst-out eyeball staring up from the seat beside him.

Herries climbed erect. He saw his torn-off machine-gun lying in the mud. A hundred yards off, at the jungle edge, the tyrannosaur fought the jeeps. It made clumsy rushes, which they sideswerved, and they spat at it and gnawed at it. Herries thought in a dull, remote fashion: *This can go on forever. A man is easy to kill, one swipe of a tail and all his songs are a red smear in the rain. But a reptile dies hard, being less alive to start with. I can't see an end to this fight.*

The Number Four jeep rushed in. A man sprang from it and it darted back in reverse from the monster's charge. The man – 'Stop that, you idiot,' whispered Herries into a dead microphone, 'stop it, you fool' – plunged between the huge legs. He moved sluggishly enough with clay on his boots, but he was impossibly fleet and beautiful under that jerking bulk. Herries recognized Worth. He carried a grenade in his hand. He pulled the pin and dodged claws for a moment. The flabby, bleeding stomach made a roof over his head. Jaws searched blindly above him. He hurled the grenade and ran. It exploded against the tyrannosaur's belly. The monster screamed. One foot rose and came down. The talons merely clipped Worth, but he went spinning, fell in the gumbo ten feet away and tried weakly to rise but couldn't.

The tyrannosaur staggered in the other direction, spilling its entrails. Its screams took on a ghastly human note. Somebody stopped and picked up Worth. Somebody else came to Herries and gabbled at him. The tyrannosaur stumbled in yards of gut, fell slowly, and struggled, entangling itself.

Even so, it was hard to kill. The cars battered it for half an hour as it lay there, and it hissed at them and beat the ground with its tail. Herries was not sure it had died when he and his men finally left. But the insects had long been busy, and a few of the bones already stood forth clean white.

The phone jangled on Herries' desk. He picked it up. 'Yeh?'

'Yamaguchi in sickbay,' said the voice. 'Thought you'd want to know about Worth.'

'Well?'

'Broken lumbar vertebra. He'll live, possibly without permanent paralysis, but he'll have to go back for treatment.'

'And be held incommunicado a year, till his contract's up. I wonder how much of a patriot he'll be by that time.'

'What?'

'Nothing. Can it wait till tomorrow? Everything's so disorganized right now, I'd hate to activate the projector.'

'Oh, yes. He's under sedation anyway.' Yamaguchi paused. 'And the man who died—'

'Sure. We'll ship him back too. The government will even supply a nice coffin. I'm sure his girl friend will appreciate that.'

'Do you feel well?' asked Yamaguchi sharply.

'They were going to be married,' said Herries. He took another pull from the fifth of bourbon on his desk. It was getting almost too dark to see the bottle. 'Since patriotism nowadays . . . in the future, I mean . . . in our own home, sweet home . . . since patriotism is necessarily equated with necrophilia, in that the loyal citizen is expected to rejoice every time his government comes up with a newer gadget for mass-producing corpses . . . I am sure the young lady will just love to have a pretty coffin. So much nicer than a mere husband. I'm sure the coffin will be chrome plated.'

'Wait a minute—'

'With tail fins.'

'Look here,' said the doctor, 'you're acting like a case of combat fatigue. I know you've had a shock today. Come see me and I'll give you a tranquilizer.'

'Thanks,' said Herries. 'I've got one.' He took another swig and forced briskness into his tone. 'We'll send 'em back tomorrow morning, then. Now don't bother me. I'm composing a letter to explain to the great white father that this wouldn't have happened if we'd been allowed one stinking little atomic howitzer. Not that I expect to get any results. It's policy that we aren't allowed heavy weapons

27

down here, and who ever heard of facts affecting a policy? Why, facts might be unAmerican.'

He hung up, put the bottle on his lap and his feet on the desk, lit a cigarette and stared out the window. Darkness came sneaking across the compound like smoke. The rain had stopped for a while, and lamps and windows threw broken yellow gleams off puddles, but somehow the gathering night was so thick that each light seemed quite alone. There was no one else in the headquarters shack at this hour. Herries had not turned on his lights.

To hell with it, he thought. *To hell with it.*

His cigarette tip waxed and waned as he puffed, like a small dying star. But the smoke didn't taste right when invisible. Or had he put away so many toasts to dead men that his tongue was numbed? He wasn't sure. It hardly mattered.

The phone shrilled again. He picked it up, fumble-handed in the murk. 'Chief of operations,' he said pleasantly. 'To hell with *you.*'

'What?' Symonds' voice rattled a bare bit. Then: 'I have been trying to find you. What are you doing there this late?'

'I'll give you three guesses. Playing pinochle? No. Carrying on a sordid affair with a lady iguanodon? No. None of your business? Right! *Give* that gentleman a box of see-gars.'

'Look here, Mr Herries,' wasped Symonds, 'this is no time for levity. I understand that Matthew Worth was seriously injured today. He was supposed to be on guard duty tonight – the secret shipment. This has disarranged all my plans.'

'Tsk-tsk-tsk. My nose bleeds for you.'

'The schedule of duties must be revised. According to my notes, Worth would have been on guard from midnight until 4 A.M. Since I do not know precisely what other jobs his fellows are assigned to, I cannot single any one of them out to replace him. Will you do so? Select a man who can then sleep later tomorrow morning?'

'Why?' asked Herries.

'Why? Because – because—'

'I know. Because Washington said so. Washington is afraid some nasty dinosaur from what is going to be Russia will sneak in and look at an unguarded crate and hurry home with the information. Sure, I'll do it. I just wanted to hear you sputter.'

Herries thought he made out an indignant breath sucked past an upper plate. 'Very good,' said the clerk. 'Make the necessary arrangements for tonight, and we will work out a new rotation of watches tomorrow.'

Herries put the receiver back.

The list of tight-lipped, tight-minded types was somewhere in his desk, he knew vaguely. A copy, rather. Symonds had a copy, and no doubt there would be copies going to the Pentagon and the FBI and the Transoco personnel office and – Well, look at the list, compare it with the work schedule, see who wouldn't be doing anything of critical importance tomorrow forenoon, and put him on a bit of sentry-go. Simple.

Herries took another swig. He could resign, he thought. He could back out of the whole fantastically stupid, fantastically meaningless operation. He wasn't compelled to work. Of course, they could hold him for the rest of his contract. It would be a lonesome year. Or maybe not; maybe a few others would trickle in to keep him company. To be sure, he'd then be under surveillance the rest of his life. But who wasn't, in a century divided between two garrisons?

The trouble was, he thought, *there was nothing a man could do about the situation*. You could become a peace-at-any-cost pacifist and thereby, effectively, league yourself with the enemy; and the enemy had carried out too many cold massacres for any halfway sane man to stomach. Or you could fight back (thus becoming more and more what you fought) and hazard planetary incineration against the possibility of a tolerable outcome. It only took one to make a quarrel, and the enemy had long ago elected himself that one. Now, it was probably too late to patch up the quarrel.

29

Even if important men on both sides wished for a disengagement, what could they do against their own fanatics, vested interests, terrified common people . . . against the whole momentum of history?

Hell, take it, thought Herries, *we may be damned but why must we be fools into the bargain?*

Somewhere a brontosaur hooted, witlessly plowing through a night swamp.

Well, I'd better – No!

Herries stared at the end of his cigarette. It was almost scorching his fingers. At least, he thought, at least he could find out what he was supposed to condone. A look into those crates, which should have held the guns he had begged for, and perhaps some orchestral and scientific instruments . . . and instead held God knew what piece of Pentagonal-brained idiocy . . . a look would be more than a blow in Symonds' smug eye. It would be an assertion that he was Herries, a free man, whose existence had not yet been pointlessly spilled from a splintered skull. He, the individual, would know what the Team planned; and if it turned out to be a crime against reason, he could at the very least resign and sit out whatever followed.

Yes. By the dubious existence of divine mercy, yes.

Again a little rain, just a small warm touch on his face, like tears. Herries splashed to the transceiver building and stood quietly in the sudden flashlight glare. At last, out of blackness, the sentry's voice came: 'Oh, it's you, sir.'

'Uh-huh. You know Worth got hurt today? I'm taking his watch.'

'What? But I thought—'

'Policy,' said Herries.

The incantation seemed to suffice. The other man shuffled forth and laid his rifle in the engineer's hands. 'And here's the glim,' he added. 'Nobody came by while I was on duty.'

'What would you have done if somebody'd tried to get in?'

'Why, stopped them, of course.'

'And if they didn't stop?'

The dim face under the dripping hat turned puzzledly toward Herries. The engineer sighed. 'I'm sorry, Thornton. It's too late to raise philosophical questions. Run along to bed.'

He stood in front of the door, smoking a damp cigarette, and watched the man trudge away. All the lights were out now, except overhead lamps here and there. They were brilliant, but remote; he stood in a pit of shadow and wondered what the phase of the Moon was and what kind of constellations the stars made nowadays.

He watched. There was time enough for his rebellion. Too much time, really. A man stood in rain, fog about his feet and a reptile smell in his nose, and he remembered anemones in springtime, strewn under trees still cold and leafless, with here and there a little snow between the roots. Or he remembered drinking beer in a New England country inn one fall day, when the door stood open to red sumac and yellow beech and a far blue wandering sky. Or he remembered a man snatched under black Jurassic quagmires, a man stepped into red ruin, a man sitting in a jeep and bleeding brains down onto the picture of the girl he had planned to marry. And then he started wondering what the point of it all was, and decided that it was either without any point whatsoever or else had the purpose of obliterating anemones and quiet country inns, and he was forced to dissent somehow.

When Thornton's wet footsteps were lost in the dark, Herries unlocked the shed door and went through. It was smotheringly hot inside. Sweat sprang forth underneath his raincoat as he closed the door again and turned on his flashlight. Rain tapped loudly on the roof. The crates loomed over him, box upon box, many of them large enough to hold a dinosaur. It had taken a lot of power to ship all that

31

tonnage into the past. No wonder taxes were high. And what might the stuff be? A herd of tanks, possibly ... some knocked-down bombers ... Lord knew what concept the men who lived in offices, insulated from the sky, would come up with. And Symonds had implied it was just a beginning; there would be more shipments when this had been stored out of the way, and more, and more.

Herries found a workbench and helped himself to tools. He would have to be careful; no sense in going to jail. He laid the flashlight on a handy barrel and stooped down by one of the crates. It was of strong wood, securely screwed together. But while that would make it harder to dismantle, it could be reassembled without leaving a trace. Maybe. Of course, it might be booby trapped. No telling how far the religion of secrecy could lead the office men.

Oh, well, if I'm blown up I haven't lost much. Herries peeled off his slicker. His shirt clung to his body. He squatted and began to work.

It went slowly. After taking off several boards, he saw a regular manufacturer's crate, openslatted. Something within was wrapped in burlap. A single curved metal surface projected slightly. What the devil? Herries got a crowbar and pried one slat loose. The nails shrieked. He stooped rigid for a while, listening, but there was only the rain, grown more noisy. He reached in and fumbled with the padding ... God, it was hot!

Only when he had freed the entire blade did he recognize what it was. And then his mind would not quite function; he gaped a long while before the word registered.

A plowshare.

'But they don't know what to do with the farm surpluses at home,' he said aloud, inanely.

Like a stranger's, his hands began to repair what he had torn apart. He couldn't understand it. Nothing seemed altogether real any more. Of course, he thought in a dim way, theoretically anything might be in the other boxes, but

32

he suspected more plows, tractors, discs, combines . . . why not bags of seeds . . .? *What were they planning to do?*

'Ah.'

Herries whirled. The flashlight beam caught him like a spear.

He grabbed blindly for his rifle. A dry little voice behind the blaze said: 'I would not recommend violence.' Herries let the rifle fall. It thudded.

Symonds closed the shed door behind him and stepped forward in his mincing fashion, another shadow among bobbing misshapen shadows. He had simply flung on shirt and pants, but bands of night across them suggested necktie, vest, and coat.

'You see,' he explained without passion, 'all the guards were instructed *sub rosa* to notify me if there was anything unusual, even when it did not seem to warrant action on their part.' He gestured at the crate. 'Please continue reassembling it.'

Herries crouched down again. There was a hollowness in him, his only wonder was how best to die. For if he were sent back to the twentieth century, surely, surely they would lock him up and lose the key, and the sunlessness of death was better than that. It was strange, he thought, how his fingers used the tools with untrembling skill.

Symonds stood behind him and held his light on the work. After a long while he asked primly, 'Why did you break in like this?'

I could kill him, thought Herries. *He's unarmed. I could wring his scrawny neck between these two hands, and take a gun, and go into the swamp to live for a few days. . . . But it might be easier all around just to turn the rifle on myself.*

He sought words with care, for he must decide what to do, even though it seemed remote and scarcely important. 'That's not an easy question to answer,' he said.

'The significant ones never are.'

Astonished, Herries jerked a glance upward and back.

(And was the more surprised that he could still know surprise.) But the little man's face was in darkness. Herries saw only a wan blank glitter off the glasses.

He said, 'Let's put it this way. There are limits even to the right of self-defense. If a killer attacks me, I can fight back with anything I've got. But I wouldn't be justified in grabbing some passing child for a shield.'

'So you wished to make sure that nothing you would consider illegitimate was in those boxes?' asked Symonds academically.

'I don't know. What is illegitimate, these days? I was . . . I was disgusted. I liked Greenstein, and he died because Washington had decided we couldn't have bombs or atomic shells. I just didn't know how much more I could consent to. I had to find out.'

'I see.' The clerk nodded. 'For your information, it is *all* agricultural equipment. Later shipments will include industrial and scientific material, a large reserve of canned food, and as much of the world's culture as it proves possible to microfilm.'

Herries stopped working, turned around and rose. His knees would not hold him. He leaned against the crate and it was a minute before he could get out: 'Why?'

Symonds did not respond at once. He reached forth a precise hand and took up the flashlight Herries had left on the barrel. Then he sat down there himself, with the two glowing tubes in his lap. The light from below ridged his face in shadows, and his glasses made blind circles. He said, as if ticking off the points of the agenda.

'You would have been informed of the facts in due course, when the next five hundred people arrive. Now you have brought on yourself the burden of knowing what you would otherwise have been ignorant of for months yet. I think it may safely be assumed that you will keep the secret and not be broken by it. At least, the assumption is necessary.'

Herries heard his own breath harsh in his throat. 'Who are these people?'

The papery half-seen countenance did not look at him, but into the pit-like reaches of the shed. 'You have committed a common error,' said Symonds, as if to a student. 'You have assumed that because men are constrained by circumstances to act in certain ways, they must be evil or stupid. I assure you, Senator Wien and the few others responsible for this are neither. They must keep the truth even from those officials within the project whose reaction would be rage or panic instead of a sober attempt at salvage. Nor do they have unlimited powers. Therefore, rather than indulge in tantrums about the existing situation, they use it. The very compartmentalization of effort and knowledge enforced by Security helps conceal their purposes and mislead those who must be given some information.'

Symonds paused. A little frown crossed his forehead, and he tapped an impatient fingernail on a flashlight casing. 'Do not misunderstand,' he went on. 'Senator Wien and his associates have not forgotten their oaths of office, nor are they trying to play God. Their primary effort goes, as it must, to a straightforward dealing with the problems of the twentieth century. It is not they who are withholding the one significant datum – a datum which, incidentally, any informed person could reason out for himself if he cared to. It is properly constituted authority, using powers legally granted to stamp certain reports Top Secret. Of course, the Senator has used his considerable influence to bring about the present eventuality, but that is normal politics.'

Herries growled: 'Get to the point, damn you! What are you talking about?'

Symonds shook his thin gray head. 'You are afraid to know, are you not?' he asked quietly.

'I—' Herries turned about, faced the crate and beat it with his fist. The parched voice in the night continued to punish him:

35

'You know that a time-projector can go into the future about a hundred years at a jump, but can only go pastward in jumps of approximately one hundred megayears. You have spoken of a simple way to explore certain sections of the historical past, in spite of this handicap, by making enough century hops forward before the one long hop backward. But can you tell me how to predict the historical future? Say, a century hence? Come, come, you are an intelligent man. Answer me.'

'Yeah,' said Herries. 'I get the idea. Leave me alone.'

'Team A, a group of well-equipped volunteers, went into the twenty-first century,' pursued Symonds. 'They recorded what they observed and placed the data in a chemically inert box within a large block of reinforced concrete erected at an agreed-on location: one which a previous expedition to circa 100,000,000 A.D. had confirmed would remain stable. I presume they also mixed radioactive materials of long half-life into the concrete, to aid in finding the site. Of course, the bracketing of time jumps is such that they cannot now get back to the twentieth century. But Team B went a full hundred-megayear jump into the future, excavated the data, and returned home.'

Herries squared his body and faced back to the small man. He was drained, so weary that it was all he could do to keep on his feet. 'What did they find?' he asked. There was no tone in his voice or in him.

'There have actually been several expeditions to 100,000,000,' said Symonds. 'Energy requirements for a visit to 200,000,000 – A.D. or B.C. – were considered prohibitive. But in 100,000,000, life is re-evolving on Earth. However, as yet the plants have not liberated enough oxygen for the atmosphere to be breathable. You see, oxygen reacts with exposed rock, so that if no biological processes exist to replace it continuously – But you have a better technical education than I.'

'Okay,' said Herries, flat and hard. 'Earth was sterile for a long time in the future. Including the twenty-first century?'

'Yes. The radioactivity had died down enough so that Team A reported no danger to itself, but some of the longer-lived isotopes were still measurably present. By making differential measurements of abundance, Team A was able to estimate rather closely when the bombs had gone off.'

'And?'

'Approximately one year from the twentieth-century base date we are presently using.'

'One year . . . from now.' Herries stared upward. Blackness met him. He heard the Jurassic rain on the iron roof, like drums.

'Possibly less,' Symonds told him. 'There is a factor of uncertainty. This project must be completed well within the safety margin before the war comes.'

'The war comes,' Herries repeated . . . 'Does it have to come? Fixed time line or not, does it have to come? Couldn't the enemy leaders be shown the facts – couldn't our side, even, capitulate—'

'Every effort is being made,' said Symonds like a machine. 'Quite apart from the theory of rigid time, it seems unlikely that they will succeed. The situation is too unstable. One man, losing his head and pressing the wrong button, can write the end; and there are so many buttons. The very revelation of the truth, to a few chosen leaders or to the world public, would make some of them panicky. Who can tell what a man in panic will do? That is what I mean when I said that Senator Wien and his co-workers have not forgotten their oaths of office. They have no thought of taking refuge, they know they are old men. To the end, they will try to save the twentieth century. But they do not expect it; so they are also trying to save the human race.'

Herries pushed up from the crate he had been leaning against. 'Those five hundred who're coming,' he whispered. 'Women?'

'Yes. If there is still time to rescue a few more, after the ones you are preparing for have gone through, it will be done. But there will be at least a thousand young, healthy adults here, in the Jurassic. You face a difficult time, when

37

the truth must be told them: you can see why the secret must be kept until then. It is quite possible that someone here will lose his head. That is why no heavy weapons have been sent: a single deranged person must not be able to destroy everyone. But *you* will recover. You must.'

Herries jerked the door open and stared out into the roaring darkness. 'But there are no traces of us . . . in the future,' he said, hearing his voice high and hurt like a child's.

'How much trace do you expect would remain after geological eras?' answered Symonds. He was still the reproving schoolmaster; but he sat on the barrel and faced the great moving shadows in a corner. 'It is assumed that you will remain here for several generations, until your numbers and resources have been expanded sufficiently. The Team A I spoke of will join you a century hence. It is also, I might add, composed of young men and women in equal numbers. But this planet in this age is not a good home. We trust that your descendants will perfect the spaceships we know to be possible, and take possession of the stars instead.'

Herries leaned in the doorway, sagging with tiredness and the monstrous duty to survive. A gust of wind threw rain into his eyes. He heard dragons calling in the night.

'And you?' he said, for no good reason.

'I shall convey any final messages you may wish to send home,' said the dried-out voice.

Neat little footsteps clicked across the floor until the clerk paused beside the engineer. There was silence, except for the rain.

'Surely I will deserve to go home,' said Symonds.

And suddenly the breath whistled inward between teeth which had snapped together. He raised his hands, claw-fingered, and screamed aloud: 'You can let me go home *then!*'

He began running toward the supervisors' barge. The sound of him was soon lost. Herries stood for a time yet in the door.

Welcome

Barlow's first astonishment was at how little different the future seemed. He had thought that five hundred years would change every detail beyond imagination. To be sure, nothing was quite like the twentieth-century United States; but contemporary Mexico had been a good deal more exotic than the North American Federation of the United World Republics looked.

Several persons awaited him when he emerged from the superenergy state. All but one were men, ranging from boyish to middle-aged: two Orientals, a Negro, the others white. They wore shirts, trousers, and fabric shoes, of synthetic material in subdued colors, cut much like Barlow's. One had a sleek pistol-like weapon in a holster, but left it there, unafraid of the newcomer. They all gathered around, made sympathetic noises in accented but recognizable English, led him to a couch and gave him a drink. The room was windowless, with a fluorescent ceiling and ventilator grilles. A workbench supported miscellaneous scientific equipment, most of which Barlow could identify.

'Heh, now, buddow, swallow this an' you'll feel better.'

Barlow obeyed mechanically. He had a bad case of the shakes. A gentle, relaxing warmth spread through him. Within minutes he could regard his situation as calmly as if it were someone else's. He felt happy, his mind clearer and quicker than usual. And yet, he thought, this was not so different from the tranquilizers of his era.

'I guess he's 'kay now, Joe,' said a young man.

The oldest, who appeared to be the leader, nodded.

'How're you?' he smiled, offering his hand. 'I'm Joe Grozen. Here's my primary daughter Amily. She 'nsisted on seeing you arrive. I won' ask you to 'member any other names right off.'

'Tom Barlow.' He was much taken with Amily, who was tall and well-formed, with dark hair falling past a heartshaped blue-eyed face and halfway down her back. She wore sandals, shorts, a kind of tee shirt, and a friendly expression. 'What, uh, what year is this?'

'Twen'y-four nine'y-seven,' she replied. 'The twelfth April. Your calculations were very close. This place was readied special for your coming.'

He had to ask it, with his heart in his throat despite all soothing drugs: 'Is there any way for me to return?'

Joe Grozen's broad red visage grew sober. 'No,' he muttered. ''Fraid not.'

Barlow sighed. 'Never mind. I didn't expect it. Travel into the past, an obvious absurdity. All I did was give myself a jolt of energy, a vector along the time axis rather than through space, and so increased my rate of existence several millionfold . . . But you know all about that.' He fumbled after a cigarette.

'Oh, yes,' said an Oriental. 'The phenomenon's well un'erstood today.' He bowed. 'Though 's an honor to meet its first discoverer. So youthful you are, too.'

'Sam's chief o' the technics department,' explained Amily. 'Natur'lly he'd be mos' in'erested in the science aspect. An' Phil here.' She laid a hand briefly on the shoulder of the Negro. 'He'll want to ask you all sorts of questions 'bout the past.'

'You'll have the status all your life in my department, if you wish,' Phil assured Barlow. 'Special lecturer, consultant, whatever you want to call it. We're missing so much information about everything prior to the Atomic Wars.'

'Shut up, you damn scientists,' said Joe good-naturedly. 'Our frien' Tom is first of all a free human being. You can

40

quiz him later, but give the poor tovarsh time to get used to us first. How y' feeling now, Tom?'

'Okay.' Barlow drew heavily on his cigarette. It might have been the drug, or simply the conviction, now proven, that his farewells in the twentieth century had been final. But whatever the cause, that era already seemed remote – though he had departed it less than half an hour ago, as far as his conscious mind knew. His fears had not materialized: emergence in a desert, or an Orwellian dictatorship, or something equally horrible. He'd gambled on finding a world where his own romantic advent would give him a head start in establishing himself. (Surely, even in the course of five hundred years, there had not been many time leapers. The messages he left, sealed into marked blocks of concrete, had been carefully designed to arouse the curiosity of future humankind about Thomas Barlow.) These easy-going, familiar-looking people dissolved the tension in him. His gamble had paid off.

'Sure, I'm fine,' he said. 'Tired, is all.'

Joe nodded. 'That I un'erstan'. We got a home all prepared for you. You can rest up there. I'd like to give you a welcoming banquet this evening, though. Lots o' people want to meet you.'

'I don't need—' Barlow was interrupted as Amily took him by the hand.

'You come with me,' she said. 'I'll take you to your place. On the way I can give you a lining o' what the world's like these days.'

'Now, wait,' objected Phil.

'Wait yourself,' she chuckled. 'I know you, you ol' professor. You'd stuff him so full o' precise information he wouldn' know his charge from a Dirac hole. What he needs right now is facts, not data.'

'An' someone to snuggle with,' Sam teased.

She made a face at him. Joe grinned. 'What's the use o' being the Pres'dent's daughter, Tom, if she can' get to know

41

you ahead of all the other girls?' he said. 'You're going to be the most chased bachelor on this planet, in case you hadn' guessed.'

As a matter of fact, Barlow had guessed, but it was pleasant to have his anticipations borne out.

There was a little more conversation, then he left the room with the young woman. They went through a very ordinary door and down a very ordinary hall to an underground garage. Gray-clad men, shaven-headed, bowed to Amily with extreme deference and wheeled forth a small, brightly colored, teardrop-shaped machine. The seats, within a transparent canopy, were luxurious. She punched controls and leaned back. Under some kind of automatic piloting, the vehicle whirred up a ramp and into the air.

From above, Barlow saw endless miles of buildings. The effect was more like Chicago than any futuristic megalopolis: drab, dirty cubicles, with nearly solid streams of pedestrians moving through the canyons between. Enormous vehicles, freight and passenger, rumbled on elevated ways which sometimes ducked below ground. Only a few private cars were to be seen, flitting like the one which bore him over the city.

'What's the population?' he asked slowly.

Amily shrugged. 'Who knows? For the whole world, maybe fifteen billion.'

He whistled. A fifth of that number had been obscene enough when he departed his own century. However, progress must have been made in food production: algae, ocean farming, and whatnot. He was pleased to note that the air was free of smog. Probably exhaustion of chemical fuels had forced total conversion to atomic-electrical power.

Still, fifteen billion! He asked about other planets, and was a trifle saddened, but not surprised, to hear that they were visited about as often and as significantly as Pago Pago or Antarctica had been in his day.

'What sort of government do you have?' he inquired.

Amily's laugh was as musical a sound as he had ever heard. 'True scientist, you! First you find out 'bout Mars, then 'bout affairs at home! Well, if I 'member my hist'ry right, you had many sep'rate countries in the twentieth century. That was before the Atomic Wars, no? All one country now, the United World Republics. How else could fifteen billion people survive?'

'And I suppose all the races are equal?'

'What? I don' un'erstan'.'

With some effort, he got across to her the idea that secondary physical characteristics had once been considered important. She was as startled and amused to hear of race riots as he had once been to learn of blood spilled by early Christians over the *iota* distinguishing homoousian from homoiousian.

'That's cheering,' he said. 'As I'd hoped.'

She regarded him closely, for minutes, while the aircar whispered through an April sky the color of her eyes. 'Your message was never clear as to why you left,' she said.

He looked away, down to the brick and concrete earth, up again to clouds. 'It's hard to explain. Disgust would be the simplest word. I had no close personal ties after my mother died. And I saw freedom being crushed in most of the world, rotted and vulgarized in my own country; I read interviews with allegedly sane leaders, who spoke calmly of incinerating some tens of millions of women and children, if national policy so demanded. What had I to lose?'

She grimaced. 'You did wisely, Tom. I won'er why so few others did the same. But then, there were the Atomic Wars, an' all their aftermath. Not much chance for escape. Nowadays, not much incentive. Who, with access to a time accelerator, 'd want to leave this world?'

He watched her, healthy, serene, and beautiful, and thought: Who, indeed? Of course he hadn't found any Utopia, but he hadn't been so naive as to expect that. It was enough to have found hope. He took out another cigarette, offered her one, and was politely refused. 'Very few people use tobacco,' she said. 'Maybe jus' 'cause how expensive 'tis. But if you want, 's your own affair.'

'The supremely civilized art,' he said. 'Minding one's own business.'

She gave him a long, sidewise look. 'Could be my business too,' she murmured. 'You're a han'some buddo, Tom.'

The drug didn't slow down his pulse much.

He steered the conversation toward herself. She told him she was interested in sports and theatricals. Another bit of semantic confusion straightened itself out after he realized that 'amateur performances' would have been a redundant phrase. All art nowadays was amateur, in the sense of being done for love (and, admittedly, social prestige) by people who had no need to do it for money. The mass-produced entertainment of Barlow's birthcentury was long forgotten. He was not displeased to learn that scientific research, as opposed to technology and engineering, was classed among the arts. Amily voiced a few opinions on Shakespeare's real intent in *Hamlet* and *Lear*, which might be banal to her contemporaries but to Barlow were so novel and perceptive that he felt this would prove one of the great artistic eras.

'But I did expect more change,' he said. 'More inventions, especially. What I've seen looks less than fifty years in advance of my period. No offense,' he hastened to add.

Her expression was puzzled rather than hurt. 'Why should there be change? Isn' this aircar good enough?'

Perhaps these folk were only rationalizing a static technology forced on them by swollen population and dwindled resources. Obviously capitalism such as Barlow's America had known, with its inherent need to innovate, was extinct. But he didn't mind. So much so-called progress had been sheer hokum anyhow. Let the world take a thousand years to digest the authentic advances of the Industrial Revolution; give the simple grace of living a chance to catch up.

The car glided down to a platform on the fiftieth floor of a skyscraper. The surrounding buildings were as hideous as most of the continent-wide city; but this tower stood clean and proud, its starkness relieved by colorful beds of mutated flowers on each terrace. 'So many men wanted to sponsor you, we set up a fund an' got a special place,' said Amily. She squeezed his arm. 'But I saw you first, 'member.'

With that buildup, he was surprised at the modesty of the apartment: two smallish rooms, plus bath and kitchenette. Amily showed him how to operate the gadgets, which were little different from those he knew. He was more interested in the quiet good taste of the interior decoration. The bookshelves were filled with finer volumes than he was accustomed to, most of them handbound. He wouldn't have much trouble getting used to the spelling, he saw. A music library ranged from medieval chants to modern symphonies almost as foreign to his ear; but in between he found many old friends, and when he tried out part of the Beethoven Ninth, he had never heard it better performed.

'I think you're hungry,' said the girl. She opened a built-in refrigerator. 'Lemme make you a san'wich.' The meat was exotic, the bread far tastier than that library paste sold under the name in Barlow's milieu. He ate with pleasure, downing a bottle of excellent beer.

'Might be best you nap now,' she said. 'Been a strain, I know.'

'I feel fine,' he said, rising.

'Tha's jus' the tranquitism,' she warned. 'Tonight'll be a big do. Last till all hours.'

He edged closer. She stayed where she was. Her eyelashes fluttered, long and smokey against smooth sunbrowned cheeks. 'I can rest tomorrow,' he said.

'Sure. You're your own master here, Tom. Later Dad'll find some status position for you, but tha's nominal. An' no hurry 'bout it.'

He stopped, struck by a thought. In all this bewilderment

45

of newness, it hadn't occured to him before. But if he really was such a wonder, he had been received with extraordinary quietness and informality. 'What does your father do?' he asked.

'Why, Joe's the Pres'dent o' the world. Didn' you realize?' She laughed afresh. 'I s'pose not. We all get so used to each other, all good frien's not standin' on ceremony, we plain forgot – Oh, yes, Joe's the Pres'dent. Sam Wong heads the World Department o' Technics, Phil Faubus is chief sociohistorian, Ivan – No matter.'

He needed a while to shed his preconceptions. That the chief executive of fifteen billion people could be so human seemed almost a contradiction in terms. He noticed he'd stepped back from Amily.

She noticed too, seized both his hands and pulled him closer. 'Don' be scared,' she said merrily. 'Jus' 'cause I'm the Pres'dent's daughter, I won't eat you. Got other plans.'

Barlow decided to take things as they came. 'I told you before,' he said. 'Please don't rush off.'

'Well,' she answered, low-voiced, 'I'm not in that much of a hurry . . .'

An hour or two later, when she declared that now he did need a rest and he was inclined to agree, he asked casually if she had any brothers or sisters.

'Sure. Lots of 'em.' She kept her eyes on the mirror, before which she sat combing her hair. 'Rozh'd like to've met you when you came, but he's been too busy studying. 'S not all fun, being President.'

'Rozh? A brother? But you said your father—'

'Well, Joe won' live forever, you know. Rozh has to be prepared.'

'But this – hey wait!'

She gave him a direct glance. 'Don' you un'erstan'? Rozh is Joe's oldes' son by his chief orthowife. So he'll be the next Pres'dent.'

'Oh.' Barlow sat for a while. At last: 'Is the succession like that in all the other offices?'

'What else? It'd be an unnatural father who didn' han' on his position to his heirs, wouldn't it?' Amily finished combing her locks, sprang up, and blew him a kiss. 'I *mus*' run. 'Bye, darling.' She hurried from the room. A moment later he heard her aircar take off.

Alone, he fretted for a while. But after all, he told himself, in the total context of history, hereditary government was the norm, elective government the deviation. Given proper training . . . modern genetics also, no doubt, and medicine, so there were no defectives . . . the same family might provide wise rulers for hundreds of years.

He was too tired to think further. Sleep swooped on him.

Soft music awoke him at dusk. A man entered, bearing a tray with tea and cookies. He was a burly fellow, with shaven pate and gray clothes like the garage attendants. His face was expressionless. He set the tray on the bed and prostrated himself.

After he had lain there for a number of seconds, Barlow snapped nervously, 'Well, what's the matter with you?'

'My owner hasn' commanded me t' arise,' responded a dead voice.

'Huh?'

Another man drifted in. He was more gaily clad, in some kind of livery, but his skull was as bare as the other's. 'If my owner please,' he said, 'his bath an' garments 're ready. It's soon time for the banquet.'

Barlow swung his feet to the carpet. 'Good Lord!' he exploded. His tea spilled on the prostrate man, and it was hot, but there was no stir or whimper.

When he had argued his way to comprehension – which was not easy, both his chattels being invincibly stupid – Barlow stood for a long while staring at the wall. Well, he told himself at last, in a remote fashion, when fifteen billion people are jammed together on one impoverished planet, they are bound to become a cheap commodity.

With the help of some more tranquilizer, he made a

creditable entrance with many of Earth's rulers. Their total number was small, and he learned they were careful to restrict their own reproduction, lest the power they had be divided. However, they were no more conscious of tyrannizing the unfree than a rancher would be of unfairly dominating his cattle. Their welcome to Barlow was warm and genuine. When Amily took his arm and led the procession into the dining room, he began to feel that he had come home.

The hors d'oeuvres, soup, and salad were delicious. Then, proud and fond, Amily's father stood up to do the honors as the main course was brought in: roast suckling coolie.

The Nest

I'd been out hunting all day, in the reeds and thickets and tall grass of the bottom-lands down by the Styx, and luck had been bad. The heat and mugginess bothered me worse than it should have, after all these years in the Nest, and the flies were a small hell, and there was no game to speak of. We'd killed it all off, I suppose. Once I did spot the sabertooth which had been hanging around the cattle pens, and shot at him, but he got away. While chasing him, I went head over heels into a mudhole and lost my powderhorn and two good flints, besides ruining my shirt. So I came back toward evening in a devil of a temper, which is probably what started the trouble.

There was a sort of quiet golden light all over the world as I rode homeward, filling the air and the wide grasslands and the forest. Pretty. But I was thinking bitterly about the cave and The Men and a wet cold wind blowing off the glaciers of home and roaring in the pines. I wondered why the hell I hadn't had the brains to stay where I was well off. You got rich, working out of the Nest, if you lived, but was it worth the trouble?

Iggy's feet scrunched on gravel as we came onto the road. A lot of the boys have kidded me about riding a dinosaur, when a horse is so much faster and smarter. But what the hell, a young iguanodon goes quickly enough for me, and the flies don't bother him. And if the need arises, he's like a small tank – as I was very shortly going to learn.

I plodded along, swaying in the saddle, ten feet up in the air on Iggy's shoulders. The fields stretched around me now, hundreds of acres of wheat and rye and maize, with the orchards dark against the yellowing sky. The slaves were still at work, cultivating, and a couple of overseers waved to me from their horses. But I was feeling too grouchy to reply; I sat hunched over pitying myself.

A screen of trees and hedges marked off the fields; beyond, the road went through gardens that blazed with color, all around the Nest. Roses and poppies like fresh blood, white and tiger tawny lilies, royally purple violets – sure, Duke Hugo was a free-wheeling buzzard, but he did know flowers. Ahead of me, I could see the peaked roofs of the houses, the slave pens beyond them, and the castle black over all. I thought of a hot shower and clicked my tongue at Iggy, to make him step faster.

That was where the fight began.

The girl burst out a clump of cherry trees in blossom, screaming as she saw me. It was a small dry scream, as if she'd already burned out her throat. I only had time to see that she was young and dark and pretty, then she swerved around to dodge me. Her foot slipped and she went down in a heap. I don't know exactly why I grabbed my ax and jumped to the ground. Maybe the long red weals across her naked back had something to do with it.

She tried to scramble up, I put my foot on her back and held her down. As she looked up, I saw big dark eyes, a small curved nose, a wide full mouth, and a hell of a big bruise on one cheek. 'What's the hurry, sis?' I asked.

She cried something, I didn't know the language but there was a terrible begging in her voice. A runaway slave – well, let her run. The sabertooth would be better for her than her owner, judging by those marks. I lifted my foot and bent over and helped the girl rise.

Too late. The man came out through the trees after her. He was a young fellow, short but strongly built, and mad as a Zulu. He wore a gray uniform, a square helmet, and a swastika armband – a Nazi, then – but his only weapons were a broadsword and the long whip in one hand.

The girl screamed once more and took off again. He snarled, and snapped the whip. It was a murderous Boer sjambok; its heavy length coiled around her ankles and she stumbled and fell.

I suppose it was my bad luck that day which flared up in me. I had no business interfering, but I didn't like Nazis much. I put a hand on his chest and shoved. Down he went.

He scrambled up, bellowing in excellent Norman French. I hefted my ax. 'Not so fast, chum,' I answered.

'Get out of the way!' He lunged past me toward the girl, who was lying there crying, out of hope, out of tears. I got him by the collar and spun him around, flat on his back.

'I rank thee, friend, in spite of that fancy uniform,' I told him. 'I rate a flintlock, and thou'st only got that pigsticker. Now behave thyself!'

Sure, I was looking for a fight. It's the best way there is to work off your temper.

'*Thou bloody swine—*' He got up again, slowly, and his face was strange. It was a look I'd only seen before on children and kings, just about to throw a tantrum. I didn't recognize him, never having had much truck with the Nazis or their friends. Suddenly he lashed out with the whip. It caught me across the chest like a white-hot wire.

That did it. No damned swordsman was going to hit me that way. I didn't even stop to think before my ax bounced off his helmet.

The clang sent him lurching back, but the steel held firm. He screamed, then, and drew his sword and sprang for me. I met the whistling blow in midair. Sparks showered, and our weapons were nearly torn loose.

He growled and tried to thrust, but a broadsword is no good for that. I knocked the blade aside, and my ax whirred down. He was fast, jumped back. I furrowed his shoulder.

'The devil damn thee!' He got two hands on his sword and it flamed against my bare head. I caught the blow on my ax handle, swept it aside, and took one step inward. A sidewise chop, and his head was rolling in the gravel.

Most people think a battle-ax is a clumsy weapon. It isn't. I'll take it for close quarters over any weapon except a .45 or a carbine, which I didn't rate. His pretty sword went spinning as he fell, flashing the sunlight into my eyes like a last thrust.

Breathing hard, I looked around me. I was a little surprised that the girl was still crouched there, but maybe she was too tired and scared to run any more. She was a stranger to me, and I'd have noticed anyone that nice-looking, so I decided she must have been captured just lately. She'd been horribly treated.

'Who art thou, sis?' I asked, trying to be gentle. I asked it in French, English, Latin, Greek, and whatever other languages I had a smattering of – even tried the language of The Men, just for the hell of it. Her eyes were wide and blank, without understanding.

'Well—' I scratched my head, not knowing exactly what to do next. It was decided for me. I heard a barking curse and the sound of hoofs, and looked up to see a dozen Huns charging.

I've no particular race prejudices, not like some of The Men. I'm about a quarter Neanderthal myself, and proud of it – that's where I get my red hair and strong back. We'll say nothing about the brains. Otherwise, of course, I'm a Man. But where it comes to Huns, well, I just don't like the greasy little devils. That was beside the point right now, though. They were after my skull. I didn't know what business of theirs the fight was, and didn't stop to think why. No time. Not even time to get mad again. The lead man's lance was almost in my throat.

I skipped aside, chopping low, at the horse's forelegs. The poor beast screamed as it fell. The Hun sprang lightly free, but I'd sheared his arm off before he hit the ground. The next one had his sword out, hewing at me. I turned the blow and chopped at his waist, but he was wearing chain mail. He grunted and swung once more, raking my cheek. Then they were all about me, cutting loose.

I scrambled toward Iggy, where the big stupid brute stood calmly watching. The Huns yammered and crowded their ponies in close. Reaching up in an overhand sweep, I split one brown monkey-face. A sword from behind struck at my neck. I ducked as it whistled over me, and thought in a queer short flash that this was the end of Trebuen.

'*Chinga los heréticos!*'

The tall horse had come thundering from the Nest and hit the pack like a cyclone. Don Miguel Pedro Esteban Francisco de Utrillo y Gutierrez flashed like a sun in his armor. His lance had already spitted one Hun and his sword sent another toppling. Now he reared the Arab back, and the slamming forefeet made a third man's pony yell and buck. The Huns howled and turned to meet him, giving me a chance to cross steel with one at a time.

Slash and bang! We were fighting merrily when a shot cracked in the air, and another and another. That was the signal of the bosses. We broke off and drew away from each other, still growling. There were five dead on the road, too trampled to be recognized. I drew air into lungs that seemed on fire and looked up to the new rider. She'd come galloping from the Nest, not even stopping to saddle her horse.

'Ah, Señorita Olga!' Don Miguel rose in his stirrups and swept her a bow till the plumes on his helmet brushed his horse's mane. He was always polite to women, even to Captain Olga Borisovna Rakitin, who by his lights was not only a heretic but unmaidenly.

I sort of agreed with him there. She was a big woman, as big as most men, and beautifully formed. The tight gray-green uniform of the Martian Soviet left no doubt of that. Under the peaked, red-starred cap, her face was straight, finely cut, with high cheekbones and big gray eyes, and it was a sin the way she cropped her bronze-colored hair. But she was a human icicle; or maybe a chilled-steel punching ram would be better.

She holstered her pistol with a clank and looked us over with eyes like the wind off a glacier. 'What is the meaning of this brawl?' She had a nice low voice, but spoke French like a clicking trigger.

Don Miguel's bearded hawk face broke into the famous smile that had made him the terror of husbands and fathers from Lagash to London. 'Señorita,' he said gently, 'when I see my good friend Trebuen set on by pagans and in danger of death before his conversion to the true faith is completed, there is only one thing which any hidalgo can do. Surely a lady will understand.'

'And why did ye fight?' she went on, looking at me and the Huns.

One of the horsemen pointed to the battered Nazi body. None of them spoke French very well, so they wouldn't talk it at all if they could help it. It was plain I'd killed a particular pal of theirs. Well, any friend of the Huns is an enemy of mine.

'And thou, Trebuen?' she asked. 'I've had about enough of thy Stone Age cannibalism. Thou'rt the worst trouble-maker in the Nest.'

That wasn't true, and she knew it. The Huns and the Nazis were forever brawling, and the Normans were even worse – though as they owned the place, I suppose they had the right. And I resented her crack about my people. The Men aren't ·cannibals, they're peaceful hunters, minding their own business. I'd never heard about war before being recruited into the Nest. That was when I chanced to meet a mammoth-hunting party, guided them, and had one of the Duke's sons take a fancy to me. They could always use tall husky men here.

'I didn't like his face,' I snapped. 'So I took it off.'

'This girl—' She looked at the plump, dark little chick, who had huddled up close to me.

'My property.'

'I didn't know even thou went in for slave-beating,' she sneered.

'I didn't do that!' I shouted.

Don Miguel had noticed the girl by now. He beamed at her, because she was certainly a knockout. Then he swept off his cloak and threw it over her shoulders. She drew it close around her and gave him a funny look, like a kicked dog that somebody finally pets. One small hand stole toward mine, and I took it.

By this time the cops had arrived, twenty of them marching in double-time from the Nest. The setting sun glared off their helmets, armor, and shields. They broke formation at their leader's command – he was a centurion, I noticed – and closed in around us, their short swords bare and sharp-looking.

'There've been enough brawls here,' said Captain Olga. 'This calls for an inquiry. Maybe a hanging or two.'

'Señorita,' said Don Miguel, very, very softly, his black eyes narrowed on her, 'the law of the Nest permits gentlemen to duel. Any subsequent quarrel is between the victor and the dead man's friends.'

'We'll see what the Duke has to say about it!' she snapped, and wheeled her horse around.

'Come on, friend,' said the centurion. 'Up to the castle.'

I shifted my ax. 'Are we under arrest?' I asked, putting a bite in the words. Cops have to be kept in their place.

'Er – not exactly, I guess,' said the centurion. 'But you'd better stay inside the castle walls until the Duke settles your case.'

I shrugged. Killing a man here wasn't a crime – there were plenty more where they came from. I might have to pay a fine, and perhaps some weregild to a few Huns and Nazis. That griped me, but I could afford it.

55

That's what I thought – then.

I clicked my tongue at Iggy, who stooped over so I could scramble aboard. I took the girl in front of me, which made the ride a pleasant one. She was horribly scared, and clung close to me. Iggy rose back up on his hind legs and stalked alongside Don Miguel's horse. The Huns trotted sulkily in the rear, twittering in their own language. The cops enclosed all of us and marched steadily down the road. They weren't really Romans, most of them were barbaric riffraff from Germany and Thrace, but their discipline was beautiful.

Don Miguel looked up at me. 'Who is the young woman?' he asked. 'Where is she from?'

'I don't know,' I said. 'Looks Semitic, but that could mean almost anything.'

'Well,' he said, 'we'll take her to the Wisdom and find out.'

'Uh—' I stumbled awkwardly. 'I don't know how to thank thee for—'

'*De nada, amigo.*' He waved a long, lily-white hand. 'It was a pleasure. Quite apart from the fact that I have to save thy heathenish soul before thou departest this world, unworthy apostle though I am, there is this question: Where else in the Nest would I find a man who could keep up with me in a drinking bout?'

'Well, there is that,' I agreed.

We entered on the Via Appia. There was pavement within the bounds of the Nest, beautifully laid – but a lot can be done when you have all the slave labor you want. Small houses lay on either side of the broad street, surrounded by gardens and bowers – the homes of the ordinary warriors. Slaves and naked children stopped to gape at us as we went by. We saw a few friends in the streets or in front of their homes: Thorkel the Berserk, all tricked out in Italian silks; the Mongol Belgutai, swapping small talk with Amir Hassan of Baghdad; the old sea dog Sir Henry Martingale, smoking in his garden while his concubines fanned him and played music. They hailed us cheerfully, not knowing what we had coming to us. But then, neither did we.

The cops' footfalls slammed on the pavement, a dull drumbeat between the fantastic houses. There were about a thousand homes in the Nest, each built according to the owner's fancy. A half-timbered Tudor cottage nestled between a French château and a swoop-roofed Chinese affair with one of their silly-looking dragons out in front; across from it were a miniature Moorish palace and one of those adobe huts the Greeks insisted on kenneling in. We turned at the fountain in the Place de l'Etoile – a lovely piece of Renaissance work, through it had gotten somewhat knocked up en route to us – and crossed London Bridge to the Street of St Mark. The town muezzin was calling Moslems to prayer as we climbed the hill on which the castle stood.

Its gray stone battlements threw a nightlike shadow over us. Looking around, I could see the slave pens on the other side of town; overseers were herding the field workers back, and such of the city's slaves as worked by day were trotting obediently toward the same place. Not many ever tried to get away – there was no place to go, and if a sabertooth or nimravus didn't get you first, the Normans would hunt you down with dogs. They thought that was rare sport.

We went through the gate into the flagged courtyard, past the guards – those were specially trusted Janissaries, armed with repeater rifles. 'Get on down,' said the centurion. 'I'll take your mounts to the stables.'

'Okay,' I said, 'but if they don't give Iggy enough to drink there, thou'lt hear from me. He needs lots of water.'

We stood in the courtyard. A couple of big mastiffs growled at us. There was a small group of Normans breaking up an outdoor poker game as it got too dark to see – some of the Duke's many sons and grandsons. They swaggered past us into the main keep. Most of them were dressed in Renaissance style, though one wore a Chinese mandarin's robe. Some, the older ones, carried pistols as well as swords.

'I suppose we wait here till the Duke summons us. I hope it won't be long – I'm hungry.' Don Miguel spoke to the Nubian porter: 'If we are called for, we will be in the Wisdom's chamber, or else in the main gaming room.'

The girl shuddered as we walked into the keep. Don Miguel laid a brotherly arm not quite about her waist. 'There, there,' he said. 'We shall find out who thou art, and then we will get thee some wine and dress those hurts.'

'How about the rest of her?' I asked.

'Oh, there is no hurry about that,' he answered.

I felt a tinge of jealousy. Just lately, I'd lost my concubine in a crap game to Ethelwulf the Saxon – I'm not a harem keeper, I believe in one at a time – and had been thinking that this wench would make a nice replacement when she was patched up. But if a man's saved your life – oh, well. She kept looking in my direction anyway.

We went down long, stony corridors, hung with rich tapestries; the electric lights didn't drive away the gloom and chill, somehow. Now and then we'd pass a slave or a warrior, but no one paid any attention to us, in spite of the fact that I was only wearing breeks and that Don Miguel and I were both spattered with red. You got used to almost anything in the Nest.

'I thought the Duke was away this afternoon?' I said.

'He is. Off to survey the Danelaw. I fear me the poor English will be missing more than the Vikings ever took.'

'Well,' I said, 'it's about time for another expedition anyway. The boys are getting restless.' As a warrior third class – technically a musketeer – I had my own responsibilities and command. 'And there ought to be good pickings in Saxon England; the Romano-Britons certainly had some fine things.'

58

Don Miguel shrugged delicately. 'I wish, my friend, thou wouldst not be quite so blunt about it,' he said. 'At any rate, Duke Hugo and his party should be back in time for dinner. They took the Rover out this morning.'

The Normans were often pretty stupid. They could have brought the Rover back within a second of its leaving the Nest, no matter how long they stayed in the Danelaw, but no, they were too superstitious for that, they had to be gone all day. In fact, they'd never done any of the things they could have done with the machine, except just transport themselves and us. Oh, well, it was theirs.

We came to the fork in the hall. One branch of it went off toward the eating and gaming rooms, another to the guarded door beyond which was the Rover's place. We took the third branch, toward the harem. That was guarded too, of course, by slaves whose sizes and strength hadn't been hurt much by Hugo's following the quaint custom of his father, Duke Roger of Sicily; but we didn't go that far. The girl shuddered and moaned as we started up a long stair, into the north tower.

A fancy bronze door at its top opened into the Wisdom's laboratory. I slammed the rather gruesome knocker down, and pretty soon his dusty voice said to come in.

The lab was a huge room, most of it filled with bookshelves; an arched doorway led into a still bigger library. One end of the lab, though, was given over to grimoires, wands, skulls, a stuffed crocodile, bottles and flasks, an alembic, a spectroscope, and an induction furnace, for the Wisdom dabbled in alchemy. He came toward us, his long black robe sweeping the ground, his hairless head bent forward as he peered near-sightedly at us. 'Ah,' he murmured. 'The Cro-Magnon and the hidalgo. What can I do for you, gentlemen?'

I never knew just where the Wisdom came from. Some said he was Victorian English, some said he was Reformation German, but my private guess is Byzantine Greek.

He was here because of his impossibly good memory and scholar's brain. I don't think there ever was a book he couldn't translate or a language he couldn't soon learn, and if you gave him time and references, he'd tell you what you wanted to know about any sector. It saved a lot of firsthand casing of many joints. Then he was our interpreter and teacher of new arrivals. I didn't like him – nobody did – nasty cold-blooded snake – but we could hardly do without that big head of his.

'We got into a fight about this girl,' I said. 'Where's she from and so on?'

He blinked at her, touched her with long skinny fingers, tilted her head this way and that. She moaned again and shrank close to me. Finally he began to talk to her, trying this language and that. At one, she brightened a little, under the dirt and tears, and began to jabber back.

He nodded, rubbing his hands together with a dry scaly sound. 'The daughter of a Babylonian merchant,' he said. 'Seventeen years old, carefully brought up. Some of our men snatched her during Assurbanipal's sack and brought her here. She resisted the attentions of the 'one in gray' as she calls him – a Nazi? – broke out of his house, and ran in terror. Then you rescued her. That is all.'

'The poor child,' said Don Miguel. There was a world of pity on his face. 'I fear I shall burn a long time for belonging to the Nest.'

'What's her name?' I inquired.

'Oh – that.' The Wisdom asked her. 'Inini. Is that important?'

'Yes,' said Don Miguel stiffly. 'She is a human soul, not an animal.'

'There is a difference?' The Wisdom shrugged. 'Was there anything else?'

'No,' I said. 'No, I guess not. Thanks. Let's go get some chow.'

Don Miguel was still biting his lip. He got those guilty

spells now and then, though why he should blame himself, I don't know. He'd been in trouble with the Governor of Mexico when he was located by one of our recruiters, and it was as much as his handsome head was worth to go home.

Now I don't mind a good healthy fight at all. When we took Knossos – yes, we were the ones who did that – or helped in any of several times from Brennus to Charles V, or worked in a hundred other wars, it was good honest battle and we earned our loot. You could say that when we lifted that Prussian city just ahead of the Soviet soldiers, we deserved its loot more than they. And my year of hijacking in Prohibition America – the only time I was ever allowed to carry a real firearm – was just clean fun. But in nearly ten years of the Nest and the Rover, I'd seen a lot of other things that turned my guts. Like this.

'Come on, Inini,' I said. 'Thou'rt among friends now.' She managed a small trembling smile.

We were going out when the door opened before us. Captain Olga Rakitin stood there. Her gun came out as she saw us. 'There ye are,' she said, slowly. Her lips were drawn back, and her face was very white.

'Uh-huh,' I answered. 'What of it? Been looking for us?'

'Yes. Drop that ax! Drop it or I'll shoot!' Her voice rose high.

'What the holy hell—'

'Thou knowest who thou killed, Trebuen?' she asked shrilly.

'Some damn Nazi,' I answered. My spine prickled, looking down the barrel of that gun. It threw explosive shells.

'No. Not a Nazi. Just a young fellow who admired them, liked to strut around in their costume. He didn't rate a gun yet, but his birth – Trebuen, that was Reginald du Arronde! A grandson of the Duke!'

There was a long thundering silence. Then Inini shrank

back with a little scream, not knowing what went on but seeing death here. '*Nombre de Dios!*' muttered Don Miguel. 'Judas priest!' I said.

It felt like a blow in the belly. Duke Hugo had some first-class torturers.

Olga's voice was still wobbly. I'd never heard it that way before. 'Come on,' she said. 'The others will find out any moment. Thou mightest as well come quietly with me.'

I shook myself. My hands were cold and numb, and I had trouble talking. 'No,' I said. 'Nothing doing, iceberg.' I took a step toward her.

'Back!' she screamed. 'Back or I'll shoot!'

'Go ahead,' I answered. 'Think I want to be boiled alongside my own stuffed skin?'

I took another step toward her, very slow and easy. The gun shook. '*Gospody!*' she yelled. 'I *will* shoot, *me Hercule!*'

I sprang then, hitting her low. The gun went off like thunder and tore a hole in the ceiling. We fell with a crash. She hit me with her free hand, cursing in Russian. I wrenched the gun loose. She tried to knee me as I scrambled away. I got up and stood over her. She glared at me through tangled ruddy hair and spat like a wildcat.

Don Miguel had his sword out, the point just touching the Wisdom's throat. 'Make one sound, *señor*,' he purred, 'and I trust you will be able to find a suitable guide into the lower regions.'

The gun felt odd in my hand, lighter than the American rods. Those Martians built them good, though. I went to the door and peered out. A sound of voices came from below.

'They heard,' I grunted. 'Coming up the stairs. Gives merry hell now.'

'Bar the door,' snapped Don Miguel. He pricked the Wisdom's neck a little harder. 'Dog of a heathen, I want rope. Swiftly!'

There was a trampling and clanking outside. The

knocker banged, and fists thumped on the door. 'Go away,' quavered the Wisdom at Don Miguel's sharp insistence. 'I am working. There is nothing here.'

'Open up!' roared a voice. 'We seek Trebuen and de Utrillo for the Duke's justice!'

The Wisdom was pulling lengths of cord from a chest and knotting them together. From the edge of an eye, I saw Inini creep timidly forth and test the knots. Smart girl. She didn't know the score, but she knew we had to take it on the lam quick.

'Open, I say!' bellowed the man outside. Other voices clamored behind him. 'Open or we break in!'

I took my ax up in one hand, held the pistol in the other, and stood waiting. The door shook. I heard the hinge-rivets pulling loose. 'Hurry that rope up, hidalgo,' I said.

'It's not long enough yet – a frightful jump down to the courtyard – More rope, thou devil, or I'll see thy liver!'

The door buckled.

There was a green-gray blur beside me. Olga's fist came down on my arm. I'd forgotten her! She yanked the gun from me and jumped back, gasping. I whirled to face her, and looked down its barrel. Inini screamed. Don Miguel ripped out a cussword that would cost him another year in Purgatory.

I looked at Olga. She was crouched, shaking, a blindness in her eyes. My brain felt cold and clear. I remembered something that had just happened, when I took the gun from her.

'Okay, iceberg, you win,' I said. 'I hope you enjoy watching us fry. That's your style, isn't it?' I said it in French, and used *vous* though we'd been *tu* before like the other warriors.

The door crashed down. A tall Norman burst in, with a tommy gun in his hands and hell in his face. I saw spears and swords behind him.

Olga gave a queer, strangled little noise and shot the Norman in the belly.

He pitched over, his gun clattering at my feet. No time to pick it up. I jumped across his body and split the skull of the Papuan behind him. As he fell, I smashed down the sword of a Tartar. A

Goth stabbed at my back. I brought the ax around backhanded, catching him with the spike.

'Get out!' yelled Olga. 'Get out! I'll hold them!' She fired into the mass of the men. I sent another head jumping free, whirled the ax around, and hit a *Pickelhaube*. My blade glanced off, but bit into the Uhlan's shoulder. A Vandal hollered and swung at me. I caught his blade in the notch I have in my haft, twisted it out of his hands, and cut him down.

They backed away then, snarling at us. There'd be men with guns any second. 'Go, Trebuen,' cried Don Miguel. 'Get free!'

No time to argue with his Spanish pride. I had to be first, because only Olga and I really knew how to leap, and she had the gun. The rope was dangling out the window, knotted to a gargoyle. I took it in my hand and slid into the big darkness below. It scorched my palm.

When its end slipped away, I fell free, not knowing how far. I dropped the ax straight down, relaxed cat-fashion, and hit the stone flags hard enough to knock the wind out of me. About fifteen feet of drop. Staggering up, I yelled to the lighted window.

A dark shape showed against the tower wall – I could barely see it. Inini fell into my arms. *Real* smart girl – she'd snatched up that tommy gun. But it smashed across my mouth.

Olga came down under her own power. We both caught Don Miguel. Ever catch a man in helmet and corselet? I groaned and fumbled around for my ax while Olga shot at the figures peering out the window.

'This way,' I said. 'To the stables.'

We ran around the high keep, toward the rear. The yard wasn't lit, it was all shadows under the stars. But a party of cops was coming around the other side of the donjon. I grabbed the tommy gun from Inini and gave them a burst. Just like hijacking days. A couple of javelins whizzed wickedly near me, then the cops retreated.

To the stables! Their long forms were like hills of night. I opened the door and went in. A slave groom whimpered and shrank into the straw. 'Hold the door, Olga,' I said.

'*Da, kommissar.*' Was it a chuckle in her voice? No time for laughter. I switched on the lights and went down the rows of stalls. The place smelled nice and clean, hay and horses.

But it was good old Iggy and his rank alligator stink I was after. I found him at the end of the stalls, next to the Duke's armored jeep and his one tank. I wished we could take a machine, but the Duke had the keys. Anyway, a dinosaur can go where a tank can't. I thumped Iggy on his stupid snout till he bent over and I got the special saddle on his back.

Olga's gun was barking at the entrance. I heard other shots, rifles. When they brought up the big .50-caliber machine-guns, that was the end of us. Don Miguel had saddled his Arab by the time I was done.

His face was pretty grim. 'I fear we are surrounded,' he said. 'Can we break through?'

'We can try,' I said. 'Olga and I will lead on Iggy. You take Inini.' I wished he could use the tommy gun – it was easy enough, but his stallion would bolt. The brute's eyes were already rolling. Praise be, dinosaurs are too dumb to know fear.

I led Iggy toward the door, where Olga was firing through the crack. 'Hop on, icicle,' I said.

Her face was a dim shadow and a few soft highlights as she turned to me. 'What will we do?' she whispered. 'What will we do but die?'

'I don't know. Let's find out.' I scrambled into the saddle while she slammed and bolted the door. She jumped up in front of me; the seat was big enough for that, and we crouched there waiting.

The door shook and cracked and went down. 'Whoop!' I yelled. 'Giddap, boy!'

Iggy straightened, almost taking my head off as he went through the door. Olga had holstered her pistol and grabbed the tommy gun. She sprayed the mob before us. Iggy plowed right through them, trampling any that didn't get out of the way in time. Spears and swords and arrows bit at him, but he didn't mind, and his tall form shielded us.

Across the courtyard! Iggy broke into an earthshaking run as I spurred him with the ax spike. Don Miguel's horse galloped beside us. The moon was just starting to rise, shadows and white light weird between the high walls. A machine-gun opened up, hunting for us with fingers of fire.

They were closing the portcullis as we reached the main gate. Don Miguel darted ahead, the iron teeth clashing behind him. 'Hang on!' I yelled. 'Hang on! Go it, Iggy!'

The dinosaur grunted as he hit the barrier. The shock damn near threw me loose. I jammed my feet into the stirrups and clutched Olga to me. A ragged piece of iron furrowed my scalp. Then the portcullis tore loose and Iggy walked over it and on down the Street of St Mark.

'This way!' cried Don Miguel, wheeling about. 'Out of the Nest!'

We shook the ground on our way. Turning at Zulu House – Lobengula's exiled warriors still preferred barracks – we came out on Broadway and went down it to the Street of the Fishing Cat. Across Moloch Plaza, through an alley where Iggy scraped the walls, through an orchard that scattered like matchwood, and then we were out and away.

The Oligocene night was warm around us. A wet wind blew from across the great river, smell of reeds and muck and green water, the strong wild perfume of flowers that died with the glaciers. The low moon was orange-colored, huge on the rim of the world. I heard a nimravus screeching out in the dark, and the grunt and splash of some big mammal. Grass whispered around our mount's legs. Looking behind me, I saw the castle all one blaze of light. It was the only building with electricity – the rest of them huddled in darkness, showing red and yellow fire-gleams. But there were torches bobbing in the streets.

Don Miguel edged closer to me. His face was a blur under the moonlit shimmer of his helmet. 'Where do we go now, Trebuen?' he asked.

We had gotten away. Somehow, in some crazy fashion, we'd cut our way out. But before long, the Normans would be after us with dogs. They could trail us anywhere.

Swim the river – with the kind of fish they had there? I'd sooner take a few more Normans to hell with me.

'I think—' Olga's voice was as cool as it had always been. 'I think they will not start hunting us before dawn. We are too dangerous in the dark. Perhaps we can put a good distance between in the meantime.'

'Not too good,' I answered. 'The horse is carrying double, and Iggy just won't go very far; he'll lie down and go on strike after a few more miles. But yeah, I do think we have a breather. Let's rest.'

We got off, tethered our mounts to a clump of trees, and sat down. The grass was cool and damp, and the earth smelled rich. Inini crept into my arms like a frightened little kid, and I held her close without thinking much about it. Mostly, I was drawing air into my lungs, looking at the stars and the rising moon, and thinking that life was pretty good. I'd be sorry to leave it.

Don Miguel spoke out of the shadow that was his face. 'Señorita Olga,' he said, 'we owe our lives to thy kindness. Thou hast a Christian soul.'

'*Tchort!*' She spoke coldly. I sat watching the moonlight shimmer on her hair. 'I've had enough of the Nest, that's all.'

I smiled to myself, just a little. I knew better, though maybe she didn't herself.

'How long hast thou been with us, iceberg?' I asked. 'Five years, isn't it? Why didst thou enlist?'

She shrugged. 'I was in trouble,' she said. 'I spoke my mind too freely. The Martian government resented it. I stole a spaceship and got to Earth, where I was not especially welcome either. While I was dodging Martian agents, I met one of Hugo's recruiters. What else could I do but join? I didn't like the 22nd Century much anyway.'

I could understand that. And it wasn't strange she'd been picked up, out of all the reaches of time. Recruiters visited places where there were pirates and warriors, or else where there was an underworld. Olga would naturally have had something to do with the latter, she'd have had no choice with Soviet assassins after her. And she'd be wanted here for her technical knowledge, which was scarce in the Nest.

'Has the Duke or his men ever explored beyond thy century?' asked Don Miguel idly. A proper caballero wouldn't be thinking of his own coming death, he'd hold polite chit-chat going till the end.

'No, I think not,' she answered. 'They would be afraid that the true owners of the Rover would detect them. It is in the anarchic periods where they can operate safely.'

I wondered, not for the first time, what those builders were like, and where they were from. It must have been a pretty gentle, guileless culture, by all accounts. Some twenty historians and sociologists, making the mistake of dropping in on the court of Duke Roger of Sicily. But even though Roger himself had been off in Italy at the time, they might have foreseen that one of his illegitimate sons, young Hugo, would suspect these strangers weren't all they seemed. Just because a man is ignorant of science, he isn't necessarily stupid, but the time travelers overlooked that – which was costly for them when Hugo and some of his bravos grabbed them, tortured the facts out of them, and knocked them off. Of course, once that had happened, anyone could have predicted that those few Normans would take the Rover and go happily off to plunder through all space – on Earth, at least – and all time – short of some era where the Builders could find them; and that they'd slowly build up their forces by recruiting through the ages, until now—

'I wonder if the Builders ever *will* find us,' mused Don Miguel.

'Hardly,' said Olga. 'Or they'd have been here before now. It seems pretty silly to hide out way back in the American Oligocene. But I must say the operations are shrewdly planned. No anachronistic weapons used, no possible historical record of our appearances – oh, yes.'

'This era has a good climate, and no humans to give trouble,' I said. 'That's probably why Hugo picked it.'

Inini murmured wearily. Her dark hair flowed softly over my arms as she stirred. Poor kid. Poor scared kid, snatched out of home and time into horror. 'Look,' I said, 'are we just going to sit and take it? Can't we think of a way to hit back where it'll really hurt?'

It was funny how fast we'd all switched loyalties. None of us had ever much liked Duke Hugo or the company he kept, but the bandit's life had been a high and handsome one. In many ways, those had been good years. Only now – It was, somehow, more than the fact Hugo was out to fry our gizzards. That was just the little nudge which had overturned some kind of mountain inside us.

Olga spoke like a machine. 'We are three – well, four, I suppose – possessed of two working guns, a sword, an ax, a horse, and a dinosaur. Against us are a good thousand fighting men, of whom a hundred or so possess firearms. Perhaps a few of our friends might swing to our side, out of comradeship or to sack the castle, but still the odds are ridiculous.' She chuckled, a low pleasant sound in the murmuring night. 'And as a Martian, I am Dostoyevskian enough to enjoy the fact a trifle.'

Inini whispered something and raised her face. I bent my head and brushed her lips. Poor little slave! I wished she'd been mine from the start – everything would have been so much simpler.

69

Slaves!

I sat bolt upright, spilling Inini to the grass. By the horns of Pan and the eye of Odin – slaves!

'Five thousand slaves!'

'Eh?' Don Miguel came over to pick up the girl. 'Thou'rt most unknightly at times, *amigo* . . . There, there, my little partridge, all is well, be calm . . .'

Olga got it right away. I heard her fist slam the ground. 'By Lenin! I think thou'st got it, Trebuen!'

Five thousand slaves, mostly male, penned up in a wire stockade, not very heavily guarded – swiftly, we settled the plan of action. I showed Inini how to operate the tommy gun; she caught on fast and laughed savagely in the dark. I hoped she wouldn't shoot the wrong people. Then we mounted and trotted back toward the Nest, changing women passengers this time.

The moon had now cleared the eastern forests and was flooding the plain. It was a white, cold, unreal light, dripping from the grass, spattering the trees, gleaming off water and Don Miguel's armor. I swore at it. Damn the moon, anyway! We needed darkness.

We swung far around the Nest, to approach it from the side of the slave pens. Luckily, there was a lot of orchard there. Trees grew fast in the Oligocene, these were tall ones. Twigs and leaves brushed my face, branches creaked and snapped as Iggy went through them, speckles of light broke the thick shadows. I halted on the edge of the shelter and looked across a hundred feet toward the pens. The castle beyond was black against the high stars, most of its lights turned off again. The hunt for us must have died down in the hour or two we'd been gone.

The pens were a long double row of wooden barracks, fenced in with charged wire. There was a wooden guard tower, about thirty feet high, on each side, with searchlights and machine-guns on top; but there'd only be a few men on each. Olga slid off the horse – her gun would frighten it too much – but Inini stayed with me, sitting in front and cradling her weapon. Nothing moved. It was all black and white and silence there under the moon. I licked my lips; they felt like sandpaper, and my heart was thumping. Two minutes from now, we might be so much cold meat.

'Okay, Iggy.' I nudged him with my heels, trying to hold my voice hard. 'Let's go. *Giddap!*'

He broke into that lumbering run of his. The shock of his footfalls jarred back into me. Someone yelled, far and faint. The searchlights glared out, grabbing after me. I heard the machine-gun begin stuttering, and crouched low behind Iggy's neck. He grunted as the slugs hit him. Then he got mad.

We hit the tower full on, and I nearly pitched out of the saddle. Wood thundered and crashed around me. The machine-gunners screamed and tried to drag their weapon over to the parapet. Iggy heaved against the walls; they buckled, and the lights went out. Then the tower caved in around us. Something hit me, stars exploded, and I hung on in a whirling darkness.

Iggy was trampling the beams underfoot. Wires snapped, and the juice in them blazed and crackled. One of the guards, still on his feet, tried to run for help. Inini cut him down.

The gun on the other side of the stockade began hammering. I shook my head, trying to clear it. 'Go get 'em, Iggy! Goddam thee, go get that gunner!' He was too busy stamping on the tower we'd just demolished to notice. His breath was hissing as he wrecked it.

Olga dashed past us on foot, shooting at the other post. She was hard to see in that tricky light. The tracer bullets marked the gun for her. Bullets were sleeting around me now. A few slaves began coming out of the barracks, yelling their panic.

Iggy finally made up his stupid mind that the slugs still

hitting him now and then were from the other tall shape. He turned and ran to do battle. Inini fired ahead of us as we charged. Olga had to jump to get out of the way. Iggy started pulling down the tower.

Don Miguel was shouting to the slaves as they boiled out of their houses. 'Forward, comrades! On to liberty! Kill your oppressors!' They gaped at his sword. God! Wouldn't they ever catch on?

Men must be pouring from the Nest now. I kicked and cursed, trying to face my idiotic mount around to meet them. The tower began crumpling. It went down in a slow heave of timbers and splinters. Don Miguel was still haranguing the slaves. Trouble was, about the only ones who knew much Norman French had been here so long the spirit was beaten out of them. The newcomers, who might fight, didn't know what he was talking of.

A horn blew from the castle hill. Turning my face from where Iggy stood over the ruins, I saw metal flash in the moonlight. Hoofs rolled their noise through the ground. Cavalry! And if the Duke got his armored vehicles going—

Olga darted almost under Iggy's feet, to where the machine-gun lay on its splintered platform. She heaved it back into position and crouched over it. As the horsemen entered the stockade, she cut loose.

They broke, screaming. Huns and Tartars, mostly, with some mounted Normans and others. Bullets whined from their side, badly aimed in the confusion.

I heard a slow drawl from down under me. Looking, I saw a tall man in the tattered leavings of a gray uniform. 'So that's the idee,' he called. 'Whah, stranger, you should'a said so the fuhst time.'

'Who the hell are you?' I found time to gasp in English.

'Captain Jebel Morrison, late o' the Red Horse Cavalry, Confederate States of America, at yo' suhvice. The buzzahds grabbed me an' mah boys when we was on patrol in Tennessee – All right, y'all!' He turned back to the milling, muttering slaves and shouted: 'Kill the Yankees!'

There was a scattering of rebel yells, and some other men came running out toward him. They snatched swords and spears from the riders we'd cut down, let out that blood-freezing screech once more, and trotted toward the entrance of the pen.

'So 'tis smite the Papists, eh?' roared an English voice. 'Truly the hand of the Lord is on us!' And a bull-necked Roundhead darted after the Southerners.

'*Allah akbar!*' – '*Vive la republique!*' – '*Ho la, Odin!*' – '*St George for merrie England!*' '*Ave, Caesar!*' – The mob spirit caught them, and the huge dark mass of men surged forth toward the Nest. About half the slaves, the rest were still afraid, and they were unarmed and unprotected – but God, how they hated!

Don Miguel galloped forth to put himself at their head. I cursed Iggy and beat him on the snout till he turned around and lumbered after them. Inini laughed shrilly and waved her tommy gun in the air. We broke out of the pen and rolled in one swarm against the enemy.

Somebody reached up to touch my leg. I saw Olga trotting beside me; she'd grabbed one of those Hunnish ponies stampeding around the pen. 'I didn't know thou wert a cowboy!' I yelled at her.

'Neither did I!' Her teeth gleamed in the moonlight as she laughed back at me. 'But I'd better learn fast!' She snubbed in the pony's neck as it skittered. I suppose her interplanetary flying had trained nerve and muscle—

It must have been bare minutes from the time we first charged the stockade. Only the castle guard had been ready to fight us. But now as we entered the streets, going down long white lanes of moon between the black forms of houses, I saw the bandits rallying. Shots began to crack again. Men crumpled in our ranks. We had to hit them before they got organized.

We went over one thin line of Romans with a rush, grabbing

up their weapons. Circling the castle hill, we began mounting it on the side of the broken portcullis. Men were streaming from the houses and dashing toward our host. It was a bad light for shooting guns or arrows, but plenty bright enough for a sword.

Inini and Olga blazed at them as they came up the Street of St Mark. No one could miss a bunch of men, and both sides were having heavy losses; but individuals, like myself, were hard to hit. I saw the attackers recoil and churn about, waiting for reinforcements. We struggled on up the hill, in the face of gunfire from the castle.

The bandits behind us were piling up now, into a solid wall of armed men across the street. I lifted my voice and bellowed: 'Who wants to overthrow the castle?'

They hesitated, swaying back and forth. Suddenly a shout rose. 'By Tyr! I do!' A couple of men pitched aside as Thorkel the Berserk darted toward us. Inini fired at him. I slapped her gun aside. 'Not him, wench!'

Hoofs clattered on the street. I saw moonlight like water on the lacquered leather breastplates of Belgutai's Mongol troop. *God help us now*, I thought, and then the Mongols crashed into the other bandits. Belgutai had always been a good friend of mine.

Steel hammered on steel as they fought. I knew that a lot of these wolves would switch to our side if they thought we had a fair chance of winning. Hugo had trained them to steal anything that wasn't welded down, and then stuffed his own home with loot – a mistake, that! But we had to take the castle before we could count on turncoats to help us.

We were up under the walls now, out of reach of the tower guns, but our numbers were fearfully reduced. The slaves weren't running forth so fast now, they were beginning to be afraid. I jabbed Iggy with my ax, driving him forward against the gate and its rifle-armed defenders. We hit them like a tornado, and they fled.

I was hardly in the courtyard before a new bellowing lifted. The tank was coming around the keep. It was a light one, 1918 model, but it could easily stop our whole force. For a minute, my world caved in around me.

The tank's machine-guns opened up on Iggy. He'd already been wounded, and this must have hurt. He hissed and charged. I saw what was coming, dropped my ax, and jumped to the ground. Inini followed me. We hit the pavement and rolled over and bounced up again.

Iggy was crawling on top of the tank, trying to rip steel apart. His blood streamed over the metal, he was dying, but the poor brave brute was too dumb to know it. The tank growled, backing up. Iggy slapped his big stiff tail into the treads. The tank choked to a halt. Its cannon burped at us. The shell exploded against the gateway arch. Iggy stamped a foot down on the barrel and it twisted. Someone opened the turret and threw out a grenade. It burst against Iggy's throat. He got his taloned forepaws into the turret and began pulling things into chunks. Even a dying dinosaur is no safe playmate.

There was fighting all around the courtyard. A lot of the men with guns must have been disposed of by now. Those of the slaves who knew how to use firearms were grabbing them out of the hands of bandits who'd been mobbed, and turning them on the Normans. The rest of our boys were seizing axes, spears, swords, and chopping loose. Captain Morrison had somehow – God knows how – managed to hold them more or less together. The Normans and their cohorts charging out of the keep joined forces and hit that little army. It became hand-to-hand, and murder.

I was only hazily aware of all that. Olga came running up to me as I got on my feet. Her pony must have been shot from under her. 'What now?' she cried. 'What should we do?'

'Get to the Rover,' I said. 'It's the only way – they're better armed than we, they'll finish us unless—'

Don Miguel was fighting a mounted knight. He cut him down and clattered over to us as we and Inini ran for the keep. 'With ye, my friends,' he cried gaily. I imagine this work was taking a lot of guilt off his conscience. Maybe that was one reason why some of the other bandits, down in the street, had thrown in with us.

We ran along the hallway. It was empty except for some terrified women. Around a bend of the forbidden corridor was the Rover. I skidded to a halt. Machine-gunners watched over it. 'Gimme that!' I snatched the tommy gun from Inini and burst around the corner, firing. The two Mamelukes dropped.

The door was locked. I took my ax this time, and battered at it. Wood splintered before me. I turned at Olga's yell and the bark of her gun. A party of Normans, a good dozen of them, was attacking. I saw Duke Hugo's burly white-haired form in the lead. They must have heard the racket and—

They were on us before we could use our guns to stop them. A sword whistled above my head as I ducked. I reached up and cut at the hands. As the man fell against me, screaming, I flung him into another chain-mailed figure. They went down with a clash. Two-handed, I bashed in a skull. Hugo had a revolver almost in my belly. I slewed the ax around and knocked it from him with the flat of the weapon. His sword hissed free before I could brain him. It raked me down the side as I dodged. I smashed at his unhelmeted head, but he turned the blow.

'*Haro!*' he yelled. Edged metal whined down against my haft. I twisted the ax, forcing his blade aside. My left fist jumped out into his face. He staggered back, and I killed him.

Don Miguel's horse was pulled down and slain, but he was laying merrily around him. We cleared a space between us. Then Olga and Inini could use their guns.

I went back to the door and smashed it in. We broke into the high chamber. The Rover lay there, a tapered hundred-foot cylinder. Inside, I knew it was mostly empty space, with a few simple dials and studs. I'd watched it being operated.

Don Miguel grabbed my arm as I entered. 'We can't leave our comrades out there, Trebuen!' he gasped. 'As soon as the Normans get organized, it will be slaughter.'

'I know,' I said. 'Come on inside, though, all of you.'

When I turned a certain dial, the Rover moved. There was no sense of it within us, only a glowing light told us we were on our way through time. A thousand years in the future.

Hugo had never checked his own tomorrows, and wouldn't let anyone else do it. That was understandable, I guess, especially if you were a medieval man. I couldn't resist looking out. The chamber was still there, but it was dark and still, thick with dust, and some animal which had made its lair here scrambled away in alarm. The castle was empty. In a million years or so of rain and wind, and finally the glaciers grinding down over it, no trace would be left.

I drew a shuddering sigh into the stillness. But I knew I was going back. We'd left a lot of friends back there in the mess of the Nest. And besides, I'd always had an idea about the Rover. Those Normans had been too superstitious to try it, but it should work. Don Miguel swore, but agreed. And Olga helped me work out the details. Then we took off.

The verniers were marked in strange numerals, but you could read them all right, once you'd figured them out. And the Rover was accurate to a second or less. We jumped back to within one second of our departure time.

The rest of the fight is blurred. I don't *want* to remember the next twenty minutes – or twenty-four hours, depending on how you look at it. We stepped out of the machine. We turned and went quickly from the chamber. As we reached its door, the machine appeared again, next to itself, and three dim figures came out. I looked away from my own face. Soon there was a mob of ourselves there.

We stuck together, running out and firing. Twenty minutes later, each time we finished, we'd dart back to the Rover, jump it into the future, and return within one second and some feet of our last departure point. There were a good three hundred of us, all brought to the same time, approximately. And in a group like that, we had fire power. It was too much for the enemy. Screaming about witchcraft, they finally threw down their weapons and ran. I hate to think about seventy-five of myself acting as targets at the same time, though. It would only have needed one bullet.

But twenty minutes after the last trip, our messed-up time lines straightened out, and the four of us were all there – victors.

I stood on the castle walls, looking over the Nest as sunrise climbed into the sky. Places were burning here and there, and bodies were strewn across the ground. The bandits who'd fought with us or surrendered were holed up in a tower, guarding themselves against the slaves who were running wild as they celebrated their freedom. I only allowed firearms to those people I could trust, so now I was king of the Nest.

Olga came to me where I stood. The damp morning wind ruffled her hair, and her eyes were bright in spite of the weariness in us all. She'd changed her ragged uniform for a Grecian dress, and its white simplicity was beautiful on her.

We stood side by side for a while, not speaking. Finally I shook my head. 'I don't feel too happy about this, iceberg,' I said. 'In its own way, the Nest was something glorious.'

'Was?' she asked softly.

'Sure. We can't start it up again – at least I can't, after this night. I've seen enough bloodshed for the rest of my life. We'll have to organize things here, and return everyone to whatever time they pick; not all of them will want to go home, I suppose. I don't think I will. Life with The Men would be sort of – limited, after this.'

She nodded. 'I can do without my own century too,' she said. 'It could be fun to keep on exploring in time for awhile, till I find some era I really want to settle down in.'

I looked at her, and slowly the darkness lifted from me. 'Till *we* do,' I said.

'We?' She frowned. 'Don't get ideas, Sir Caveman.' Her lips trembled. 'Thou and th-th-thy Babylonian wench!'

'Oh, Inini's sweet,' I grinned. 'Don Miguel was giving her the old line when I saw them last, and she seemed to enjoy it. But she'd be kind of dull for me.'

'Of all the insufferable, conceited—!'

'Look,' I said patiently, 'thou couldst easily have shot me when I first grabbed for thy gun. But underneath, thou didn't want to – be honest, now! – so thou missed. And I don't think thou changed sides a little later because of a sudden attack of conscience, any more than the rest of us, iceberg.' I switched into Americanese, with Elizabethan overtones. 'C'mere, youse, and let me clutch thee!'

She did.

Eutopia

'Gif thit nafn!'

The Danska words barked from the car radio as a jet whine cut across the hum of motor and tires. 'Identify yourself!' Iason Philippou cast a look skyward through the bubbletop. He saw a strip of blue between two ragged green walls where pine forest lined the road. Sunlight struck off the flanks of the killer machine up there. It wailed, came about, and made a circle over him.

Sweat started cold from his armpits and ran down his ribs. *I must not panic*, he thought in a corner of his brain. *May the God help me now*. But it was his training he invoked. Psychosomatics: control the symptoms, keep the breath steady, command the pulse to slow, and the fear of death becomes something you can handle. He was young, and thus had much to lose. But the philosophers of Eutopia schooled well the children given into their care. You will be a man, they had told him, and the pride of humanity is that we are not bound by instinct and reflex; we are free because we can master ourselves.

He couldn't pass as an ordinary citizen (no, they said mootman here) of Norland. If nothing else, his Hellenic accent was too strong. But he might fool yonder pilot, for just a few minutes, into believing he was from some other domain of this history. He roughened his tone, as a partial disguise, and assumed the expected arrogance.

'Who are you? What do you want?'

'Runolf Einarsson, captain in the hird of Ottar Thorkelsson, the Lawman of Norland. I pursue one who has brought feud on his own head. Give me your name.'

Runolf, Iason thought. *Why, yes, I remember you well, dark and erect with the Tyrker side of your heritage, but you have blue eyes that came long ago from Thule.* In that detached part of him which stood aside watching: *No, here I scramble my histories. I would call the autochthons Erythrai, and you call the country of your European ancestors Danarik.*

'I hight Xipec, a trader from Meyaco,' he said. He did not slow down. The border was not many stadia away, so furiously had he driven through the night since he escaped from the Lawman's castle. He had small hope of getting that far, but each turn of the wheels brought him nearer. The forest was blurred with his speed.

'If so be, of course I am sorry to halt you,' Runolf's voice crackled. 'Call the Lawman and he will send swift gild for the overtreading of your rights. Yet I must have you stop and leave your car, so I may turn the farseer on your face.'

'Why?' Another second or two gained.

'There was a visitor from Homeland' – Europe – 'who came to Ernvik. Ottar Thorkelsson guested him freely. In return, he did a thing that only his death can made clean again. Rather than meet Ottar on the Valfield, he stole a car, the same make as yours, and fled.'

'Would it not serve to call him a nithing before the folk?' *I have learned this much of their barbaric customs, anyhow!*

'Now that is a strange thing for a Meyacan to say. Stop at once and get out, or I open fire.'

Iason realized his teeth were clenched till they hurt. How in Hades could a man remember the hundreds of little regions, each with its own ways, into which the continent lay divided? Westfall was a more fantastic jumble than all Earth in that history where they called the place America. *Well,* he thought, *now we discover what the odds are of my hearing it named Eutopia again.*

'Very well,' he said. 'You leave me no choice. But I shall indeed want compensation for this insult.'

He braked as slowly as he dared. The road was a hard

black ribbon before him, slashed through an immensity of trees. He didn't know if these woods had ever been logged. Perhaps so, when white men first sailed through the Pentalimne (calling them the Five Seas) to found Ernvik where Duluth stood in America and Lykopolis in Eutopia. In those days Norland had spread mightily across the lake country. But then came wars with Dakotas and Magyars, to set a limit; and the development of trade – more recently of synthetics – enabled the people to use their hinterland for the hunting they so savagely loved. Three hundred years could re-establish a climax forest.

Sharply before him stood the vision of this area as he had known it at home: ordered groves and gardens, villages planned for beauty as well as use, lithe brown bodies on the athletic fields, music under moonlight . . . Even America the Dreadful was more human than a wilderness.

They were gone, lost in the multiple dimensions of space-time, he was alone and death walked the sky. *And no self-pity, you idiot! Spend energy for survival.*

The car stopped, hard by the road edge. Iason gathered his thews, opened the door, and sprang.

Perhaps the radio behind him uttered a curse. The jet slewed around and swooped like a hawk. Bullets sleeted at his heels.

Then he was in among the trees. They roofed him with sun-speckled shadow. Their trunks stood in massive masculine strength, their branches breathed fragrance a woman might envy. Fallen needles softened his foot-thud, a thrush warbled, a light wind cooled his cheeks. He threw himself beneath the shelter of one bole and lay in it gasping with a heartbeat which all but drowned the sinister whistle above.

Presently it went away. Runolf must have called back to his lord. Ottar would fly horses and hounds to this place, the only way of pursuit. But Iason had a few hours' grace.

After that – He rallied his training, sat up and thought. If

Socrates, feeling the hemlock's chill, could speak wisdom to the young men of Athens, Iason Philippou could assess his own chances. For he wasn't dead yet.

He numbered his assets. A pistol of the local slug-throwing type; a compass; a pocketful of gold and silver coins; a cloak that might double as a blanket, above the tunic-trousers-boots costume of central Westfall. And himself, the ultimate instrument. His body was tall and broad – together with fair hair and short nose, an inheritance from Gallic ancestors – and had been trained by men who won wreaths at the Olympeion. His mind, his entire nervous system, counted for still more. The pedagogues of Eutopia had made logic, semantic consciousness, perspective as natural to him as breathing; his memory was under such control that he had no need of a map; despite one calamitous mistake, he knew he was trained to deal with the most outlandish manifestations of the human spirit.

And, yes, before all else, he had reason to live. It went beyond any blind wish to continue an identity; that was only something the DNA molecule had elaborated in order to make more DNA molecules. He had his beloved to return to. He had his country: Eutopia, the Good Land, which his people had founded two thousand years ago on a new continent, leaving behind the hatreds and horrors of Europe, taking along the work of Aristotle, and writing at last in their Syntagma, 'The national purpose is the attainment of universal sanity.'

Iason Philippou was bound home.

He rose and started walking south.

That was on Tetrade, which his hunters called Onsdag. Some thirty-six hours later, he knew he was not in Pentade but near sunset of Thorsdag. For he lurched through the wood, mouth filled with mummy dust, belly a cavern of emptiness, knees shaking beneath him, flies a thundercloud about the sweat dried on his skin, and heard the distant belling of hounds.

A horn responded, long brazen snarl through the leaf arches. They had gotten his scent, he could not outrun horsemen and he would not see stars again.

One hand dropped to his gun. *I'll take a couple of them with me . . . No.* He was still a Hellene, who did not kill uselessly, not even barbarians who meant to slay him because he had broken a taboo of theirs. *I will stand under an open sky, take their bullets, and go down into darkness remembering Eutopia and all my friends and Niki whom I love.*

Realization came, dimly, that he had left the pine forest and was in a second growth of beeches. Light gilded their leaves and caressed the slim white trunks. And what was that growl up ahead?

He stopped. A portal might remain. He had driven himself near collapse; but the organism has a reserve which the fully integrated man may call upon. From consciousness he abolished the sound of dogs, every ache and exhaustion. He drew breath after breath of air, noting its calm and purity, visualizing the oxygen atoms that poured through his starved tissues. He made the heartbeat quit racketing, go over to a deep slow pulse; he tensed and relaxed muscles until each functioned smoothly again; pain ceased to feed on itself and died away; despair gave place to calm and calculation. He trod forth.

Plowlands rolled southward before him, their young grain vivid in the light that slanted gold from the west. Not far off stood a cluster of farm buildings, long, low, and peak-roofed. Chimney smoke stained heaven. But his eyes went first to the man closer by. The fellow was cultivating with a tractor. Though the dielectric motor had been invented in this world, its use had not yet spread this far north, and gasoline fumes caught at Iason's nostrils. He had thought that stench one of the worst abominations in America – that hogpen they called Los Angeles! – but now it came to him clean and strong, for it was his hope.

84

The driver saw him, halted, and unshipped a rifle. Iason approached with palms held forward in token of peace. The driver relaxed. He was a typical Magyar: burly, high in the cheekbones, his beard braided, his tunic colorfully embroidered. *So I did cross the border!* Iason exulted. *I'm out of Norland and into the Voivodate of Dakoty.*

Before they sent him here, the anthropologists of the Parachronic Research Institute had of course given him an electrochemical inculcation in the principal languages of Westfall. (Pity they hadn't been more thorough about teaching him the mores. But then, he had been hastily recruited for the Norland post after Megasthenes' accidental death; and it was assumed that his experience in America gave him special qualifications for this history, which was also non-Alexandrine; and, to be sure, the whole object of missions like his was to learn just how societies on the different Earths did vary.) He formed the Ural-Altaic words with ease:

'Greeting to you. I come as a supplicant.'

The farmer sat quiet, tense, looking down on him and listening to the dogs far off in the forest. His rifle stayed ready. 'Are you an outlaw?' he asked.

'Not in this realm, freeman.' (Still another name and concept for 'citizen'!) 'I was a peaceful trader from Home-land, visiting Lawman Ottar Thorkelsson in Ernvik. His anger fell upon me, so great that he broke sacred hospitality and sought the life of me, his guest. Now his hunters are on my trail. You hear them yonder.'

'Norlanders? But this is Dakoty.'

Iason nodded. He let his teeth show, in the grime and stubble of his face. 'Right. They've entered your country without so much as a by-your-leave. If you stand idle, they'll ride onto your freehold and slay me, who asks your help.'

The farmer hefted his gun. 'How do I know you speak truth?'

'Take me to the Voivode,' Iason said. 'Thus you keep

both the law and your honor.' Very carefully, he unholstered his pistol and offered it butt foremost. 'I am forever your debtor.'

Doubt, fear and anger pursued each other across the face of the man on the tractor. He did not take the weapon. Iason waited. *If I've read him correctly, I've gained some hours of life. Perhaps more. That will depend on the Voivode. My whole chance lies in using their own barbarism – their division into petty states, their crazy idea of honor, their fetish of property and privacy – to harness them.*

If I fail, then I shall die like a civilized man. That they cannot take away from me.

'The hounds have winded you. They'll be here before we can escape,' said the Magyar uneasily.

Relief made Iason dizzy. He fought down the reaction and said: 'We can take care of them for a time. Let me have some gasoline.'

'Ah . . . thus!' The other man chuckled and jumped to earth. 'Good thinking, stranger. And thanks, by the way. Life has been dull hereabouts for too many years.'

He had a spare can of fuel on his machine. They lugged it back along Iason's trail for a considerable distance, dousing soil and trees. If that didn't throw the pack off, nothing would.

'Now, hurry!' The Magyar led the way at a trot.

His farmstead was built around an open courtyard. Sweet scents of hay and livestock came from the barns. Several children ran forth to gape. The wife shooed them back inside, took her husband's rifle, and mounted guard at the door with small change of expression.

Their house was solid, roomy, aesthetically pleasing if you could accept the unrestrained tapestries and painted pillars. Above the fireplace was a niche for a family altar. Though most people in Westfall had left myth long behind them, these peasants still seemed to adore the Triple God Odin-Attila-Manitou. But the man went to a sophisticated radiophone. 'I don't have an aircraft myself,' he said, 'but I can get one.'

Iason sat down to wait. A girl neared him shyly with a beaker of beer and a slab of cheese on coarse dark bread. 'Be you guest-holy,' she said.

'May my blood be yours,' Iason answered by rote. He managed to take the refreshment not quite like a wolf.

The farmer came back. 'A few more minutes,' he said. 'I am Arpad, son of Kalman.'

'Iason Philippou.' It seemed wrong to give a false name. The hand he clasped was hard and warm.

'What made you fall afoul of old Ottar?' Arpad inquired.

'I was lured,' Iason said bitterly. 'Seeing how free the unwed women were—'

'Ah, indeed. They're a lickerish lot, those Danskar. Nigh as shameless as Tyrkers.' Arpad got pipe and tobacco pouch off a shelf. 'Smoke?'

'No, thank you.' *We don't degrade ourselves with drugs in Eutopia.*

The hounds drew close. Their chant broke into confused yelps. Horns shrilled. Arpad stuffed his pipe as coolly as if this were a show. 'How they must be swearing!' he grinned. 'I'll give the Danskar credit for being poets, also in their oaths. And brave men, to be sure. I was up that way ten years back, when Voivode Bela sent people to help them after the floods they'd suffered. I saw them laugh as they fought the wild water. And then, their sort gave us a hard time in the old wars.'

'Do you think there will ever be wars again?' Iason asked. Mostly he wanted to avoid speaking further of his troubles. He wasn't sure how his host might react.

'Not in Westfall. Too much work to do. If young blood isn't cooled enough by a duel now and then, why, there're wars to hire out for, among the barbarians overseas. Or else the planets. My oldest boy champs to go there.'

Iason recalled that several realms further south were

pooling their resources for astronautical work. Being approximately at the technological level of the American history, and not required to maintain huge military or social programs, they had put a base on the moon and sent expeditions to Ares. In time, he supposed, they would do what the Hellenes had done a thousand years ago, and make Aphrodite into a new Earth. But would they have a true civilization – be rational men in a rationally planned society – by then? Wearily, he doubted it.

A roar outside brought Arpad to his feet. 'There's your wagon,' he said. 'Best you go. Red Horse will fly you to Varady.'

'The Danskar will surely come here soon,' Iason worried.

'Let them,' Arpad shrugged. 'I'll alert the neighborhood, and they're not so stupid that they won't know I have. We'll hold a slanging match, and then I'll order them off my land. Farewell, guest.'

'I . . . I wish I could repay your kindness.'

'Bah! Was fun. Also, a chance to be a man before my sons.'

Iason went out. The aircraft was a helicopter – they hadn't discovered gravitics here – piloted by a taciturn young autochthon. He explained that he was a stock-breeder, and that he was conveying the stranger less as a favor to Arpad than as an answer to the Norlander impudence of entering Dakoty unbidden. Iason was just as happy to be free of conversation.

The machine whirred aloft. As it drove south he saw clustered hamlets, the occasional hall of some magnate, otherwise only rich undulant plains. They kept the population within bounds in Westfall as in Eutopia. But not because they knew that men need space and clean air, Iason thought. No, they acted from greed on behalf of the reified family. A father did not wish to divide his possessions among many children.

The sun went down and a nearly full moon climbed huge

and pumpkin-colored over the eastern rim of the world. Iason sat back, feeling the engine's throb in his bones, almost savoring his fatigue, and watched. No sign of the lunar base was visible. He must return home before he could see the moon glitter with cities.

And home was more than infinitely remote. He could travel to the farthest of those stars which had begun twinkling forth against purple dusk – were it possible to exceed the speed of light – and not find Eutopia. It lay sundered from him by dimensions and destiny. Nothing but the warpfields of a parachronion might take him across the time lines to his own.

He wondered about the why. That was an empty speculation, but his tired brain found relief in childishness. Why had the God willed that time branch and rebranch, enormous, shadowy, bearing universes like the Yggdrasil of Danskar legend? Was it so that man could realize every potentiality there was in him?

Surely not. So many of them were utter horror.

Suppose Alexander the Conqueror had not recovered from the fever that smote him in Babylon. Suppose, instead of being chastened thereby, so that he spent the rest of a long life making firm the foundations of his empire – suppose he had died?

Well, it *did* happen, and probably in more histories than not. There the empire went down in mad-dog wars of succession. Hellas and the Orient broke apart. Nascent science withered away into metaphysics, eventually outright mysticism. A convulsed Mediterranean world was swept up piecemeal by the Romans: cold, cruel, uncreative, claiming to be the heirs of Hellas even as they destroyed Corinth. A heretical Jewish prophet founded a mystery cult which took root everywhere, for men despaired of this life. And that cult knew not the name of tolerance. Its priests denied all but one of the manifold ways in which the God is seen; they cut down the holy groves, took from the house its humble idols, and martyred the last men whose souls were free.

89

Oh yes, Iason thought, *in time they lost their grip. Science could be born, almost two millennia later than ours. But the poison remained: the idea that men must conform not only in behavior but in belief. Now, in America, they call it totalitarianism. And because of it, the nuclear rockets have had their nightmare hatching.*

I hated that history, its filth, its waste, its ugliness, its restriction, its hypocrisy, its insanity. I will never have a harder task than when I pretended to be an American that I might see from within how they thought they were ordering their lives. But tonight . . . I pity you, poor raped world. I do not know whether to wish you soon dead, as you likeliest will be, or hope that one day your descendants can struggle to what we achieved an age ago.

They were luckier here. I must admit that. Christendom fell before the onslaught of Arab, Viking and Magyar. Afterward the Islamic Empire killed itself in civil wars and the barbarians of Europe could go their own way. When they crossed the Atlantic, a thousand years back, they had not the power to commit genocide on the natives; they must come to terms. They had not the industry, then, to gut the hemisphere; perforce they grew into the land slowly, taking it as a man takes his bride.

But those vast dark forests, mournful plains, unpeopled deserts and mountains where the wild goats run . . . those entered their souls. They will always, inwardly, be savages.

He sighed, settled down, and made himself sleep. Niki haunted his dreams.

Where a waterfall marked the head of navigation on that great river known variously as the Zeus, Mississippi and Longflood, a basically agricultural people who had not developed air transport as far as in Eutopia were sure to build a city. Trade and military power brought with them government, art, science and education. Varady housed a hundred thousand or so – they didn't take censuses in Westfall – whose inward-turning homes surrounded the castle towers of the Voivode. Waking, Iason walked out on his balcony and heard the traffic rumble. Beyond roofs lay the defensive outworks. He wondered if a peace founded on the balance of power between statelets could endure.

But the morning was too cool and bright for such musings. He was here, safe, cleansed and rested. There had been little talk when he arrived. Seeing the condition of the fugitive who sought him, Bela Zsolt's son had given him dinner and sent him to bed.

Soon we'll confer, Iason understood, *and I'll have to be most careful if I'm to live.* But the health which had been restored to him glowed so strong that he felt no need to suppress worry.

A bell chimed within. He re-entered the room, which was spacious and airy however overornamented. Recalling that custom disapproved of nudity, he threw on a robe, not without wincing at its zigzag pattern. 'Be welcome,' he called in Magyar.

The door opened and a young woman wheeled in his breakfast. 'Good luck to you, guest,' she said with an accent; she was a Tyrker, and even wore the beaded and fringed dress of her people. 'Did you sleep well?'

'Like Coyote after a prank,' he laughed.

She smiled back, pleased at his reference, and set a table. She joined him too. Guests did not eat alone. He found venison a rather strong dish this early in the day, but the coffee was delicious and the girl chattered charmingly. She was employed as a maid, she told him, and saving her money for a marriage portion when she returned to Cherokee land.

'Will the Voivode see me?' Iason asked after they had finished.

'He awaits your pleasure.' Her lashes fluttered. 'But we have no haste.' She began to untie her belt.

Hospitality so lavish must be the result of customal superimposition, the easygoing Danskar and still freer Tyrker mores influencing the austere Magyars. Iason felt almost as if he were now home, in a world where individuals found delight in each other as they saw fit. He was tempted, too – that broad smooth brow reminded him of Niki. But no. He had little time. Unless he established his position unbreakably firm before Ottar thought to call Bela, he was trapped.

He leaned across the table and patted one small hand. 'I thank you, lovely,' he said, 'but I am under vow.'

She took the answer as naturally as she had posed the question. This world, which had the means to unify, chose as if deliberately to remain in shards of separate culture. Something of his alienation came back to him as he watched her sway out the door. For he had only glimpsed a small liberty. Life in the Westfall remained a labyrinth of tradition, manner, law and taboo.

Which had well-nigh cost him his life, he reflected; and might yet. Best hurry!

He tumbled into the clothes laid out for him and made his way down long stone halls. Another servant directed him to the Voivode's seat. Several people waited outside to have complaints heard or disputes adjudicated. But when he announced himself, Iason was passed through immediately.

The room beyond was the most ancient part of the building. Age-cracked timber columns, grotesquely carved with gods and heroes, upheld a low roof. A fire pit in the floor curled smoke toward a hole; enough stayed behind for Iason's eyes to sting. They could easily have given their chief magistrate a modern office, he thought – but no, because his ancestors had judged in this kennel, so must he.

Light filtering through slit windows touched the craggy features of Bela and lost itself in shadow. The Voivode was thickset and gray-haired; his features bespoke a considerable admixture of Tyrker chromosomes. He sat on a wooden throne, his body wrapped in a blanket, horns and feathers on his head. His left hand bore a horse-tailed staff and a drawn saber was laid across his lap.

'Greeting, Iason Philippou,' he said gravely. He gestured at a stool. 'Be seated.'

'I thank my lord.' The Eutopian remembered how his own people had outgrown titles.

'Are you prepared to speak truth?'

'Yes.'

'Good.' Abruptly the figure relaxed, crossed legs and extracted a cigar from beneath the blanket. 'Smoke? No? Well, I will.' A smile meshed the leathery face in wrinkles. 'You being a foreigner, I needn't keep up this damned ceremony.'

Iason tried to reply in kind. 'That's a relief. We haven't much in the Peloponnesian Republic.'

'Your home country, eh? I hear things aren't going so well there.'

'No. Homeland grows old. We look to Westfall for our tomorrows.'

'You said last night that you came to Norland as a trader.'

'To negotiate a commercial agreement.' Iason was staying as near his cover story as possible. You couldn't tell different histories that the Hellenes had invented the para-chronion. Besides changing the very conditions that were being studied, it would be too cruel to let men know that other men lived in perfection. 'My country is interested in buying lumber and furs.'

'Hm. So Ottar invited you to stay with him. I can grasp why. We don't see many Homelanders. But one day he was after your blood. What happened?'

Iason might have claimed privacy, but that wouldn't have sat well. And an outright lie was dangerous; before this throne, one was automatically under oath. 'To a degree, no doubt, the fault was mine,' he said. 'One of his family, almost grown, was attracted to me and – I had been long away from my wife, and everyone had told me the Danskar hold with freedom before marriage, and – well, I meant no harm. I merely encouraged – but Ottar found out, and challenged me.'

'Why did you not meet him?'

No use to say that a civilized man did not engage in violence when any alternative existed. 'Consider, my lord,' Iason said. 'If I lost, I'd be dead. If I won, that would be the end of my company's project. The Ottarssons would never have taken weregild, would they? No, at the bare least they'd ban us all from their land. And Peloponnesus needs that timber. I thought I'd do best to escape. Later my associates could disown me before Norland.'

'M-m . . . strange reasoning. But you're loyal, anyhow. What do you ask of me?'

'Only safe conduct to – Steinvik.' Iason almost said 'Neathenai.' He checked his eagerness. 'We have a factor there, and a ship.'

Bela streamed smoke from his mouth and scowled at the glowing cigar end. 'I'd like to know why Ottar grew wrathful. Doesn't sound like him. Though I suppose, when a man's daughter is involved, he doesn't feel so lenient.' He hunched forward. 'For me,' he said harshly, 'the important thing is that armed Norlanders crossed my border without asking.'

'A grievous violation of your rights, true.'

Bela uttered a horseman's obscenity. 'You don't understand, you. Borders aren't sacred because Attila wills it, whatever the shamans prate. They're sacred because that's the only way to keep the peace. If I don't openly resent this crossing, and punish Ottar for it, some hothead might well someday be tempted; and now everyone has nuclear weapons.'

'I don't want war on my account!' Iason exclaimed, appalled. 'Send me back to him first!'

'Oh no, no such nonsense. Ottar's punishment shall be that I deny him his revenge, regardless of the rights and wrongs of your case. He'll swallow that.'

Bela rose. He put his cigar in an ashtray, lifted the saber, and all at once he was transfigured. A heathen god might have spoken: 'Henceforward, Iason Philippou, you are peace-holy in Dakoty. While you remain beneath our shield, ill done you is ill done me, my house and my people. So help me the Three!'

Self-command broke down. Iason went on his knees and gasped his thanks.

'Enough,' Bela grunted. 'Let's arrange for your transportation as fast as may be. I'll send you by air, with a military squadron. But of course I'll need permission from the realms you'll cross. That will take time. Go back, relax, I'll have you called when everything's ready.'

Iason left, still shivering.

He spent a pleasant couple of hours adrift in the castle and in its courtyards. The young men of Bela's retinue were eager to show off before a Homelander. He had to grant the picturesqueness of their riding, wrestling, shooting and riddling contests; something stirred in him as he listened to tales of faring over the plains and into the forests and by river to Unnborg's fabled metropolis; the chant of a bard awakened glories which went deeper than the history told, down to the instincts of man the killer ape.

But these are precisely the bright temptations that we have turned our backs on in Eutopia. For we deny that we are apes. We are men who can reason. In that lies our manhood.

I am going home. I am going home.

A servant tapped his arm. 'The Voivode wants you.' It was a frightened voice.

Iason hastened back. What had gone wrong? He was not taken to the room of the high seat. Instead, Bela awaited him on a parapet. Two men-at-arms stood at attention behind, faces blank under the plumed helmets.

The day and the breeze were mocked by Bela's look. He spat on Iason's feet. 'Ottar has called me,' he said.

'I – Did he say—'

'And I thought you were only trying to bed a girl. Not seeking to destroy the house that befriended you!'

'My lord—'

95

'Have no fears. You sucked my oath out of me. Now I must spend years trying to make amends to Ottar for cheating him.'

'But—' *Calm! Calm! You might have expected this.*

'You will not ride in a warcraft. You'll have your escort, yes. But the machine that carries you must be burned afterward. Now go wait by the stables, next to the dung heap, till we're ready.'

'I meant no harm,' Iason protested. 'I did not know.'

'Take him away before I kill him,' Bela ordered.

Steinvik was old. These narrow cobbled streets, these gaunt houses, had seen dragon ships. But the same wind blew off the Atlantic, salt and fresh, to drive from Iason the last hurt of that sullenness which had ridden here with him. He pushed whistling through the crowds.

A man of Westfall, or America, would have slunk back. Had he not failed? Must he not be replaced by someone whose cover story bore no hint of Hellas? But they saw with clear eyes in Eutopia. His failure was due to an honest mistake: a mistake he would not have made had they taught him more carefully before sending him out. One learns by error.

The memory of people in Ernvik and Varady – gutsy, generous people whose friendship he would have liked to keep – had nagged him awhile. But he put that aside too. There were other worlds, an endlessness of them.

A signboard creaked in the wind. The Brotherhood of Hunyadi and Ivar, Shipfolk. Good camouflage, that, in a town where every second enterprise was bent seaward. He ran to the second floor. The stairs clattered under his boots.

He spread his palm before a chart on the wall. A hidden scanner identified his finger-patterns and a hidden door opened. The room beyond was wainscoted in local fashion. But its clean proportions spoke of home; and a Nike statuette spread wings on a shelf.

Nike . . . Niki . . . I'm coming back to you! The heart leaped in him.

Daimonax Aristides looked up from his desk. Iason sometimes wondered if anything could rock the calm of that man. 'Rejoice!' the deep voice boomed. 'What brings you here?'

'Bad news, I'm afraid.'

'So? Your attitude suggests the matter isn't catastrophic.' Daimonax's big frame left his chair, went to the wine cabinet, filled a pair of chaste and beautiful goblets, and relaxed on a couch. 'Come, tell me.'

Iason joined him. 'Unknowingly,' he said, 'I violated what appears to be a prime taboo. I was lucky to get away alive.'

'Eh.' Daimonax stroked his iron-gray beard. 'Not the first such turn, or the last. We fumble our way toward knowledge, but reality will always surprise us ... Well, congratulations on your whole skin. I'd have hated to mourn you.'

Solemnly, they poured a libation before they drank. The rational man recognizes his own need for ceremony; and why not draw it from otherwise outgrown myth? Besides, the floor was stainproof.

'Do you feel ready to report?' Daimonax asked.

'Yes, I ordered the data in my head on the way here.'

Daimonax switched on a recorder, spoke a few cataloguing words and said, 'Proceed.

Iason flattered himself that his statement was well arranged: clear, frank and full. But as he spoke, against his will experience came back to him, not in the brain but in the guts. He saw waves sparkle on that greatest of the Pentalimne; he walked the halls of Ernvik castle with eager and wondering young Leif; he faced an Ottar become beast; he stole from the keep and overpowered a guard and by-passed the controls of a car with shaking fingers; he fled down an empty road and stumbled through an empty forest; Bela spat and his triumph was suddenly ashen. At the end, he could not refrain:

'Why wasn't I informed? I'd have taken care. But they

said this was a free and healthy folk, before marriage anyway. How could I know?'

'An oversight,' Daimonax agreed. 'But we haven't been in this business so long that we don't still tend to take too much for granted.'

'Why are we here? What have we to learn from these barbarians? With infinity to explore, why are we wasting ourselves on the second most ghastly world we've found?'

Daimonax turned off the recorder. For a time there was silence between the men. Wheels trundled outside, laughter and a snatch of song drifted through the window, the ocean blazed under a low sun.

'You do not know?' Daimonax asked at last, softly.

'Well . . . scientific interest, of course—' Iason swallowed. 'I'm sorry. The Institute works for sound reasons. In the American history we're observing ways that man can go wrong. I suppose here also.'

Daimonax shook his head. 'No.'

'What?'

'We are learning something far too precious to give up,' Daimonax said. 'The lesson is humbling, but our smug Eutopia will be the better for some humility. You weren't aware of it, because to date we haven't sufficient hard facts to publish any conclusions. And then, you are new in the profession, and your first assignment was elsewhen. But you see, we have excellent reason to believe that Westfall is also the Good Land.'

'Impossible,' Iason whispered.

Daimonax smiled and took a sip of wine. 'Think,' he said. 'What does man require? First, the biological necessities, food, shelter, medicine, sex, a healthful and reasonably safe environment in which to raise his children. Second, the special human need to strive, learn, create. Well, don't they have these things here?'

'One could say the same for any Stone Age tribe. You can't equate contentment with happiness.'

98

'Of course not. And, if anything, is not ordered, unified, planned Eutopia the country of the cows? We have ended every conflict, to the very conflict of man with his own soul; we have mastered the planets; the stars are too distant; were the God not so good as to make possible the parachronion, what would be left for us?'

'Do you mean—' Iason groped after words. He reminded himself that it was not sane to take umbrage at any mere statement, however outrageous. 'Without fighting, clannishness, superstition, ritual and taboo . . . man has nothing?'

'More or less that. Society must have structure and meaning. But nature does not dictate what structure or what meaning. Our rationalism is a non-rational choice. Our leashing of the purely animal within us is simply another taboo. We may love as we please, but not hate as we please. So are we more free than men in Westfall?'

'But surely some cultures are better than others!'

'I do not deny that,' Daimonax said; 'I only point out that each has its price. For what we enjoy at home, we pay dearly. We do not allow ourselves a single unthinking, merely felt impulse. By excluding danger and hardship, by eliminating distinctions between men, we leave no hopes of victory. Worst, perhaps, is this: that we have become pure individuals. We belong to no one. Our sole obligation is negative, not to compel any other individual. The state – an engineered organization, a faceless undemanding mechanism – takes care of each need and each hurt. Where is loyalty unto death? Where is the intimacy of an entire shared lifetime? We play at ceremonies, but because we know they are arbitrary gestures, what is their value? Because we have made our world one, where are color and contrast, where is pride in being peculiarly ourselves?

'Now these Westfall people, with all their faults, do know who they are, what they are, what they belong to and what belongs to them. Tradition is not buried in books but is part of life; and so their dead remain with them in loving memory. Their problems are real; hence their successes are real. They believe in their rites. The family, the kingdom, the race is something to live and die for. They use their brains less, perhaps – though even that I am not certain of – but they use nerves, glands, muscles more. So they know an aspect of being human which our careful world has denied itself.

'If they have kept this while creating science and machine technology, should we not try to learn from them?'

Iason had no answer.

Eventually Daimonax said he might as well return to Eutopia. After a vacation, he could be reassigned to some history he might find more congenial. They parted in friendly wise.

The parachronion hummed. Energies pulsed between the universes. The gate opened and Iason stepped through.

He entered a glazed colonnade. White Neathenai swept in grace and serenity down to the water. The man who received him was a philosopher. Decent tunic and sandals hung ready to be donned. From somewhere resounded a lyre.

Joy trembled in Iason. Leif Ottarsson fell out of memory. He had only been tempted in his loneliness by a chance resemblance to his beloved. Now he was home. And Niki waited for him, Nikias Demostheneou, most beautiful and enchanting of boys.

Afterword

Readers ought to know that writers are not responsible for the opinions and behavior of their characters. But many people don't. In consequence, I, for instance, have been called a fascist to my face. Doubtless the present story will get me accused of worse. And I only wanted to spin a yarn!

Well, perhaps a bit more. That can't be helped. Everybody views the world from his particular philosophical platform. Hence any writer who tries to report what he sees is, inevitably, propagandizing. But as a rule the propaganda lies below the surface. This is twice true of science fiction, which begins by transmuting reality to frank unreality.

So what have I been advocating here? Not any particular form of society. On the contrary, humankind seems to me so splendidly and ironically variable that there can be no perfect social order. I do suspect that few people are biologically adapted to civilization; consider its repeated collapses. This idea could be wrong, of course. Even if true, it may just be another factor which our planning should take into account. But the mutability of man is hardly open to question.

Thus each arrangement he makes will have its flaws, which in the end bring it to ruin; but each will also have its virtues. I myself don't think here-and-now is such a bad place to live. But others might. In fact, others do. At the same time, we cannot deny that *some* ways of life are, on balance, evil. The worst and most dangerous are those which cannot tolerate anything different from themselves.

So in an age of conflict we need a clear understanding of our own values – and the enemy's. Likewise we have to see with equal clarity the drawbacks of both cultures. This is less a moral than a strategic imperative. Only on such a basis can we know what we ought to do and what is possible for us to do.

For we are not caught in a meaningless nightmare. We are inhabiting a real world where events have understandable causes and causes have effects. We were never given any sacred mission, and it would be fatal to believe otherwise. We do, though, have the right of self-preservation. Let us know what it is we want to preserve. Then common sense and old-fashioned guts will probably get us through.

This is rather a heavy sermon to load on a story which was, after all, meant as entertainment. The point was made far better by Robinson Jeffers:

'Long live freedom and damn the ideologies.'

The Little Monster

Throughout that terrible end-of-night, Jerry Parker kept his head. Once he even called skyward, 'Hey, Mr Matthews, if I last this thing out, I ought to make Eagle, huh?' But his Scoutmaster was a million and a half years away in time. So were Dad, Mother, Sis . . .

A long-drawn roar coughed and thundered over plains white beneath a sinking moon under stars wheeling, frosty, in nameless constellations. The noise was followed by a series of yelps, a cackling scream. Unseen wings were ghostly above him. If nothing of him came home, except his clean-picked bones . . .

He hunched, hugging himself, in what little shelter from the cold a spiny bush offered. His clothes were only sport shirt, lightweight slacks, sneakers. Teeth clattered in his head. Spain of the Pliocene Period – No, wait; this land didn't look right for Spain – not the topography nor the wildlife nor – Well, Europe was supposed to be warmer now than in 1995. The Ice Age hadn't begun. If Earth had any polar caps at all, they were not large. That meant less rainfall in these parts, and no forests. Open grasslands would get hot enough by day but chill off fast after sundown.

Was this also true in Ohio, which didn't yet exist? He couldn't tell. He was no geologist; he was only a boy who, for a twelfth birthday present, had been (would be?) sent to spend a summer with the family of his Spanish mother's brother.

Ohio . . . Dad, Mother, Sis, the dogs, his friends and schoolmates, his teachers and Scout troop, his books and carpentry bench . . . gentle countrysides, gleaming cities, aircars murmuring through the heavens . . . a vacation trip to Rio and a telecast from Mars – all unborn, nonexistent, unimaginable. He couldn't even call any of them very clearly to mind. How could the image of his father strengthen or the image of his mother comfort, when they would not even *be* for fifteen thousand centuries?

Somehow, Jerry found, he could more readily hark back to his uncle's laboratory, though, in a way, that crowded apparatus, those oracular meters, the technicians at their enigmatic work, seemed as alien as the land which now held him.

'Never mind the physics of it,' Antonio Viana said. He spoke excellent English; but then, he was world-renowned for his contribution in bringing Mitsuhito's theory of temporal relativistics into engineering practice. 'Come back when you know tensor calculus, and I'll explain to you about n-dimensional forces and the warping of world lines. Today I thought you would simply like to visit the shop.'

'Oh, gee, would I ever!' Jerry breathed. He hesitated. 'Of course, I've read a lot about time projection, and I've seen things on TV, but your place never was mentioned. I've never actually been in a lab . . .'

A smile flashed through Uncle Antonio's beard. 'True, we have attracted no foreign newsmen, but ours is a small, rather specialized part of an international effort. We have had no spectacular results so far – or, rather, the anthropologists we have been sending back have had none.'

'They haven't seen any, uh, cavemen?' Jerry asked.

Uncle Antonio chuckled. 'Not hereabouts. Besides, no one ever will, strictly speaking, unless we can find a way to enter the past at a later date than about one million B.C. There were no men that early – only ancestral half-apes.' He shrugged. 'Not that I am an anthropologist myself. I am just a physicist and engineer, but, helping to send expeditions back, I grew interested. I asked questions and read books.'

'Well, how come they haven't even met any, uh, half-apes?'

'A protohuman, or the original Homo sapiens, for that matter, was a rare animal, Jerry. Suppose you, today, had about thirty hours to fish off the coast of Africa. How likely would you be to catch a coelacanth?' The man paused. 'Besides, the temporal inertia effect does more than bar us from the closer past and bar us completely from the future. It also causes great uncertainty about arrival dates. As near as can be checked by astronomical instruments – not very near, considering how the skies change over so much time – no two expeditions have landed even within thousands of years of each other. We know, from fossils, that premen once lived in this neighborhood, but we don't know exactly when, and we have never happened to hit it right. You cannot possibly hope to search a wide area in thirty hours, either.'

'Will they ever manage to improve that?' Jerry wondered.

'Well, we are trying,' Uncle Antonio said. 'You see us experimenting, hoping to get more precision. I do not think we will lengthen the time span that can be spent in the past. What we send is snapped back to here and now after thirty hours, because of built-up stresses in the continuum. That is also the reason our people cannot bring anything home with them except photographs, notes – essentially the same matter as they took along.'

'Hey, look,' Jerry protested, since this had never been made clear to him, 'the men you've sent have sampled water and fruits and all kinds of things in the past. They've certainly breathed the air. What about the atoms their bodies took up and the other atoms they got rid of?'

The man rumpled the boy's brown hair. 'A good brain under that mop,' he said, laughing. Again he shrugged, in his very Latin way. 'I think maybe the intermolecular forces account for it – that people do come back whole, with full lungs and so on, I mean. Maybe this will give us an approach to collecting objects, live plants, animals. Temporalistics is still such a new science. Many unknowns.'

They had stopped before a burnished steel cylinder, studded with instruments and controls, on which a pair of technicians labored. A window showed a bare interior. 'We project the travelers from this,' Uncle Antonio said. 'Would you like to step inside?'

A thrill ran through Jerry. 'Gosh, thanks!' He darted through the open door.

The chamber was narrow and cheerless – but nevertheless exciting to Jerry. Trying to capture a sense of really going off on a time voyage, he started to close the door.

He barely glimpsed a horrified face in the window, barely heard a screamed '*No, no!*' He couldn't stop his motion fast enough. The heavy metal door clanged shut.

Then came the flash, the whirling, the . . .

First light. Wind cold over skin, ruffle hair, whistle from gray-before-sun till stars go. Dew shiny on thorn wall, tree leaf; wet smell. Nest rustle soggy. Warm bodies, flesh smell, dry grass smell, mold-underneath smell.

Lion smell!

Last night lion prowl outside thorn wall. Roar. Lion alone. Hes wake, grab spears, jump around shes and cubs, scream, show teeth. Lion go. Helion; see mane under moon. Lame. Big, big, big. Come back tonight? Help, Old Father!

Get up. Cubs cry; mothers give milk. Thirsty. Hungry. Lion . . . Thirsty. Hungry. Go to water hole. Go hunt.

Old Father's pole bent over outside thorn wall. Lion hit it with clawpaw. Untangle branches. Scratch. Blood on skin. Go out. Straighten pole. Reach; daub blood from scratch onto Old Father's teeth. Howl for Old Father; dance before his hollow eyes. All hes howl, dance. Old Father, do not call lion back! We need you!

Ung-ng-n-n-n. To water hole. Hes outside band, with sharpstones and spears. Half-cubs inside hes, with rocks and clubs. Inside them, shes and cubs. Flesh smell. Breathing, chattering, shoving. Walk through tall, whispery yellow grass to water hole.

Sunup. Sky, hills blue. Antelope herd far off by mimosa trees. Pride of lions come back from kill. Quick, make ring – spears outward, jump, bellow, bristle hair, whiskers! Lions look sleepy at us; go on. Hale lion not hunt man. Limping lion hunt man.

These lions kill last night. Leave carcass. Where? Look. Vultures coming down yonder. Quick, before hyenas. Hurry to water hole.

Khr-r-rarr. Mastodon drinking. Must wait in woods. Hear splash, slurp, belly-rumble. Find grubs in rotten log. Sweet. Groom each other. Catch fleas; crack between teeth.

Mastodon go away; hill-high. Branches swish around flanks. Out on savannah, mastodons' hair red under sun, tusks old-bone-white. Smell rank. Grass crushed under feet smell sweet.

To water hole. Muddy. Taste, smell like bottom ooze. Drink fast; aaaahh! Not stop to chase frogs. Carcass waiting.

Back to thorn wall. Shes, cubs, half-cubs stay near here; search for roots, worms, grasshoppers; maybe knock over hare with flung stone. Old Father, keep lame lion asleep by day!

Hes go to kill of lions. Lope over plain. Hot. Grass brush skin, rustle, ripple. Breeze bring meat smell. Vultures, flies thick ahead. Big Kill. Horse? Elk? Hold sharpstone tight. Sharpstones to rip skin, cut carcass apart. Hes to bring home bones, to cut off meat, lovely fat. To crack bones with rock, suck lovely marrow . . .

Vultures flap away.

Howls like laughing. Harsh smell. Shaggy, high-shouldered bodies. Hyena pack on way.

Skulk off. Man band can't fight hyenas. Look for small

game. Spear can't break thick skins like lion claw, leopard jaw, sabertooth. Man band hunt anteater, hare, coney, snake, lizard; maybe catch young of big game.

Carcass smell lovely. Hyenas laugh. Man band go.

Hungry, hungry.

Dawn stole up above eastern hills. Jerry stretched stiffened limbs and jogged around the bush to start his blood moving warmly.

With waxing daylight, nightmarishness faded. He could understand what had happened. Probably the workers had had the main circuits closed but the fail-safe devices disconnected while they tinkered, and they had neglected to tell their chief. Closing the door had tripped the last switch needed to activate the projector.

You couldn't blame the technicians too much; they had assumed that whoever entered that chamber would know. Also, he, Jerry, should have asked before touching anything.

'Well, never mind whose fault it was,' he said aloud into the wind. 'I'm here – or should I say I'm *now?*'

The area was a suburb of Valladolid, A.D. 1995, but in present reality, it was dry savannah under a cruelly bright sun, 1,500,000 B.C. give or take enough millennia that there was no possibility of sending him help.

In thirty-odd hours, minus the few he'd already spent, he would return to 1995. It would be not only to almost the exact moment of departure, but also to the exact spot, even if he wandered around in the meantime – so he might as well.

In fact, he'd better. Some of those animals in the dark had sounded awfully mean. He had no shelter here, no tree to climb, no weapon better than his Scout knife.

Suppose he died. His body would still return. Suppose it were eaten. Would anything enter the chamber except bones? Jerry shivered and struck off northward, merely because that kept the low sun out of his eyes.

It rose as he walked, and the heat increased. Crickets leaped and chirped. The land reached on and on, in billows of tawny grass that soughed in the faint breezes. At a distance, he spied an immense, earth-darkening herd. He couldn't make out what kinds of animals were in it – more than one kind, surely – apart from a few that were elephants, but not quite. These trumpeted, a somehow shrill bass that rolled across the grassland. The cloudless, pale blue sky filled with wings and became clamorous with voices.

Thirst nagged Jerry. He said aloud, just to hear something human, 'That much life has to have water. I can last without it, but a drink'd be nice. Mainly, though, a river or a spring ought to mean trees that I could roost in after sundown . . .'

When at last, afar, he saw low, scattered growths, it was noon. He rested. Peering northeast, he made out a dim line on the horizon. A grove? Worth trying. He trudged on through late afternoon.

Yes, those were stunted trees with dusty green foliage, clustered around what must be a water hole. Individual trees were strung out across the plain. One of them, some two miles from the woods, stood by itself but was fairly tall. It seemed to be surrounded by – Was it a lot of the scrubby thornbush that grew everywhere about? No, not exactly. Hard to tell, with this early evening light, these long shadows, his own thirst and hunger and weariness . . .

A line of animals was headed toward it, evidently returning from a drink. They were silhouetted black against the fading light. Jerry gulped and pulled out his knife. He couldn't really see them in detail, but didn't they walk upright?

A wind gusted at his back. Suddenly a chorus of harsh yells burst over him. Members of the band came leaping, howling, chattering their teeth. Their bodies were the bodies of small, dark, wiry, naked men, and they brandished crudely shaped sticks and stones. Their heads were the heads of beasts.

Stop! What? Man smell?

Man coming yonder?

No strange man on our grounds! Drive outsider away! Hes lope close, yell, jump around, make afraid. Kyaa, kyaa, kyaa!

No man, this. No ape – two legs. No man. Smell wrong. Look wrong. Bigger than a she, not as big as a he. Short hair, no whiskers, flat face, thin jaw, no fangs. Hand hold shiny sharpstone. Backing off. Sweating in chill breeze. Stinking of fear.

Kyaa, kyaa, kyaa! Food!

Rush. Monster turn around, run. Hear breath sob in, out. Slow he run. Throw sharpstone. *Thunk* between shoulders! Monster stumble, fall. Surround. Move in for kill.

Monster spring up. Rush in under spear. Shriek. Slash. Shiny sharpstone cut arm open to bone. Blood, hurt, yammer. Monster has sharp, sharp sharpstone. Monster slash next he.

Draw back. Bristle, spread lips, clack teeth, growl, beat breast. Monster stand fast. Smell monster's fear. Throw another stone. Monster catch with free hand, throw back. Owwww! Blood-run into eyes, mouth. Hot, salt-sweet.

Monster retreat. Hes not follow. Shes, cubs yelling, scared. Sun on world edge. Lame lion come soon? Move backward, shake weapons, growl, flash teeth at standing monster.

Monster follow, not close. Stop again. Here thorn wall. Part branches. Scratches? Not like sharp, sharp sharpstone! Everybody go inside. Passing by Old Father, crawl. Old Father, help! Drive away big lion, little monster.

Close thorn wall. Keep watch. Hack day's catch apart. Coney, snake, lizard, field mouse, field mouse, field mouse, toad, handful crickets. Hungry tonight. Lion pride not hungry. Hyenas not hungry. Man band not have sharp claws, big jaws. Hes, shes, half-cubs hungry. Lame lion hungry. Old Father, help!

Peer out through dusk. Monster by tree yonder. Pulling

110

grass? Breaking branches? Squat and chip rock? Hard to see. Dark getting thick.

Lion roar, boom-boom-br-r-room.

By monster – red, yellow, crackle, smoke sting. *Fire!* Howl fear. Old Father, Old Father!

Pithecanthropus, Jerry thought. And again, aloud, out of a dry mouth into a gathering wind and deepening shadows: 'I had to be the one to stumble on preman. Not a scientific expedition, but me – and I p-p-pretty near got killed and eaten, I guess.'

His self-defensive fight had been sheer terror reflex. It was blurred in his memory. He didn't know why the males hadn't pressed their attack. They could have taken him. His knife had inflicted no serious wounds. He wasn't able to field every thrown rock. Those pointed sticks weren't much as spears, but they'd have hurt him, and once he was down, he could have been clubbed to death.

Maybe his strangeness had made them hold back. From Scouting and natural history books, he knew that carnivores don't look for unnecessary trouble. Courage is a human invention. Beasts of prey want nothing except to stay alive; they seldom tangle with any creature that has a chance to harm them. And you couldn't call those – those monsters there – human!

Besides, they'd seemed anxious to get themselves and their mates and young inside that crude low-wall of thorny boughs. They probably didn't dare to get caught in the open after dark. A big cat . . .

'And you'd better not loaf around, either,' Jerry told himself. 'Pick a tree, while you've still got light to see by.' There would be a moon, but not till an hour or two after sunset, and meanwhile dimness stole out of the west. Sometime tomorrow morning, the stresses were supposed to discharge and carry him home – but he had to last until then.

He threw a tortured glance toward the water hole. No telling what might lurk in that now-gloomy grove. Parched tongue and painfully empty stomach he could tough out. Be nice to have a fire, though. Protection, too.

No really good refuge tree was in reach before nightfall, except the one the ape-folk had taken. Jerry chose the best of a bad lot, a gnarled thing whose twigs ripped at him when he tested climbing it. He got about thirteen feet aloft before the limbs grew too weak. That was useless against an arboreal hunter like a leopard; even a determined lion might leap high enough to pluck him down. 'Better build a fire – fast!' he muttered.

Luckily, fuel lay around: punk for tinder, bark and grass for kindling, larger wood from a nearby dead tree, ample dry dung. To start a fire without matches was a problem. Jerry scurried around, squinting into the dusk, which relentlessly closed around him.

He found a good many smallish stones. Most were shards or other stones bearing signs of workmanship. The ape-folk did chip an edge and a rough shape from a rock. The result was an unspecialized tool, equally useful (or semiuseful) for casting as a weapon, for butchering prey, and for scraping out a point of sorts on a stick, which would then serve as a blunt, soft spear.

Through gray blueness that hid the horizon, a roaring drummed. Jerry heard an answering clamor, high and terrified, from behind the ring of thorn branches. Iciness crawled up his own spine and over his scalp. Somehow he forced himself to continue his search in the grass.

There – what he'd hoped for! Not flint, to use with the steel of his pocketknife, but at least a chunk of pyrite, its golden hue barely visible in the last illumination. Squatting by his tinder, he held it in his left hand and clashed another stone against it. For a moment his heart halted; nothing had happened. He began to tremble. 'Stop that!' he told himself and gave another, more glancing blow. Sparks flew, as brilliant as hope.

He managed a strained grin. 'Thanks, Mr Matthews,' he whispered, as if his scoutmaster were there and could hear. Woodcraft; primitive lore, including ways of fire making; the incidental information that pyrite was abundant in Spain . . .

Crouch close, smite shower after shower of sparks onto the tinder. See one catch and glow, ever so faintly. Puff. Too hard; out it went. Try again.

When the first twigs crackled, when his fire really was started, Jerry cried. He couldn't help himself.

The lion bawled again, closer. Invisible, save as a bulk of blackness underneath early stars, the ape-folk's camp chattered forlorn defiance. Jerry threw a glance their way.

'I hope he d-d-does eat you,' he half sobbed. 'You filthy cannibals!'

Then somehow the thought that these were *his, Jerry Parker's*, noble ancestors, or so close as to make no difference, and that he might have become their dinner, struck him as insanely funny. He shrieked laughter, until renewed lion thunder brought him up short with the knowledge of how near to hysteria he had come.

'A spear is a great idea,' he breathed shakily. From his tree, he cut a stout, not too crooked branch, almost as long as he was. It took time, even with a steel blade, but he had nothing else to do.

Often he needed to pause to feed the fire, which had become sizable – his friend, dancing, sputtering, casting a smoky glow toward the stars . . . many-colored flames that sang and drove the night back into demon-shaped shadows.

Cross-legged, Jerry whittled a point on the stave and reasonable straightness into its length. Next he fire-hardened the point, turning it round and round over the coals till the wood dried to black toughness. Always he was aware of unseen eyes watching from behind the thorns.

His thoughts ran on as if he still spoke to himself or to Uncle Antonio or his father: *I sure understand why people used*

*to hate to think they were descended from creatures like those. I
don't care much for the idea, either.*

In body they were human enough, erect and not
especially hairy. Of course, they were runts, the biggest
adult male little more than about five feet tall. Their nude
hides were weathered to a leathery brown; on some, in that
first flashing instant of encounter, he had noticed signs of
skin disease. Their heads, topped by greasy black manes,
were small, with little brow but with thick ridges over the
eyes. They had flat noses and powerful-looking jaws. The
males' beards and throat ruffs concealed what was obvious
on the females and the young: that there was little or no
chin.

The band numbered perhaps ten adults of each sex and
twenty half-grown offspring. Three or four of the females
had clutched infants. The infant mortality must be too high
to bear thinking about (Jerry didn't suppose the ape-folk
were capable of thinking about it), and certainly no one lived
to be old. Doubtless this band were as many as the whole
grim country within sight would support.

'I guess you can't blame them for trying to drive a
stranger out of their territory,' Jerry said to himself. 'But
they didn't just make a threat display, as normal animals
would. They wanted to kill me. They're cannibals! Why else
do they keep outside that fence, on a pole, the skull of one of
their own kind?'

He shuddered and longed miserably for dawn. Only the
moon rose, cold and lopsided above the swiftly chilling air.
It turned the grasslands hoar, save where bushes and trees
made misshapen darknesses, the ape-folk's camp a bigger
one. Jerry huddled closer to his fire. Its heat was like a
caress. He was tired, so tired; drowsiness rolled over him in
thick, soft waves; he'd better climb . . .

The lion woke him.

He was into his tree before the roar and the shrieks had

114

fully registered. Clinging to a limb, he stared across fifty yards, his vision sharpened by terror.

His fire had burned low, to a mere heap of sullen red and tiny bluish flickers. Nonetheless, it had doubtless made the beast avoid him. Moonlight and uncountable stars turned the savannah into an ice-colored lake. His heart pounding uncontrollably, Jerry imagined that he could actually count the ribs of the lion.

The animal was truly gaunt – a male whose mane was ragged and whose coat was mangy. He limped, his right hind paw a mass of infection from some injury. His voice boomed, hollow and desperate.

In their compound, the ape-folk yammered. From his perch, Jerry could see that the females had borne their young into the high tree. They clustered there like ungainly fruit. No room remained, save in the lowest boughs, which a lion could reach. The males stayed together on the ground, dancing, shouting, bristling, baring teeth.

A healthy cat would never have attacked through those thorns, but this one, unable to hunt or even drive the hyenas off the kills of others, no longer had a choice. Maddened by the scent of meat, he flayed himself as his forepaws scooped away the thorn wall.

'Oh, no; oh, no!' Jerry gasped. Once inside, even though he was crippled and bleeding, the beast would still overmatch ten or twelve little men with no better weapons than chipped pebbles and stone-whittled sticks. He'd scarcely stop at killing one. No, he'd lay about him, pile high the corpses, then gorge and sleep, gorge and sleep, while sunlight slashed across the women and children in their tree, beseiged.

Jerry, almost in shock, knew that he was back on the ground and that he couldn't just do nothing while the thing happened, whatever it cost him.

He felt strangely cool, as if he stood in the moonlight, apart from his body, watching and directing it according to calculation:

Poke the fire, throw on more fuel, build a goodly blaze. Take three or four long sticks, thrust them into the coals, whip them in the air till they are fluttering torches. Hold that bundle in your left hand, the hardened spear in your right. Run forward to meet the lion.

He is almost through the thorn wall but has stopped his assault to stare warily in your direction. Lightning or the friction of wind-rubbed brush must kindle grass fires often enough, devastatingly enough, that animals have a built-in dread of flame. As you come near, the bleeding lion snarls and crouches. How big are those fangs!

From the ape-folk, sudden utter stillness. White under the moon, the skull regards you from its pole.

Mowgli act, drifts crazily across your head. 'Take that, Lame Thief!' – though your outside observer knows the poor creature is only trying to survive – and you ram your torch bundle at the great maw.

Be careful. Let him make a determined advance, and you're done. You'll go down beneath a swipe of claws that can break a neck with one blow. Your fire will go out forever. Keep the man-eater in retreat. Yell, chatter, show teeth. Thrust also with your right hand that carries the spear. Ha, blood spurts out!

With a final rumble from deep in his throat, more sigh than challenge, the lame lion drags himself off into the night to die.

For a long while, Jerry stared into the murk behind the thorns. He knew he must show stark in the sight of those eyes. His torches guttered low, became embers. Silence and cold flowed back around him.

Trembling racked his frame. He retreated to his place beneath the tree, stoked his fire, and settled down to wait out the night, sobbing, now, with the terror he had refused to feel as he drove away the lion.

After the jubilation and the first blurted brief account and the medical care for minor hurts, Antonio Viana took his nephew home and put him to bed. Several hours' sleep did wonders. Awakening toward evening, Jerry learned that a family feast was being prepared to celebrate his safe return.

His uncle led him to the study and offered him a glass of sherry. 'No, thank you,' the boy said, but he appreciated the compliment. To a Spaniard, the offer was a tribute to the manhood he had shown.

Antonio smiled and gave him a soft drink instead, then filled a wineglass, and lit a cigar for himself. They settled into creaky old leather chairs that still smelled faintly of horses. Books surrounded them, save where a window gave on dusk and multitudinous twinkling lights. A warm breeze carried in odors of jasmine.

'Well,' the scientist said with a smile, 'we can relax before dinner, we two, no? Maybe we can talk over what happened in more detail. Your aunt and cousins, you must see them, of course – and tomorrow the anthropologists – but there will be so much excitement, I think you will want to take this chance to arrange your thoughts.'

'I suppose so.' Jerry frowned at the ice that tinkled in his glass. 'But I'm – well – I'm happy to be back, that's all.'

'Understood. However, in retrospect, at least, your experience was fascinating.'

'Kind of rough.' Jerry grimaced. 'I don't mean the being, uh, marooned. Sure, I'm glad to know I had the guts to survive, but those . . . pithecanthropuses . . . those little monsters . . . I don't like to think about them. Cannibals and—'

'Oh?' Antonio raised dark brows. 'Yet you rescued them.'

'Yeah. I don't know why.'

'What makes you think they were cannibals?'

'Huh?' Jerry needed a moment to get over astonishment. 'I told you; they attacked me to kill.'

'How could you expect them to know you were human? In fact, you were not, from their viewpoint.' Antonio smiled through his beard. 'As an American might say, oddness

117

works both ways.' More seriously: 'You have told how the males – no, I will say the men – were prepared to die for their women and children. Why should they be, unless they loved them?'

'But that skull – like a trophy!'

'Someone they slew? Or someone who died but was revered?' Antonio paused before he added, 'Remember how Catholics preserve the relics of saints. I think those people of the dawn already had souls, Jerry. And they endured; they actually found the strength to love. Be proud of such fore-bears.'

The boy spoke no word, because at that moment a glory was opening for him.

His uncle reached to clasp his shoulder. 'And they,' he said simply, 'could be proud of their descendant.'

Gone. Gone.

You send stranger, Old Father? Stranger *is* Old Father?

Light, wind, ripple, rustle across grasses. Clouds scud. Antelope race cloud shadows. Wings, wings, wings.

Stranger gone. Lame lion gone.

Sour gray ashes. Warm on palm of hand. Prod with stick like stranger. Blow, like stranger. Puff-ff-ff; tiny flames. Put on dry stick. Slow, careful, careful. Not to anger Old Father.

Touch stranger's spear?

Spear out of fire? Spear dark from fire, from blood of lion?

For shes, for cubs – grab spear! Lift! Shout, dance under morning sun!

Hard, sharp, black spear. Make many. Kill big beasts. No more hungry.

Fire. Light in moonless night. Scare off lion, hyena. Harden spear, spear, spear, spear, spear. Make man band strong!

Thank you, Old Father. This holy fire you have given us – we must never let it die.

118

The Light

You've got to realize this is the biggest secret since the Manhattan Project. Maybe bigger than that. Your life has been investigated since you got out of rompers and—

No, blast it! We're not a gang of power-nutty militarists. Think I wouldn't like to yell the truth to all the world?

But it might touch off the war. And everybody knows the war will mean the end of civilization.

I should think that you, as a historian, could see our reasons. Machiavelli is the symbol of cold-blooded realism . . . and you don't have to tell me that he was only an exceptionally clear-headed patriot. I've read *The Prince* and the *Discourses*.

Frankly, I'm surprised that you're surprised. Just because I know enough math and physics to be in Astro, why should I be an uncultured redneck? No, sir, I've traveled around and I spent as much time in the museums of Europe as I did in the taverns.

I'll admit my companions on the Moon trip looked a bit askance at me because of that. They weren't robots, either, but there was so much to learn, it didn't seem that one human skull could hold it all. Down underneath, I think they were afraid my memories of the *Virgin of the Rocks* – the one in London, I mean, that's the best one – would crowd out my memories of orbital functions. So I made a point of showing off all the astrogational knowledge I had, during rehearsals, and it may have antagonized Baird a little.

Not that we had any fights. We were a tightly woven team when the *Benjamin Franklin* left the space station and blow-torched for the Moon. It's just – well, maybe we were somewhat more tense than we would have been otherwise.

There were three of us, you remember. Baird was the skipper and pilot, Hernandez the engineer, and I the instrument man. A single person could have handled the ship if nothing went wrong, but three were insurance – any one of us could do any of the other jobs. Also, of course, since this was to be the first actual landing on the Moon, not merely a swing around it, we thought our numbers were peeled down to the bare minimum.

Once in orbit, we hadn't much to do for several days. We floated upward, watching Earth recede and Luna grow against the deepest, blackest, starriest night you have ever imagined. No, you haven't imagined it, either. Pictures don't convey it, the splendor and loneliness.

It was very quiet in the ship. We talked of little things, to keep that silence at arm's length. I remember one conversation pretty well and it touches on the why of all this secrecy.

Earth hung sapphire in the middle of darkness and the stars. Long white auroral streamers shook from the poles like banners. Did you know that, seen from such a distance, our planet has belts? Very much like Jupiter. It's harder than you'd believe to distinguish the continental outlines.

'I think that's Russia coming into view,' I said.

Baird glanced at the chronometers and the orbital schedule taped to the wall, and worked his slipstick a minute. 'Yeah,' he grunted. 'Siberia ought to be emerging from the terminator right about now.'

'Are they watching *us?*' murmured Hernandez.

'Sure,' I said. 'They've got a space station of their own, haven't they, and good telescopes on it?'

'Won't they grin if we barge into a meteor!' said Hernandez.

'If they haven't already arranged an accident,' grumbled Baird. 'I'm not a damn bit sure they're behind us in astronautics.'

'They wouldn't be sorry to see us come to grief,' I said,

'but I doubt if they'd actually sabotage us. Not a trip like this, with everybody watching.'

'It might start the war?' said Baird. 'Not a chance. Nobody's going to wipe out a nation – knowing his own will be clobbered, too – for three spacemen and a ten-million-dollar hunk of ship.'

'Sure,' I replied, 'but one thing can lead to another. A diplomatic note can be the first link in a chain ending at war. With the antipodal hydrogen missile available to both sides, you get an interesting state of affairs. The primary aim of national policy has become the preservation of the status quo, but at the same time the tension created makes that status quo exceedingly unstable.

'Do you think our own government would be sending us to the Moon if there were any military benefit to be gained? Hell, no! The first thing which looks as though it will tip the balance in favor of one side will make the other side go to war, and that means the probable end of civilization. We gain points – prestige – by the first Lunar landing, but not a nickel more. Even as it is, you'll note the Moon is going to be international territory directly under the U.N. That is, nobody dares claim it, because there just might be something of real strategic value there.'

'How long can such a balance exist?' wondered Hernandez.

'Till some accident – say, a hothead getting into power in Russia, or anywhere else, for that matter – touches off the attack and the retaliation,' I said. 'Or there's the faint hope that we'll come up with a gadget absolutely revolutionary – oh, a force screen able to shield a continent – before they have any inkling of it. Then we'll present the world with a *fait accompli* and the Cold War will be over.'

'Unless the Russians get that screen first,' said Hernandez. 'Then it'll be over, too, but the bad guys will have won the bloodless victory.'

'Shut up,' snapped Baird. 'You both talk too much.'

It had been the wrong thing for me to say, I knew, out there in the great quiet night. We shouldn't have carried our little hates and fears and greeds beyond the sky and out into space.

Or perhaps the fact that we can be burdened with them and still reach the Moon shows that Man is bigger than he knows. I couldn't say.

The waiting wore us down, that and the free-fall. It's easy enough to get used to zero gravity while you're awake, but your instincts aren't so docile. We'd go to sleep and have nightmares. Toward the end of the trip, it happened less often, so I suppose you can get completely adjusted in time.

But we felt no dramatic sense of pioneering when we came down. We were very tired and very tense. It was merely a hard breakneck job.

Our landing site hadn't been chosen exactly, since a small orbital error could make a big difference as far as the Lunar surface was concerned. We could only be sure that it would be near the north pole and not on one of the *maria*, which look invitingly smooth but are probably treacherous. In point of fact, as you remember, we landed at the foot of the Lunar Alps, not far from the crater Plato. It was rugged country, but our gear had been designed for such a place.

And when the thunder of blasts had faded and our deafened ears tolled slowly toward quiet, we sat. We sat for minutes without a word being spoken. My clothes were plastered to me with sweat.

'Well,' said Baird at length. 'Well, here we are.'

He unstrapped himself and reached for the mike and called the station. Hernandez and I crowded the periscopes to see what lay outside.

It was eerie. I've been in deserts on Earth, but they don't blaze so bright, they aren't so absolutely dead, and the rocks aren't so huge and razor-cornered. The southern horizon was near; I thought I could see the surface curve away and tumble off into a foam of stars.

Presently we drew lots. Hernandez got the small one and stayed inside, while I had the privilege of first setting foot on the Moon. Baird and I donned our spacesuits and clumped out through the airlock. Even on Luna, those suits weighed plenty.

We stood in the shadow of the ship, squinting through glare filters. It wasn't a totally black, knife-edged shadow – there was reflection from the ground and the hills – but it was deeper and sharper than any you'll see on Earth. Behind us, the mountains rose high and cruelly shaped. Ahead of us, the land sloped rough, cracked, ocherous toward the rim of Plato, where it shouldered above that toppling horizon. The light was too brilliant for me to see many stars.

You may recall we landed near sunset and figured to leave shortly after dawn, two weeks later. At night on the Moon, the temperature reaches 250 below zero, but the days are hot enough to fry you. And it's easier – takes less mass – to heat the ship from the pile than to install a refrigerating unit.

'Well,' said Baird, 'go ahead.'

'Go ahead and what?' I asked.

'Make the speech. You're the first man on the Moon.'

'Oh, but you're the captain,' I said. 'Wouldn't dream of – no, no, Boss. I insist.'

You probably read that speech in the papers. It was supposed to have been extemporaneous, but it was written by the wife of somebody way upstairs who believed her claim to be a poet. A verbal emetic, wasn't it? And Baird wanted *me* to deliver it!

'This is mutiny,' he grumbled.

'May I suggest that the captain write in the log that the speech was delivered?' I said.

'Judas priest!' he snarled. But he did that, later. You understand you're hearing this under the Top Secret label, don't you?

Baird remained in a foul temper. 'Get some rock samples,' he ordered, setting up the camera. 'And on the double! I'm being cooked alive.'

I picked loose some of the material, thinking that the traces I left would probably last till the Sun burned out. It seemed an act of desecration, though Lord knew this landscape was ugly enough—

No, I thought, it wasn't. It was only so foreign to us. Do you know, it was several hours before I could really *see* everything? It took that long for my brain to get used to some of those impressions and start registering them.

Baird was taking pictures. 'I wonder if this lighting can be photographed,' I remarked. 'It isn't like anything that ever shone on Earth.' And it wasn't. I can't describe the difference. Think of some of the weird illuminations we get on Earth like that brass-colored light just before a storm, things like that – and multiply the strangeness of them a millionfold.

'Of course it'll photograph,' said Baird.

'Oh, yes. In a way,' I said. 'But to get the feel of it, you'd need such a painter as hasn't lived for centuries. Rembrandt? No, it's too harsh for him, a cold light that's somehow hell-hot, too—'

'Shut up!' The radio voice nearly broke my earphones. 'You and your blasted Renaissance!'

After a while, we went inside again. Baird was still mad at me. Unreasonable, but he'd been under a breaking strain, and he still was, and perhaps this wasn't the right place to chat about art.

We fiddled around with our instruments, took what observations were possible, had a meal and a nap. The shadows crept across the land as the Sun rolled downhill. It was a very slow movement. Hernandez examined my rock samples and said that while he wasn't a geologist, this didn't look like anything on Earth. We were told later that it was new to the experts. Same minerals, but crystallized differently under those fantastic conditions.

After our rest, we noticed that the low Sun and the irregular landscape had joined to give us a broad, nearly continuous band of shade clear to Plato Crater. Hernandez suggested we use the chance to explore. It would be after sunset before we could get back, but the ground wouldn't cool off so fast that we couldn't return with the help of our battery packs. In sunless vacuum, you don't lose heat very fast by radiation; it's the Lunar rock, cold to the core, which sucks it out through your boots.

Baird argued, for the record, but he was eager himself. So, in the end, we all set out and to hell with doctrine.

I won't describe that walk in detail. I can't. It wasn't simply the landscape and the lighting. On the Moon, your weight is only one-sixth as much as on Earth, while the inertia remains the same. It feels a bit like walking under water. But you can move fast, once you get the hang of it.

When we came to the ringwall, there were still a couple of hours till sundown, and we climbed it. Tricky work in that undiffused dazzle and those solid-looking shadows, but not very hard. There was an easy slope at the spot we picked and a kind of pass on top, so we didn't have to climb the full height, which is a little under 4000 feet.

When we reached the summit, we could look down on a lava plain sixty miles across; the farther side was hidden from us. It seemed almost like polished black metal, crossed by the long shadow of the western ringwall. The downward grade was steeper, its base lost in darkness, but it could also be negotiated.

My helmet, sticking into the direct sunlight, was a Dutch oven; my feet, in the shade, were frozen clods. But I forgot all that when I saw the mist below me.

Have you heard of it? Astronomers have noticed it for a long time, what seemed to be clouds or – something – in some of the craters. Plato is one. I'd been hoping we'd solve the mystery this trip. And there, curling in ragged streamers a quarter mile below me, was the fog!

It boiled out of the murk, glowed like gold for a moment as it hit the light, and then it was gone, evaporated, but more came rolling up every minute. Not a big patch, this one couldn't have been seen from Earth, but—

I started down the wall. 'Hey!' cried Baird. 'Get back here!'

'Just a look,' I pleaded.

'And you break your leg and have to be carried home, with the night coming on? No!'

'I can't break anything in this suit,' I told him. True enough. Space armor is solid metal on the outside – even those trick expanding joints are metal – and the plastic helmet is equally strong. I suppose a man could fall hard enough to kill himself on the Moon, if he really tried, but it would take some doing.

'Come back or I'll have you court-martialed,' said Baird between his teeth.

'Show a heart, Skipper,' begged Hernandez.

Eventually he talked Baird around. It was only me the captain was irritated with. We roped ourselves together and made a cautious descent.

The mist was coming out of a fissure about halfway down the wall. Where the shadows fell, our lights showed it collecting in hoarfrost on the rocks, then boiling gently away again. After dark, it would settle as ice till dawn. What was it? Water. There's a water table of some kind, I guess, and – I don't know. It suggests there may be indigenous life on the Moon, some low form of plant life maybe, but we didn't find any while we were there. What we found was—

A broad ledge lay just beneath the fissure. We scrambled to it and stood looking up.

Now you'll have to visualize the layout. We were on this ledge, several yards across, with the ringwall jutting sheer above and a cliff falling below into blackness. Far away, I could see the steely glimmer of the crater floor. The ground was all covered with the fine meteoric dust of millions of years; I saw my footprints sharp and clear and knew they might last forever, or until thermal agitation and new dustfall blurred them.

Ten feet overhead was the fissure, like a petrified mouth, and the mist came out of it and smoked upward. It formed almost a roof, a thin ceiling between us and the sky. And the Sun was behind the upper wall, invisible to us. The peaks reflected some of its beams down through the fog.

So we stood there in a cold, faintly golden-white radiance, a fog-glow – God! There's never been such light on Earth! It seemed to pervade everything, drenching us, cold and white, like silence made luminous. It was the light of Nirvana.

And I had seen it once before.

I couldn't remember where. I stood there in that totally alien dream-light, with the mist swirling and breaking overhead, with the stillness of eternity humming in my earphones and my soul, and I forgot everything except the chill, calm, incredible loveliness of it—

But I had seen it somewhere, sometime, and I couldn't remember—

Hernandez yelled.

Baird and I jerked from our thoughts and lumbered to him. He stood crouched a few feet away, staring and staring.

I looked at the ground and something went hollow in me. There were footprints.

We didn't even ask if one of us had made them. Those weren't American spaceboots. And they had come from *below*. They had climbed the wall and stood here for a while, scuffed and paced around, and presently we located the trail going back down.

The silence felt like a fiddle string ready to snap.

Baird raised his head at last and gazed before him. The light made his face a thing of unhuman beauty, and somewhere I had seen a face lit that way. I had looked at it, losing myself, for half an hour or more, but when, in what forgotten dream?

'Who?' whispered Baird.

'There's only one country that could send a spaceship to the Moon secretly,' said Hernandez in a dead voice.

'British,' I croaked. 'French—'

127

'We'd know about it, if they had.'

'Russians. Are they still here?' I looked down into the night welling up in Plato.

'No telling,' said Baird. 'Those tracks could be five hours or five million years old.'

They were the prints of hobnailed boots. They weren't excessively large, but judging from the length of the stride, even here on the Moon, they had belonged to a tall man.

'Why haven't they told the world?' asked Hernandez wildly. 'They could brag it up so—'

'Why do you think?' rasped Baird.

I looked south. Earth was in half phase, low above the horizon, remote and infinitely fair. I thought America was facing us, but couldn't be sure.

There was only one reason to keep this trip a secret. They had found something which would upset the military balance, doubtless in their favor. At this moment, there on Earth, the Kremlin was readying the enslavement of all the human race.

'But how *could* they have done it secretly?' I protested.

'Maybe they took off in a black ship when our space station was on the other side of the planet. Shut up!' Baird stood without moving.

The Sun went lower, that eldritch light died away, and the blue radiance of Earth took its place. Our faces grew corpse-colored behind the helmets.

'Come on,' said Baird. He whirled around. 'Let's get back to the ship. They have to know about this in Washington.'

'If the Russians know we know, it may start the war,' I said.

'I've got a code.'

'Are you sure it can't be broken? That it hasn't already been?'

'You trouble-making whelp!' he shouted in a fury. 'Be quiet, I tell you!'

'We'd better have a closer look,' said Hernandez gently. 'Follow those prints and see.'

'We didn't bring any weapons,' said Baird. 'I'd be surprised if the Russians were as careless.'

I won't detail the arguments. It was finally settled that I would look further while Baird and Hernandez returned. I had about an hour to follow that trail, then must hurry home if I didn't want to freeze solid.

I looked back once and saw a space-armored shape black across the stars. There were more stars every minute as the sunlight faded and my pupils expanded. Then the shadows walled me in.

It was a rough climb, but a quick one. The stone here was dark and brittle; I could track the stranger by the lighter spots where he'd flaked off chips as he scrambled. I wondered why those spots should be lighter when there was no oxygen around, but decided a photochemical effect was involved.

It was hard to see my way in the shade. The flashbeam was only a puddle of undiffused light before me. But soon I came out in the Earth-glow, and when my eyes had adjusted, it was easy enough. In half an hour, I was on the crater floor. The Sun was behind the ringwall. Black night lay over me.

Not much time to spare. I stood on dark, slick lava and wondered whether to follow those dim footprints in the dust. It might be a long way. Then I shrugged and went bounding off, faster than the other man had gone.

My heart thudded, the suit filled with stale air, it was hard to see the trail by Earthlight. I was more aware of those discomforts than of any danger to my life.

I was a little past the limit of safety when I found the camp.

There wasn't much to see. A long track of plowed dust and chipped stone, where something with runners had landed and taken off again . . . but no sign of a rocket blast! A few scars where a pick had removed samples. Footprints. That was all.

I stood there with the crater wall a loom of night behind me and the mist rising thicker, blue-tinged now. I stood thinking about somebody who landed without needing rockets and never told anyone. I looked around the sky and saw the ruddy speck of Mars and felt cold. Had the Martians beaten us to our own Moon?

But I had to get back. Every minute I lingered whittled down the chance of my returning at all.

One more look—

There was a little outcrop of granite not far away. I thought it might be a cairn, but when I got there, I saw it was natural. I shrugged and turned to go.

Something caught my eye. I looked closer.

The rock was sleet-colored in the Earthlight. It had one flat surface, facing my planet. And there was a cross hacked into the stone.

I forgot time and the gathering cold. I stood there, thinking, wondering if the cross was merely a coincidental symbol or if there had also, on Mars or on some planet of another star, been One who—

The million suns wheeled and glittered above me.

Then I knew. I remembered where I had seen that light which lay on the wall at sundown, and I knew the truth.

I turned and started running.

I almost didn't make it. My batteries gave out five miles from the ship. I reported over the radio and continued moving to keep warm, but my feet quickly froze, I stumbled, and each minute the cold deepened.

Baird met me halfway, ripped off my pack and connected another unit.

'You moron!' he snapped. 'You blind, bloody, pudding-brained idiot! I'm going to have you up before a court-martial if—'

'Even if I tell you who that was in Plato?' I asked.

'Huh?'

We were in the ship and my toes thawing before he got me to explain. It took a lot of talking, but when he grasped the idea—

Of course, Intelligence has been working overtime ever since we came home and told them. They've established now that there was no Russian expedition. But Baird and Hernandez and I have known it ever since our first night on the Moon.

And that, Professor, is the reason you've been drafted. We're going overseas together, officially as tourists. You'll search the archives and I'll tell you if you've found anything useful. I doubt very much if you will. That secret was well kept, like the secret of the submarine, which he also thought should not be given to a warring world. But if somewhere, somehow, we find only a scribbled note, a hint, I'll be satisfied.

It couldn't have been done by rockets, you see. Even if the physics had been known, which it wasn't, the chemistry and metallurgy weren't there. But something else was stumbled on. Antigravity? Perhaps. Whatever it may be, if we can find it, the Cold War will be won . . . by free men.

Whether or not we dig up any notes, our research men are busy. Just knowing that such a gadget is possible is a tremendous boost, so you can understand why this must be kept secret.

You don't get it? Professor, I am shocked and grieved. And you a historian! A cultured man!

All right then. We'll go via London and you'll stop at the National Gallery and sit down in front of a painting called *The Virgin of the Rocks*. And you will see a light, cold and pale and utterly gentle, a light which never shone on Earth, playing over the Mother and Child. And the artist was Leonardo da Vinci.

The Discovery of the Past

Now and then in life, if a person is lucky, there comes a moment that carries the spirit beyond itself. 'Thrill' is too weak a word for that lightning-like leap and blaze, 'transcendence' is too heavy. Most often, no doubt, we know it at the height of a perfect lovemaking. Some people throughout the ages have felt it as the revealed presence of the divine. To others it has come with a sudden flash of insight – scientists, philosophers – or at the sudden demonic surge of creativity – writers, poets, composers, artists of every kind – although I think these two are, at root, the same.

Among such moments that have taken me there have been the Lunar mission liftoffs, more beautiful than seemed possible, bound not only beyond the sky but into the future . . . or so we believed at the time. But there was also the instant many years ago, on my first visit to London, when I was wandering through that charming old junkshop they call Westminster Abbey and abruptly, without warning, came upon the grave of Isaac Newton. The memory of that can still send a tingle up my spine.

It was not quite the same kind of experience, because it took longer, one morning in Brittany, September 1979; and yet it was as meaningful, and makes an even better story. My wife Karen and I had spent the night in an old fishing village, Ploumanac'h, on which the resort hotels seem the merest overlay. Next morning we drove off and, following the guidebook, turned inland at Kergentuil. (How much those Celtic names bring to mind, the fall of Rome, the migration from Britain, the resistance to Norman, Frenchman, Englishman, German. Some outlying parts of

Brittany remained pagan until the seventeenth century, and everywhere many of the horde of local saints are ancient gods in disguise.) We stopped at a farm whose buildings are surely a couple of hundred years old at least – the land itself must have been cultivated since the later Stone Age – where Grandmother in her black dress and wooden shoes was busy among loose-wandering ducks and chickens. She paid us no heed as we explored a magnificent Neolithic dolmen and passage grave on the property. A little farther on, at St Uzec, stands a particularly tall menhir from that same era, give or take several centuries; but in it, early Christians chiseled a symbol of their faith. Not far beyond that, one of the largest radomes in the world was tracking manmade satellites. All this we saw in the space of an hour or two. Works of the Middle Ages and the Renaissance were for the afternoon . . .

On a shelf in my home lies a relic of the Paleolithic, a so-called hand ax, a heavy piece of flint chipped into a sort of pear shape but once rimmed with sharp edges. I hasten to add that this is none of the archaeological plunder so notorious these days; I got it legitimately, from a French prehistorian, because stratigraphic data are lacking and hence the object has no scientific value. However, from the style it can be approximately dated. It is Middle Acheulean, made perhaps a hundred thousand years ago by a hunter whose folk were not yet quite at the Neanderthal stage of evolution. Embedded in the flint is a fossil, a sea shell laid down perhaps a hundred million years ago . . .

Alfred Korzybski, the father of general semantics, described man as 'a time-binding animal.' Our minds join past, present, and future in a way unique upon this planet, impossible and inconceivable to any of the beings that share it with us. No matter how fine the brains of the cetaceans are – and we're not really sure of that – we have no evidence of their doing this to anything like the degree that we do, throughout our lives, so ordinarily that we hardly ever consider how miraculous it is.

That shelf of mine is a small, helter-skelter museum of .

time-binding. Among the objects on it are a stone spearhead and arrowhead which I watched my prehistorian friend, the late François Bordes, make himself. He was among those who pioneered reconstruction of Paleolithic techniques. Although the pieces are beautifully done, they took him only five or ten minutes each. That alone tells us a great deal about the economy, hence the lives of our remote ancestors.

Nearby lies an obsidian knife from Mexico. It is set in a plastic handle of ugliness appropriate to the workmanship, whose crudity would have appalled the Acheulean hunter. He made his living by his tools; the modern thing is for sale to gringo tourists. I keep it because of that contrast.

On the other hand, the Egyptian scarab and Horus falcon, also modern, are good copies of Pharaonic originals. Three comic Viking figures stand above a bit of oyster shell recovered at a Viking site in York. Offside rests something perhaps comic too, an archeosaur coprolith – a fossilized dropping from a reptile ancestral to the dinosaurs – given me by a charming young lady paleontologist as a token of her esteem. There is a letter opener presented to my paternal grandfather, upon the occasion of his retiring as a sea captain on the route between Denmark and Greenland, in 1905. There is a new Greek ten-drachma coin, depicting an atom on the reverse and Democritus on the obverse, Democritus who proposed the idea of atoms some four hundred years before Christ. There is a fine statuette of a Diomedean, inhabitant of an imaginary planet of mine which was visited by human beings in the twenty-fifth century . . .

In one sense, the present is where we live, it is all that we can directly know, everything else is inference. But in another and equally true sense, the present is no more than the interface, ever changing, between past and future. Just as our Earth is a mote in the immensity of space, so is our life a glimmer in the vastness of time. Yet we can look beyond both, and be exalted thereby.

Science fiction, of course, generally turns uptime, toward the future. That is right and proper. Whether the tomorrows it imagines be hopeful or horrible, we can learn from them, prepare ourselves, become better able to bear what we must and, otherwise, endure no unnecessary evil but rather shape destiny nearer to the heart's desire.

Besides, we can enjoy. Lest the foregoing seem too pompous, let me here and now declare that no art, no literature, from Sophocles and Shakespeare on down, is any good unless it is, one way or another, fun. 'Pleasurable' might be a better word, more easily stretched to accommodate the emotions aroused by tragedy, but I'll stick to plain 'fun.'

What I would like to stress is, first, that exploring the past is every bit as enjoyable, as fascinating, as exploring the present or the future. Furthermore, as far as we know, the time stream runs in a single direction. We cannot understand, therefore we cannot cope with the present unless we have some knowledge of the past from which it comes. This is twice true in our epoch, when change goes through the world like a storm. We need to know why. We also need to know *how* to see the likeness – to former events, as well as whatever uniquenesses may have arisen. We can't even tell what is and what is not new to history, unless we are aware of what is ancient in it.

(Thus many of today's younger generation seem to believe that they invented love, peacefulness, women's liberation, communal living, concern for the environment, and contempt for the establishment. A little reading of the Classical Greeks and Romans, if of nobody else, would have shown them differently, and predicted for them what usually comes of such movements. Given that kind of information, they might conceivably find how to make their ideals viable – not otherwise. At the same time, the same studies could have made our own establishment less complacent about its automatic, indefinite survival.)

The science fiction writer, the professional futurologist, and anybody trying to plan beyond next week have special need to be familiar with the past. Else their projections will be grotesquely out of line with reality. Making them is chancy at best, without the handicap of ignorance. That includes ignorance of other histories than ours.

I can clarify this last point by an example. Once I was talking about archaeology with a friend, an intelligent and well-read man. Mention came up of the archaeology of the Americas, and he wondered why anybody bothered. Who cared? The native societies are long gone, except for a few pathetic and doomed remnants, aren't they? Their development earlier makes no difference now, nor will it ever. The mainstream of the future, as of the present and of the past since Columbus, flows from the Old World.

So he said. I tried to explain. First, I said, there does not seem to have been anything simple in the development of civilization – agriculture, towns and cities, record-keeping, metallurgy, hierarchical government, nations and empires, everything beyond the life of Paleolithic hunters and gatherers. It seems to have happened just three times, in three independent areas from which those ideas diffused. Two of them were in the New World. If we want to investigate the process, can we afford to ignore two of the only three samples in existence?

Second, the native American societies did strongly influence the Europeans, directly and indirectly. For instance, in the eighteenth century the Five Nations were a power with which the British, French, and Spanish had to reckon. Still more important were such Amerindian contributions as potatoes, tomatoes, maize, tobacco.

Third, the native societies were by no means totally overrun, nor are they all extinct or dying today. Their pervasiveness is most obvious in Mexico, a country which cannot be understood without a knowledge of them, but reaches from the Pole to Patagonia – while even in the

United States and Canada, we begin to see more and more effects as the tribes regain hopefulness.

Fourth, as Terence wrote in second-century Rome, '*Homo sum; humani nil a me alienum puto.*' I am a man; nothing human is alien to me. At least, it had better not be, if I am to have any hope of halfway comprehending this infinitely various species to which I belong. There is as much to learn about humanity – about myself and everyone else – from a Navajo herdsman or an Australian bushman, as there is from a Yankee capitalist, European socialist, Confucian scholar, or Islamic warrior.

That is the more true if we want to make guesses about what is to come. If nothing else, the past can show us how many totally unforeseeable elements have always interplayed to make history.

I have tried to illustrate that point with a parable which may as well be repeated here. Once in the Rome of Augustus Caesar, a writer hit upon the concept of science fiction. He wanted to tell a story laid a thousand years in the future. First he sat down to consider what the possibilities were.

'Maybe,' he thought, 'Roman power will keep on expanding, until in a thousand years the Empire includes the whole world. Or maybe, as Caesar's present policies suggest, the situation will not really change; a thousand years from now, the Imperial borders will still be more or less along the Rhine and the Danube, with the barbarians prowling beyond. Or maybe, pessimistically, I should assume that Rome will fall, the barbarians move in, and nothing exist at that distant time but ruins and wilderness.'

I don't know which possibility he picked, and it doesn't matter. What really happened, of course, was something he never imagined, and scarcely could have imagined. A heretical offshoot of the religion of a subjugated people, afar in a corner of the Mediterranean ambit, took over Romans and barbarians alike, completely transforming them and breeding new, utterly different civilizations.

Thus, one thing we learn from history is that she plays with wild cards. It is knowledge more than useful, necessary to keep us on the alert for surprises. Borne in mind, it helps guard us against being suckered by ideologies that purport to have the final answers, the ultimate understanding and prescription.

Yet history is not utter chaos. We have much of enduring validity to learn, and it is vitally important that we do so.

First is our heritage, the knowledge of where we came from and how. Without that, we do not know ourselves, nor have we anything to conserve and pass on to our children. From pride springs courage, the will to survive and even prevail. When Alex Haley published his book *Roots*, he did a wonderful thing for black Americans. He gave them back a vision of their ancestral past, and thereby a strengthened identity, self-esteem, independence.

Something of the kind has, happily, been occurring too for American Indians and other minorities. Admittedly, much of what one hears, many of the claims made, are bombastic nonsense. For example, the assertion that various Stone Age peoples – in Africa, Oceania, the Americas – lived in peace, love, and perfect harmony with nature, until the nasty white man arrived, bears no more relation to reality than did Nazi noises about noble blond Aryans in a pre-Christian past. (For that matter, the aboriginal Mother Goddess and matriarchy in which today's neopagans believe are a bit of sentimentalism quite unsupported by actual evidence.) However, the real achievements and the authentic identities of anyone's ancestors are supremely worth knowing.

Who will do the same service for white Americans?

How much of our culture do we still possess? In the face of threats around the globe and within our borders, how shall we mount guard if we do not realize that this country, this civilization are worth defending, that they deserve to survive – and why this is so?

One need not, in fact one should not be a chauvinist, or any other kind of supremacist. This whole essay is a call for more appreciation of the marvelous and creative diversity of mankind. But if all societies are essentially the same, if ours has no special merits of its own, why should we sacrifice to preserve it? Why should we even work to better it?

Who are *we?* And now I mean every citizen of every Western country, regardless of race, sex, faith, or condition. How many of us know? How many today have any familiarity with the Bible, European and American history, or the rules of English grammar? Precious few!

For this, modern schools must bear a major part of the blame. Not long ago, I started to write a sentence about the Gadarene progress of twentieth-century education, then recalled that the educationists have already brought us to the point where not many readers would understand me. As for the past of the United States, that intricate, colorful, raucous pageant is, at best, made so boring in the classroom that children become downright eager to forget it. At best.

Now we the people could and would have better schools if we insisted on them and were willing to pay the price. That price includes, above all, maintaining the standard, in history as well as in every other subject. We cannot value liberty unless we know what tyranny is.

Time was when nobody who called himself or herself educated lacked a good knowledge of, at least, Western history from Biblical times onward. To the extent that information about different areas was missing, this was largely because it was not available. Contact was still slight with the great civilizations of Asia, while explorers, archaeologists, and anthropologists had yet to make most of their discoveries.

But when our Founding Fathers were considering how best to organize their new nation, they did not merely look back at recent events in Europe. They drew on Greece and Rome, the medieval Venetian republic, the city-states of the

Renaissance, the wars of religion, the rise of absolute monarchies, the entire parliamentary evolution of England. They studied declines and falls even more diligently than they did eras of glory, hoping to learn lessons that would help America avoid the same mistakes. They came to realize how little rational or altruistic human beings are by nature, how crucial is the role of institutions. See their correspondence, the *Federalist Papers*, and other writings of theirs for details.

By way of comparison, not long ago a widely televised clergyman, inveighing against immorality, declared that Rome fell because of sexual misconduct around the time of Nero. He seems to have gotten his information about Roman history from Italian B movies. This would simply be laughable if we did not have such urgent need to consider the manifold real factors that have caused nations to make fatal mistakes.

Even in affairs less than apocalyptic, ignorance is hideously handicapping. French leadership might not have felt compelled to draw France, effectively, out of NATO, if Anglo-American politicians, especially the Americans, had comprehended what the Hundred Years' War meant to France, and does to this very day. The flareup in Northern Ireland is a still more clear and tragic case of forces from the past, that we had supposed we could safely forget, suddenly springing back into our lives. We see a resurgent Islam and wonder how to deal with it – and start by witlessly taking for granted that the proper article *is* 'a,' that there is just one Moslem world and they're all a bunch of Arabs.

Here at home, too, we cannot continue to enjoy freedom, tranquility, and prosperity, let alone extend them to our less privileged citizens, unless we know how we got them. They were no gift from heaven; rather, they are very rare in history, and thus far have never endured for long.

This is not the place to write political prescriptions. I don't claim any special wisdom, anyway. I can only urge you to think for yourself, and remind you that this is impossible unless you have something to think about, a fund of factual information.

As a single down-to-earth example, though, we might look at history in order to investigate why the United States has hitherto flourished so mightily, at least in material wealth. The superficial answer, that white Americans took over half a continent and exploited it ruthlessly, will not bear examination.

After all, many parts of the planet were, and some still are, better endowed. It was not greedy agribusiness with high-tech machinery that turned most of the once-Fertile Crescent in the Near East into desert, it was peasants with wooden plows and organic goats. South America, taken as a whole, has more natural resources than does North America taken as a whole. China and much of the Soviet territory are fully comparable. Indeed, a very large part of the United States has never been especially fertile.

Then we can look at similarly well-to-do nations which had a meager inheritance from nature, such as the Scandinavian and Low Countries, Switzerland, Austria, or Japan. Until approximately the nineteenth century, most of them were for the most part miserably poor. The argument that they got rich by exploiting overseas empires won't stand up, because some of them never had colonies, and as for the rest, modern studies have shown that those colonies were always net economic liabilities, not assets.

We might glance at Great Britain, too, whose chief patrimony was merely coal, and at how it became affluent but now seems on the way back to genteel poverty. We might glance at Germany, smashed flat in World War Two, afterward split into a pair of nations – and contrast the standard of living as between East and West.

It seems obvious to me that what has made these differences has been people: their institutions, attitudes, ways of going about things. What else could it be? Possession of natural resources at home was doubtless helpful in some cases, but appears to have been neither necessary nor sufficient.

What the nations that prospered in modern times have had in common, is left as an exercise for the reader. I do not suggest that the answer is simple by any means; on the contrary. I have only used a few elementary historical data to show that *one* specific answer, often given, must be wrong.

My reticence otherwise is for the sake of avoiding political polemics. Ask me privately, or read some of my writings, and you'll quickly discover that I do have pretty definite ideas, in this case and in many more. I do believe we can draw much guidance from the past. But first we must know it.

In the famous words of George Santayana, those who will not learn the past are condemned to repeat it.

Academic knowledge by itself is not enough. The average level of education was higher than it is today when George Bernard Shaw declared tartly that the only thing we learn from history is that we learn nothing from history.

More recently, the late John W. Campbell remarked that history doesn't always repeat herself. Sometimes she screams, 'Won't you ever listen to what I'm trying to tell you?' and lets fly with a club.

I myself have suggested elsewhere: 'The problem seems to be not that the lessons of history are hard to learn, but that very few people want to learn them.' Truth is not necessarily beautiful, comforting, or equally fair to everyone. The person who utters it is apt to become unpopular, therefore not to be a leader. If we do acknowledge to ourselves that a certain course of action, or inaction, has had evil consequences in the past, it is far too easy to tell ourselves that *we* are *different* – or else that we're coping with an immediate necessity, and those who come after us will somehow manage to pungle up the price.

The chronicles confirm what instinct always has said: In

the long run there is no substitute for common sense, grit, and old-fashioned fidelity.

Of course, many scholars have tried to find patterns in recorded events, a deeper meaning or rhythm. The best known of these may be Oswald Spengler and Arnold Toynbee, but one can name any number of others – as well as colleagues who scoff at all of them. Whether or not such efforts will eventually lead to an Asimovian science of 'psychohistory' remains to be seen. The subject is fascinating, but would take us too far afield here.

Meanwhile, and always, the past has far more to offer us than dry dates and dour warnings. Let me repeat, archaeology, anthropology, historiography are fun! Together, they tell the most spellbinding stories we shall ever hear.

Recalling an earlier remark, one of the prime examples of that lies right to hand. If I may put it in the idiom of the present book, the history of the United States has been a terrific science fiction story.

We can start with Columbus, who opened up for Europe the New World – an entire hemisphere full of strange peoples, natural wonders, undreamed-of openness and opportunity. Perhaps I can best illustrate the sheer marvel of it by a true anecdote.

In the year 1540, the Spanish Empire sent an expedition under Francisco Vásquez de Coronado northward from Mexico to explore the vast unknown territory yonder and, maybe, find El Dorado. The quest was an epic of daring and endurance, often a tragedy of ruthlessness, and in the end a huge irony. For he did not come upon a fabulous kingdom like Moctezuma's; what he found was far more astonishing, the bison-thunderous Great Plains; and a lieutenant of his discovered the Grand Canyon of the Colorado.

This officer, García López de Cardenas, crossed the Kaibab Plateau, a stiff trek over seemingly endless miles of flat, parched, sparsely begrown wilderness, until suddenly, unwarned, his party came to the rim of the chasm. There they stood a long while silent, looking over cliffs, crags, mesas, buttes, ravines shaped and colored like things of dream, looking a mile down and twelve miles across. Finally their leader declared: 'Something has happened here.'

(And the Everglades, the Okeefenokee Swamp, Yellowstone, the salt flats and Great Salt Lake, Death Valley, the volcanic cinder cones at Mt Lassen, the primeval redwood forests – yes, we have much in this country which a science fiction writer would be proud to have imagined for another planet.)

Socially speaking, our nation was quite futuristic in its time, among the boldest human experiments ever undertaken. To be sure, it had roots. As observed earlier, the Founding Fathers were keenly conscious of history. Today a science fiction writer tries, or ought to try, to be likewise. The more solidly timbered his created world is, the more the reader will be interested. At the same time he, like the Founding Fathers, should attempt a new synthesis, even a mutation, and see what happens. Granted, his responsibility is infinitely less than theirs. They had to live in a real world. John Campbell once pointed out that one advantage of science fiction is that in a story you can test a social system to destruction without actually killing anybody. The Founding Fathers did not have that godlike copout. They had to deal with living human beings, who were often foolish and could always be hurt. Writings of theirs show how well aware they were of this.

Not only was the Republic itself a venture into the unknown, but later countless utopian communities were established in America, some of them on very strange principles indeed. How could a science fiction writer be more original than, say, the Shakers? The most successful of these undertakings, which is still going strong, took place in Utah. I hope my Mormon friends won't mind my saying that their church, like our country, has a grand science fiction flavor about it. That ecclesiastical division into stakes and wards is pure Heinlein, isn't it? And so, by the way, is the raw courage with which their pioneers entered the wilderness.

A complaint often made against science fiction stories is that important events in them happen too fast, and are brought about by a few determined individuals. This is alleged to be unrealistic. Well, let's take a look at the historic transformations of America. From the Declaration of 1776 to the annexation of 1848 that established us on the Pacific coast was a period of seventy-two years: a single reasonable lifetime. The steam engine, the cotton gin, the combine, the railroad, the telegraph, the telephone, the electric light, the automobile, the airplane, the atomic power plant, with all their consequences for good or ill, came in at the same headlong pace; and always you can easily identify the persons responsible. We think it extraordinary that just sixty-six years elapsed between the first powered flight at Kitty Hawk and the first manned landing on the moon; yet my mother was around for both of them.

Thrilling though such great public happenings have been, and still are to those of us who relive them through reading history – nevertheless, there is more sheer fun on the human scale. The past, like the present, swarms with remarkable figures. Thought goes to David, dancing in barbaric glee before the Ark of the Lord; Confucius, setting forth an ideal of civic virtue in an age when all hell was letting out for noon, an ideal which was to outlive every imperial attempt to scrub it out, from Shi Huang-Ti to Mao Tse-Tung; Theodora, starting in whoredom, finishing under a crown, saving the East Roman Empire by the steel she put in her husband's backbone; Saladin, chivalrous nemesis of the Crusaders; Hernán Cortez, conqueror of Mexico, who ended his days trying to get decent treatment for the Mexicans, and Tomás de Torquemada, Inquisitor-General of Spain, who rescued what Mexican documents we have from being burned as the work of devil-worshippers; William Dampier, buccaneer who became a literary lion; Sacajawea, woman guide of Lewis and Clark – The tale of the names is endlessly rich.

Sometimes we are disillusioned, of course. Akhnaton, the Egyptian Pharaoh who preached monotheism, turns out to have been a dreadful wimp and a disaster to his country; the Athenians brought on themselves the Peloponnesian War that ended in their subjugation by tyrannizing over the Delian League when they led it and misappropriating its funds for such purposes as building the Parthenon; of Pope Innocent III, it has been said that his is the distinction of having presided over the destruction of three separate civilizations; Kublai Khan was no philosopher-king, but a war lord interested mainly in further conquests; the Irish remember Oliver Cromwell in much the same way that the Jews remember Hitler, and for much the same reason; Peter the Great was a clinical sadist; Andrew Jackson's pathological hatred of Indians brought about the slaughter of thousands, the dispossession of thousands more; Napoleon III provoked the Franco-Prussian War that cost his country Alsace and Lorraine; the horrors and stupidities of the twentieth century should be well known to everyone alive, though often they don't seem to be—

However, such things are a part of history too, as interesting as any other. If nothing else, a knowledge of them leads toward a healthy skepticism about today's statesmen and their plans for us.

But once again this essay is in danger of becoming deadly serious. Let's get back to the fun. Surely a good deal of that lies in the picturesque details, the things which people elsewhere and elsewhen have taken for granted but which to us are exotic. Is it not occasion for wonder to learn that the Hittites tried and failed to keep the technique of iron-smelting a military secret; that the Orthodox Jewish practice of wigs for married women and circumcision for boys goes back to ancient Egypt; that at least one Phoenician expedition circumnavigated Africa; that the Romans mass-produced cheap glassware for sale to the barbarians; that printing and publishing were important industries in tenth-century China; that a medieval European serf only had to work for his master one-fourth of the year (unlike the modern taxpayer); that the Dutch Republic was a going concern long before its former Spanish overlords recognized it; that Brazil and California got their names from imaginary countries in late medieval romances; that – on and on and on?

There have been some grand attempts to reconstruct this or that aspect of early life. I have mentioned my friend Bordes and his shaping of stone with a piece of reindeer antler. Once, while I was showing him around a state park in my home area, we stopped to rest and he turned out a spearpoint just to keep his hand in . . . then carefully swept up the chips, lest they confuse his colleagues in the future.

Sea voyages have been made in replicated ships. Thor Heyerdahl's are famous, if we can give that name to those primitive vessels. 'Primitive' may be the wrong word, though, since they have turned out to be surprisingly durable and steerable. Likewise have craft of the Viking era; before trying it, nobody had supposed that a hull with a single square sail and a shallow keel could point so high into the wind. On the other hand, the upper course of sails on later ships became known as the royals because King Charles II of England, who fancied himself an expert, insisted they be added. That much canvas was dangerous for vessels of the time, and skippers therefore only clothed those yards when His Majesty was watching. For that matter, the huge battleship *Vasa* of the same period capsized and sank on her maiden voyage because the King of Sweden had kept ordering the builders to add more gun decks.

In Denmark, near Roskilde, is an area devoted to experimentation with techniques of old. There you can see an Iron Age hamlet and a Stone Age camp. The knowledge gained is scientifically valuable. For instance, the yields obtained from Neolithic agriculture make it possible to estimate what the population was in those times. This in turn gives some insight into how the brilliant Bronze Age commenced – which depended on foreign trade, since Denmark had no copper or tin, nor any of the gold in which Ireland rejoiced. The amber traffic spread south across Europe . . .

Informal and cheerful experimentation goes on in the Society for Creative Anachronism. This organization, which has chapters all over the United States and in several other countries, devotes itself frankly to recreating the Middle Ages 'not as they were, but as they should have been.' It engages in tournaments, music, dance, ceremony, arts, crafts, an ideal of chivalrous conduct; lacking are plague, smallpox, famines, inquisitions, fleas, judicial torture, and the like. In spite of the romance, Society members are serious about their research, and have made a number of discoveries. Many facts lay buried in books, such as the evolution of heraldry or the recipes of the times. (It is not true that medieval people made heavy use of spices to disguise the taste of unrefrigerated meat. For preservation, they dried, smoked, salted, or pickled it. They simply liked their food highly flavored.) Others have emerged from practical experience, such as fighting techniques. (It is not true that a knight in armor needed a derrick to get him into his saddle, and lay helpless as an overturned beetle if he got knocked down. This notion derives from English propaganda about the French during the Hundred Years' War. Actually, a full suit of plate weighed about as much as a full backpack, and that weight was distributed over the entire body.) An Anachronist meeting is dramatic and colorful enough to prove, by itself, that history is fun.

Still, if you asked a member a question that often comes up as a sort of parlor game – 'If you could choose a period to live in, what would it be?' – he or she would probably not elect the Middle Ages, because of knowing too much about them. You might enjoy putting the same question to yourself. Many readers of science fiction do feel less than content with the present; that may be why they take such interest in the future. However, the future is unknowable. Even in the unlikely event that it proved utopian, settling down into it would involve a great deal of culture shock. Besides, the next question would remain: 'Utopian for whom?'

This is important to bear in mind if we want to make changes in society as it is, no matter how modest those reforms may look. A glance across the past will prove the point. What milieu *would* you pick? Well, who are you?

Usually unspoken is the implication that you will belong to the fortunate class. Thus I myself could have been quite happy if born about 1800; the nineteenth century was a period when the explorer, the scientist, the scholar, the artist, the entrepreneur were all active, all well regarded, sometimes combined in the same person. But this would only have worked if I had been born into a well-to-do family, of white race and Christian background, in one of a very few Western countries. Considering what medicine, dentistry, and sanitation were like, I would also have needed a naturally rugged constitution. And it would have helped mightily being male rather than female.

Indeed, women – at least, free-born women – had more rights in Viking-era Scandinavia, harsh though that age was, than they do in present-day Saudi Arabia. Otherwise I would advise a lady to choose Mycenean Greece, Heian Japan, early Ireland, or France of the Enlightenment, always assuming that she would be in the aristocracy. On balance, women have probably never been better off than they are here and now. This does not mean that further improvements cannot or should not be made.

Among men, a roughneck brawler might do pretty well in some such setting as Homeric Greece, with the same qualification of birth. As for a literary type, the English language peaked in the Elizabethan period – which, though, regarded itself as decadent. It was certainly easier to become rich by one's own efforts in America a hundred years ago than it is today, yet there was nothing automatic about it then. We could multiply examples forever, but these should be enough.

Every milieu is interesting, none is perfect. Probably you or I, if given the chance, would say of any past time, 'It's a great place to visit, but I wouldn't want to live there.'

We can visit, if not in the flesh, then in the mind – through history, contemporary writings and modern scholarship, archaeological and historical fiction, fantasy, and the time travel of science fiction. We can return pleased, refreshed, better able to understand our own age and even, it may be, the future.

Flight to Forever

CHAPTER ONE

No Return

That morning it rained, a fine, summery mist blowing over the hills and hiding the gleam of the river and the village beyond. Martin Saunders stood in the doorway letting the cool, wet air blow in his face and wondered what the weather would be like a hundred years from now.

Eve Lang came up behind him and laid a hand on his arm. He smiled down at her, thinking how lovely she was with the raindrops caught in her dark hair like small pearls. She didn't say anything; there was no need for it, and he felt grateful for silence.

He was the first to speak. 'Not long now, Eve.' And then, realizing the banality of it, he smiled. 'Only why do we have this airport feeling? It's not as if I'll be gone long.'

'A hundred years,' she said.

'Take it easy, darling. The theory is foolproof. I've been on time jaunts before, remember? Twenty years ahead and twenty years back. The projector works, it's been proven in practice. This is just a little longer trip, that's all.'

'But the automatic machines, that went a hundred years ahead, never came back—'

'Exactly. Some damn fool thing or other went wrong with them. Tubes blew their silly heads off, or some such thing. That's why Sam and I have to go, to see what went wrong. We can repair our machine. We can compensate for the well-known perversity of vacuum tubes.'

'But why the two of you? One would be enough. Sam—'

'Sam is no physicist. He might not be able to find the trouble. On the other hand, as a skilled mechanic he can do things I never could. We supplement each other.' Saunders took a deep breath. 'Look, darling—'

Sam Hull's bass shout rang out at them. 'All set folks! Any time you want to go, we can ride!'

'Coming.' Saunders took his time, bidding Eve a proper farewell, a little in advance. She followed him into the house and down to the capacious underground workshop.

The projector stood in a clutter of apparatus under the white radiance of fluorotubes. It was unimpressive from the outside, a metal cylinder some ten feet high and thirty feet long with the unfinished look of all experimental setups. The outer shell was simply protection for the battery banks and the massive dimensional projector within. A tiny space in the forward end was left for the two men.

Sam Hull gave them a gay wave. His massive form almost blotted out the gray-smocked little body of MacPherson. 'All set for a hundred years ahead,' he exclaimed. 'Two thousand seventy three, here we come!'

MacPherson blinked owlishly at them from behind thick lenses. 'It all tests out,' he said. 'Or so Sam here tells me. Personally, I wouldn't know an oscillograph from a klystron. You have an ample supply of spare parts and tools. There should be no difficulty.'

'I'm not looking for any, Doc,' said Saunders. 'Eve here won't believe we aren't going to be eaten by monsters with stalked eyes and long fangs. I keep telling her all we're going to do is check your automatic machines, if we can find them, and make a few astronomical observations, and come back.'

'There'll be people in the future,' said Eve.

'Oh, well, if they invite us in for a drink we won't say no,' shrugged Hull. 'Which reminds me—' He fished a pint out of his capacious coverall pocket. 'We ought to drink a toast or something, huh?'

Saunders frowned a little. He didn't want to add to Eve's impression of a voyage into darkness. She was worried enough, poor kid, poor, lovely kid. 'Hell,' he said, 'we've been back to nineteen fifty-three and seen the house standing. Nobody home at either time. These jaunts are too dull to rate a toast.'

'Nothing,' said Hull, 'is too dull to rate a drink.' He poured and they touched glasses, a strange little ceremony in the utterly prosaic laboratory. 'Bon voyage!'

'Bon Voyage.' Eve tried to smile, but the hand that lifted the glass to her lips trembled a little.

'Come on,' said Hull. 'Let's go, Mart. Sooner we set out, the sooner we can get back.'

'Sure.' With a gesture of decision, Saunders put down his glass and swung toward the machine. 'Good-by, Eve, I'll see you in a couple of hours – after a hundred years or so.'

'So long – Martin.' She made the name a caress.

MacPherson beamed with avuncular approval.

Saunders squeezed himself into the forward compartment with Hull. He was a big man, long-limbed and wide shouldered, with blunt, homely features under a shock of brown hair and wide-set gray eyes lined with crow's feet from much squinting in the sun. He wore only the plain blouse and slacks of his work, stained here and there with grease and acid.

The compartment was barely large enough for the two of them, and crowded with instruments – as well as the rifle and pistol they had along entirely to quiet Eve's fears. Saunders swore as the guns got in his way, and closed the door. The clang had in it an odd note of finality.

'Here goes,' said Hull unnecessarily.

Saunders nodded and started the projector warming up. Its powerful thrum filled the cabin and vibrated in his bones. Needles flickered across gauge faces, approaching stable values.

Through the single porthole he saw Eve waving. He

153

waved back and then, with an angry motion, flung down the main switch.

The machine shimmered, blurred, and was gone. Eve drew a shuddering breath and turned back to MacPherson.

Grayness swirled briefly before them, and the drone of the projectors filled the machine with an enormous song. Saunders watched the gauges, and inched back the switch which controlled their rate of time advancement. A hundred years ahead – less the number of days since they'd sent the first automatic, just so that no dunderhead in the future would find it and walk off with it . . .

He slapped down the switch and the noise and vibration came to a ringing halt.

Sunlight streamed in through the porthole. 'No house?' asked Hull.

'A century is a long time,' said Saunders. 'Come on, let's go out and have a look.'

They crawled through the door and stood erect. The machine lay in the bottom of a half-filled pit above which grasses waved. A few broken shards of stone projected from the earth. There was a bright blue sky overhead, with fluffy white clouds blowing across it.

'No automatics,' said Hull, looking around.

'That's odd. But maybe the ground-level adjustments – let's go topside.' Saunders scrambled up the sloping walls of the pit.

It was obviously the half-filled basement of the old house, which must somehow have been destroyed in the eighty years since his last visit. The ground-level machine in the projector automatically materialized it on the exact surface whenever it emerged. There would be no sudden falls or sudden burials under risen earth. Nor would there be disastrous materializations inside something solid; mass-sensitive circuits prevented the machine from halting whenever solid matter occupied its own space. Liquid or gas molecules could get out of the way fast enough.

154

Saunders stood in tall, wind-rippled grass and looked over the serene landscape of upper New York State. Nothing had changed, the river and the forested hills beyond it were the same, the sun was bright and clouds shone in the heavens.

No – no, before God! Where was the village?

House gone, town gone – what had happened? Had people simply moved away, or . . .

He looked back down to the basement. Only a few minutes ago – a hundred years in the past – he had stood there in a tangle of battered apparatus, and Doc and Eve – and now it was a pit with wild grass covering the raw earth. An odd desolation tugged at him.

Was *he* still alive today? Was – Eve? The gerontology of 1973 made it entirely possible, but one never knew. And he didn't want to find out.

'Must'a given the country back to the Indians,' grunted Sam Hull.

The prosaic wisecrack restored a sense of balance. After all, any sensible man knew that things changed with time. There would be good and evil in the future as there had been in the past. '—And they lived happily ever after' was pure myth. The important thing was change, an unending flux out of which all could come. And right now there was a job to do.

They scouted around in the grass, but there was no trace of the small automatic projectors. Hull scowled thoughtfully. 'You know,' he said, 'I think they started back and blew out on the way.'

'You must be right,' nodded Saunders. 'We can't have arrived more than a few minutes after their return-point.' He started back toward the big machine. 'Let's take our observation and get out.'

They set up their astronomical equipment and took readings on the declining sun. Waiting for night, they cooked a meal on a camp stove and sat while a cricket-chirring dusk deepened around them.

'I like this future,' said Hull. 'It's peaceful. Think I'll retire here – or now – in my old age.'

The thought of transtemporal resorts made Saunders grin. But – who knew? Maybe!

The stars wheeled grandly overhead. Saunders jotted down figures on right ascension, declination and passage times. From that, they could calculate later, almost to the minute, how far the machine had taken them. They had not moved in space at all, of course, relative to the surface of the earth. 'Absolute space' was an obsolete fiction, and as far as the projector was concerned Earth was the immobile center of the universe.

They waded through dew-wet grass back down to the machine. 'We'll try ten-year stops, looking for the automatics,' said Saunders. 'If we don't find 'em that way, to hell with them. I'm hungry.'

2063 – it was raining into the pit.

2053 – sunlight and emptiness.

2043 – the pit was fresher now, and a few rotting timbers lay half buried in the ground.

Saunders scowled at the meters. 'She's drawing more power than she should,' he said.

2023 – the house had obviously burned, charred stumps of wood were in sight. And the projector had roared with a skull-cracking insanity of power; energy drained from the batteries like water from a squeezed sponge; a resistor was beginning to glow.

They checked the circuits, inch by inch, wire by wire. Nothing was out of order.

'Let's go.' Hull's face was white.

It was a battle to leap the next ten years, it took half an hour of bawling, thundering, tortured labor for the projector to fight backward. Radiated energy made the cabin unendurably hot.

2013 – the fire-blackened basement still stood. On its floor lay two small cylinders, tarnished with some years of weathering.

'The automatics got a little further back,' said Hull. 'Then they quit, and just lay here.'

Saunders examined them. When he looked up from his instruments, his face was grim with the choking fear that was rising within him. 'Drained,' he said. 'Batteries completely dead. They used up all their energy reserves.'

'What in the devil is this?' It was almost a snarl from Hull.

'I – don't – know. There seems to be some kind of resistance which increases the further back we try to go—'

'Come on!'

'But—'

'Come on, God damn it!'

Saunders shrugged hopelessly.

It took two hours to fight back five years. Then Saunders stopped the projector. His voice shook.

'No go, Sam. We've used up three quarters of our stored energy – and the farther back we go, the more we use per year. It seems to be some sort of high-order exponential function.'

'So—'

'So we'd never make it. At this rate, our batteries will be dead before we get back another ten years.' Saunders looked ill. 'It's some effect the theory didn't allow for, some accelerating increase in power requirements the farther back into the past we go. For twenty year hops or less, the energy increases roughly as the square of the number of years traversed. But it must actually be something like an exponential curve, which starts building up fast and furious beyond a certain point. We haven't enough power left in the batteries!'

'If we could recharge them—'

'We don't have such equipment with us. But maybe—'

They climbed out of the ruined basement and looked eagerly towards the river. There was no sign of the village. It must have been torn down or otherwise destroyed still further back in the past at a point they'd been through.

'No help there,' said Saunders.

'We can look for a place. There must be people somewhere!'

'No doubt.' Saunders fought for calm. 'But we could spend a long time looking for them, you know. And—' his voice wavered. 'Sam, I'm not sure even recharging at intervals would help. It looks very much to me as if the curve of energy consumption is approaching a vertical asymptote.'

'Talk English, will you?' Hull's grin was forced.

'I mean that beyond a certain number of years an infinite amount of energy may be required. Like the Einsteinian concept of light as the limiting velocity. As you approach the speed of light, the energy needed to accelerate increases ever more rapidly. You'd need infinite energy to get beyond the speed of light – which is just a fancy way of saying you can't do it. The same thing may apply to time as well as space.'

'You mean – we can't ever get back?'

'I don't know.' Saunders looked desolately around at the smiling landscape. 'I could be wrong. But I'm horribly afraid I'm right.'

Hull swore, 'What're we going to do about it?'

'We've got two choices,' Saunders said. 'One, we can hunt for people, recharge our batteries, and keep trying. Two, we can go into the future.'

'The future!'

'Uh-huh. Sometime in the future, they ought to know more about such things than we do. They may know a way to get around this effect. Certainly they could give us a powerful enough engine so that, if energy is all that's needed, we can get back. A small atomic generator, for instance.'

Hull stood with bent head, turning the thought over in his mind. There was a meadowlark singing somewhere, maddeningly sweet.

Saunders forced a harsh laugh. 'But the very first thing on the agenda,' he said, 'is breakfast!'

CHAPTER TWO

Belgotai of Syrtis

The food was tasteless. They ate in a heavy silence, choking the stuff down. But in the end they looked at each other with a common resolution.

Hull grinned and stuck out a hairy paw. 'It's a hell of a roundabout way to get home,' he said, 'but I'm for it.'

Saunders clasped hands with him, wordlessly. They went back to the machine.

'And now where?' asked the mechanic.

'It's two thousand eight,' said Saunders. 'How about – well – two thousand five-hundred A.D.?'

'Okay. It's a nice round number. Anchors aweigh!'

The machine thrummed and shook. Saunders was gratified to notice the small power consumption as the years and decades fled by. At that rate, they had energy enough to travel to the end of the world.

Eve, Eve, I'll come back. I'll come back if I have to go ahead to Judgement Day . . .

2500 A.D. The machine blinked into materialization on top of a low hill – the pit had filled in during the intervening centuries. Pale, hurried sunlight flashed through wind-driven rain clouds into the hot interior.

'Come,' said Hull. 'We haven't got all day.'

He picked up the automatic rifle. 'What's the idea?' exclaimed Saunders.

'Eve was right the first time,' said Hull grimly. 'Buckle on that pistol, Mart.'

Saunders strapped the heavy weapon to his thigh. The metal was cold under his fingers.

They stepped out and swept the horizon. Hull's voice rose in a shout of glee. 'People!'

There was a small town beyond the river, near the site of old Hudson. Beyond it lay fields of ripening grain and clumps of trees. There was no sign of a highway. Maybe surface transportation was obsolete now.

The town looked – odd. It must have been there a long time, the houses were weathered. They were tall peak-roofed buildings, crowding narrow streets. A flashing metal tower reared some five hundred feet into the lowering sky, near the center of town.

Somehow, it didn't look the way Saunders had visualized communities of the future. It had an oddly stunted appearance, despite the high buildings and – sinister? He couldn't say. Maybe it was only his depression.

Something rose from the center of the town, a black ovoid that whipped into the sky and lined out across the river. *Reception committee*, thought Saunders. His hand fell on his pistol butt.

It was an airjet, he saw as it neared, an egg-shaped machine with stubby wings and a flaring tail. It was flying slowly now, gliding groundward toward them.

'Hallo there!' bawled Hull. He stood erect with the savage wind tossing his flame-red hair, waving. 'Hallo, people!'

The machine dove at them. Something stabbed its nose, a line of smoke – tracers!

Conditioned reflex flung Saunders to the ground. The bullets whined over his head, exploding with a vicious crash behind him. He saw Hull blown apart.

The jet rushed overhead and banked for another assault. Saunders got up and ran, crouching low, weaving back and forth. The line of bullets sprang past him again, throwing up gouts of dirt where they hit. He threw himself down again.

Another try . . . Saunders was knocked off his feet by the bursting of a shell. He rolled over and hugged the ground, hoping the grass would hide him. Dimly, he thought that the jet was too fast for strafing a single man; it overshot its mark.

He heard it whine overhead, without daring to look up. It circled vulture-like, seeking him. He had time for a rising tide of bitter hate.

Sam – they'd killed him, shot him without provocation – Sam, red-haired Sam with his laughter and his comradeship, Sam was dead and they had killed him.

He risked turning over. The jet was settling to earth; they'd hunt him from the ground. He got up and ran again.

A shot wailed past his ear. He spun around, the pistol in his hand, and snapped a return shot. There were men in black uniforms coming out of the jet. It was long range, but his gun was a heavy war model, it carried. He fired again and felt a savage joy at seeing one of the black-clad figures spin on its heels and lurch to the ground.

The time machine lay before him. No time for heroics; he had to get away – fast! Bullets were singing around him.

He burst through the door and slammed it shut. A slug whanged through the metal wall. Thank God the tubes were still warm!

He threw the main switch. As vision wavered, he saw the pursuers almost on him. One of them was aiming something like a bazooka.

They faded into grayness. He lay back, shuddering. Slowly, he grew aware that his clothes were torn and that a metal fragment had scratched his hand.

And Sam was dead. Sam was dead.

He watched the dial creep upward. Let it be 3000 A.D. Five hundred years was not too much to put between himself and the men in black.

He chose night time. A cautious look outside revealed that he was among tall tall buildings with little if any light. Good!

He spent a few moments bandaging his injury and changing into the extra clothes Eve had insisted on providing – a heavy wool shirt and breeches, boots, and a raincoat that should help make him relatively inconspicuous. The holstered pistol went along, of course, with plenty of extra cartridges. He'd have to leave the machine while he reconnoitered and chance its discovery. At least he could lock the door.

161

Outside, he found himself standing in a small cobbled courtyard between high houses and shuttered and darkened windows. Overhead was utter night, the stars must be clouded, but he saw a vague red glow to the north, pulsing and flickering. After a moment, he squared his shoulders and started down an alley that was like a cavern of blackness.

Briefly, the incredible situation rose in his mind. In less than an hour he had leaped a thousand years past his own age, had seen his friend murdered and now stood in an alien city more alone than man had ever been. *And Eve, will I see you again?*

A noiseless shadow, blacker than the night, slipped past him. The dim light shone greenly from its eyes – an alley cat! At least man still had pets. But he could have wished for a more reassuring one.

Noise came from ahead, a bobbing light flashing around at the doors of houses. He dropped a hand through the slit in his coat to grasp the pistol butt.

Black against the narrowed skyline four men came abreast, filling the street. The rhythm of their footfalls was military. A guard of some kind. He looked around for shelter; he didn't want to be taken prisoner by unknowns.

No alleys to the side – he sidled backward. The flashing beam darted ahead, crossed his body, and came back. A voice shouted something, harsh and peremptory.

Saunders turned and ran. The voice cried again behind him. He heard the slam of boots after him. Someone blew a horn, raising echoes that hooted between the high dark walls.

A black form grew out of the night. Fingers like steel wires closed on his arm, yanking him to one side. He opened his mouth, and a hand slipped across it. Before he could recover balance, he was pulled down a flight of stairs in the street.

'In heah.' The hissing whisper was taut in his ear. 'Quickly.'

A door slid open just a crack. They burst through, and the other man closed it behind them. An automatic lock clicked shut.

'Ih don' tink dey vised us,' said the man grimly. 'Dey better not ha'!'

Saunders stared at him. The other man was of medium height, with a lithe, slender build shown by the skin-tight gray clothes under his black cape. There was a gun at one hip, a pouch at the other. His face was sallow, with a yellowish tinge, and the hair was shaven. It was a lean, strong face, with high cheekbones and narrow jaw, straight nose with flaring nostrils, dark slant eyes under Mephistophelean brows. The mouth, wide and self-indulgent was drawn into a reckless grin that showed sharp white teeth. Some sort of white-Mongoloid half-breed, Saunders guessed.

'Who are *you*?' he asked roughly.

The stranger surveyed him shrewdly. 'Belgotai of Syrtis,' he said at last. 'But yuh don' belong heah.'

'I'll say I don't.' Wry humour rose in Saunders. 'Why did you snatch me that way?'

'Yuh didn' wanna fall into de Watch's hands, did yuh?' asked Belgotai. 'Don't ask mih why Ih ressued a stranger. Ih happened to come out, see yuh running, figgered anybody running fro de Watch desuhved help, an' pulled yuh back in.' He shrugged. 'Of course, if yuh don' wanna be helped, go back upstaiahs.'

'I'll stay here, of course,' he said. 'And – thanks for rescuing me.'

'*De nada*,' said Belgotai. 'Come, le's ha' a drink.'

It was a smoky, low-ceilinged room, with a few scarred wooden tables crowded about a small charcoal fire and big barrels in the rear – a tavern of some sort, an underworld hangout. Saunders reflected that he might have done worse. Crooks wouldn't be as finicky about his antecedents as officialdom might be. He could ask his way around, learn.

'I'm afraid I haven't any money,' he said. 'Unless – ' He pulled a handful of coins from his pocket.

Belgotai looked sharply at them and drew a whistling breath between his teeth. Then his face smoothed into blankness. 'Ih'll buy,' he said genially. 'Come, Hennaly, gi' us whissey.'

Belgotai drew Saunders into a dark corner seat, away from the others in the room. The landlord brought tumblers of rotgut remotely akin to whiskey, and Saunders gulped his with a feeling of need.

'Wha' name do yuh go by?' asked Belgotai.

'Saunders. Martin Saunders.'

'Glad to see yuh. Now – ' Belgotai leaned closer, and his voice dropped to a whisper – 'Now, Saunders, *when*'re yuh from?'

Saunders started. Belgotai smiled thinly. 'Be frank,' he said. 'Des're mih frien's heah. Dey'd think nawting of slitting yuh troat and dumping yuh in de alley. But Ih mean well.'

With a sudden great weariness, Saunders relaxed. What the hell, it had to come out sometime. 'Nineteen hundred seventy-three,' he said.

'Eh? De future?'

'No – the past.'

'Oh. Diff'ent chronning, den. How far back?'

'One thousand and twentyseven years.'

Belgotai whistled. 'Long ways! But Ih were sure yuh mus' be from de past. Nobody eve' came fro' de future.'

Sickly: 'You mean – its impossible?'

'Ih do' know.' Belgotai's grin was wolfish. 'Who'd visit dis era fro' de future, if dey could? But wha's yuh story?'

Saunders bristled. The whiskey was coursing hot in his veins now. 'I'll trade information,' he said coldly. 'I won't give it.'

'Faiah enawff. Blast away. Mahtin Saundahs.'

Saunders told his story in a few words. At the end,

Belgotai nodded gravely. 'Yuh ran into de Fanatics, five hundred yeahs ago,' he said. 'Dey was deat' on time travelers. Or on most people, for dat matter.'

'But what's happened? What sort of world is this, anyway?'

Belgotai's slurring accents were getting easier to follow. Pronunciation had changed a little, vowels sounded different, the 'r' had shifted to something like that in twentieth-century French or Danish, other consonants were modified. Foreign words, especially Spanish, had crept in. But it was still intelligible. Saunders listened. Belgotai was not too well versed in history, but his shrewd brain had a grasp of the more important facts.

The time of troubles had begun in the twenty-third century with the revolt of the Martian colonists against the increasingly corrupt and tyrranical Terrestrial Directorate. A century later the folk of Earth were on the move, driven by famine, pestilence and civil war, a chaos out of which rose the religious enthusiasm of the Armageddonists – the Fanatics, as they were called later. Fifty years after the massacres on Luna, Huntry was the military dictator of Earth, and the rule of the Armageddonists endured for nearly three hundred years. It was a nominal sort of rule, vast territories were always in revolt and the planetary colonists were building up a power which kept the Fanatics out of space, but wherever they did have control they ruled with utter ruthlessness.

Among other things they forbade was time travel. But it had never been popular with anyone since the Time War, when a defeated Directorate army had leaped from the twenty-third to the twenty-fourth century and wrought havoc before their attempt at conquest was smashed. Time travelers were few anyway, the future was too precarious – they were apt to be killed or enslaved in one of the more turbulent periods.

In the late twenty-seventh century, the Planetary League

165

and the African Dissenters had finally ended Fanatic rule. Out of the postwar confusion rose the Pax Africana, and for two hundred years man had enjoyed an era of comparative peace and progress which was wistfully looked back on as a golden age; indeed, modern chronology dated from the ascension of John Mteza I. Breakdown came through internal decay and the onslaughts of barbarians from the outer planets, the Solar System split into a multitude of small states and even independent cities. It was a hard, brawling period, not without a brilliance of its own, but it was drawing to a close now.

'Dis is one of de city-states,' said Belgotai. 'Liung-Wei, it's named – founded by Sinese invaders about tree centuries ago. It's under de dictatorship of Krausmann now, a stubborn old buzzard who'll no surrender dough de armies of de Atlantic Master're at ouah very gates now. Yuh see de red glow? Dat's deir projectors working on our energy screen. When dey break it down, dey'll take de city and punish it for holding out so long. Nobody looks happily to dat day.'

He added a few remarks, about himself. Belgotai was of a dying age, the past era of small states who employed mercenaries to fight their battles. Born on Mars, Belgotai had hired out all over the whole Solar System. But the little mercenary companies were helpless before the organized levies of the rising nations, and after the annihilation of his band Belgotai had fled to Earth where he dragged out a weary existence as thief and assassin. He had little to look forward to.

'Nobody wants a free comrade now,' he said ruefully. 'If de Watch don't catch me first, Ih'll hang when de Atlantics take de city.'

Saunders nodded with a certain sympathy.

Belgotai leaned close with a gleam in his slant eyes. 'But yuh can help me, Mahtin Saundahs,' he hissed. 'And help yuhself too.'

'Eh?' Saunders blinked wearily at him.

'Sure, sure. Take me wid yuh, out of dis damned time. Dey can't help yuh here, dey know no more about time travel dan yuh do – most likely dey'll trow yuh in de calabozo and smash yuh machine. Yuh have to go on. Take me!'

Saunders hesitated, warily. What did he really know? How much truth was in Belgotai's story? How far could he trust –

'Set me off in some time when a free comrade can fight again. Meanwhile Ih'll help. Ih'm a good man wid gun or vibrodagger. Yuh can't go battling alone into de future.'

Saunders wondered. But what the hell – it was plain enough that this period was of no use to him. And Belgotai had saved him, even if the Watch wasn't as bad as he claimed. And – well – he needed someone to talk to, if nothing else. Someone to help him forget Sam Hull and the gulf of centuries separating him from Eve.

Decision came. 'Okay.'

'Wonnaful! Yuh'll no be sorry, Mahtin.' Belgotai stood up. 'Come, le's be blasting off.'

'Now?'

'De sooner de better. Someone may find yuh machine. Den it's too late.'

'But – you'll want to make ready – say good-by – '

Belgotai slapped his pouch. 'All Ih own is heah.' Bitterness underlay his reckless laugh. 'Ih've none to say good-by to, except mih creditors. Come!'

Half dazed, Saunders followed him out of the tavern. This time-hopping was going too fast for him, he didn't have a chance to adjust.

For instance, if he ever got back to his own time he'd have descendants in this age. At the rate of which lines of descent spread, there would be men in each army who had his own and Eve's blood, warring on each other without thought of the tenderness which had wrought their very beings. But then, he remembered wearily, he had never considered the

167

common ancestors he must have with men he'd shot out of the sky in the war he once had fought.

Men lived in their own times, a brief flash of light ringed with an enormous dark, and it was not in their nature to think beyond that little span of years. He began to realize why time travel had never been common.

'Hist!' Belgotai drew him into the tunnel of an alley. They crouched there while four black-caped men of the Watch strode past. In the wan red light, Saunders had a glimpse of high cheekbones, half-Oriental features, the metallic gleam of guns slung over their shoulders.

They made their way to the machine where it lay between lowering houses crouched in a night of fear and waiting. Belgotai laughed again, a soft, joyous ring in the dark. 'Freedom!' he whispered.

They crawled into it and Saunders set the controls for a hundred years ahead. Belgotai scowled. 'Most like de world'll be very tame and quiet den,' he said.

'If I get a way to return,' said Saunders, 'I'll carry you on whenever you want to go.'

'Or yuh could carry me back a hundred years from now,' said the warrior. 'Blast away, den!'

3100 A.D. A waste of blackened, fused rock. Saunders switched on the Geiger counter and it clattered crazily. Radioactive! Some hellish atomic bomb had wiped Liung-Wei from existence. He leaped another century, shaking.

3200 A.D. The radioactivity was gone, but the desolation remained, a vast vitrified crater under a hot, still sky, dead and lifeless. There was little prospect of walking across it in search of man, nor did Saunders want to get far from the machine. If he should be cut off from it . . .

By 3500, soil had drifted back over the ruined land and a forest was growing. They stood in a drizzling rain and looked around them.

'Big trees,' said Saunders. 'This forest has stood for a long time without human interference.'

'Maybe man went back to de caves?' suggested Belgotai.

'I doubt it. Civilization was just too widespread for a lapse into total savagery. But it may be a long ways to a settlement.'

'Le's go ahead, den!' Belgotai's eyes gleamed with interest.

The forest still stood for centuries thereafter. Saunders scowled in worry. He didn't like this business of going farther and farther from his time, he was already too far ahead ever to get back without help. Surely, in all ages of human history –

4100 A.D. They flashed into materialization on a broad grassy sward where low, rounded buildings of something that looked like tinted plastic stood between fountains, statues, and bowers. A small aircraft whispered noiselessly overhead, no sign of motive power on its exterior.

There were humans around, young men and women who wore long colorful capes over light tunics. They crowded forward with a shout. Saunders and Belgotai stepped out, raising hands in a gesture of friendship. But the warrior kept his hands close to his gun.

The language was a flowing, musical tongue with only a baffling hint of familiarity. Had times changed that much?

They were taken to one of the buildings. Within its cool, spacious interior, a grave, bearded man in ornate red robes stood up to greet them. Someone else brought in a small machine reminiscent of an oscilloscope with microphone attachments. The man set it on the table and adjusted its dials.

He spoke again, his own unknown language rippling from his lips. But words came out of the machine – English!

'Welcome, travelers, to this branch of the American College. Please be seated.'

Saunders and Belgotai gaped. The man smiled. 'I see the

169

psychophone is new to you. It is a receiver of encephalic emissions from the speech centers. When one speaks, the corresponding thoughts are taken by the machine, greatly amplified, and beamed to the brain of the listener, who interprets them in terms of his own language.

'Permit me to introduce myself. I am Hamalon Avard; dean of this branch of the College.' He raised bushy gray eyebrows in polite inquiry.

They gave their names and Avard bowed ceremoniously. A slim girl, whose scanty dress caused Belgotai's eyes to widen, brought a tray of sandwiches and a beverage not unlike tea. Saunders suddenly realized how hungry and tired he was. He collapsed into a seat that moulded itself to his contours and looked dully at Avard.

Their story came out, and the dean nodded. 'I thought you were time travelers,' he said. 'But this is a matter of great interest. The archeology departments will want to speak to you, if you will be so kind – '

'Can you help us?' asked Saunders bluntly. 'Can you fix our machine so it will be reversed?'

'Alas, no. I am afraid our physics holds no hope for you. I can consult the experts, but I am sure there has been no change in spatiotemporal theory since Priogan's reformulation. According to it, the energy needed to travel into the past increases tremendously with the period covered. The deformation of world lines, you see. Beyond a period of about seventy years, infinite energy is required.'

Saunders nodded dully. 'I thought so. Then there's no hope?'

'Not in this time, I am afraid. But science is advancing rapidly. Contact with alien culture in the Galaxy has proved an immense stimulant – '

'Yuh have interstellar travel?' exploded Belgotai. 'Yuh can travel to the stars?'

'Yes, of course. The faster-than-light drive has worked out over five hundred years ago on the basis of Priogan's

170

modified relativity theory. It involves warping through higher dimensions – But you have more urgent problems – than scientific theories.'

'Not Ih!' said Belgotai fiercely. 'If Ih can get put among the stars – dere must be wars dere – '

'Alas, yes, the rapid expansion of the frontier has thrown the Galaxy into chaos. But I do not think you could get passage on a spaceship. In fact, the Council will probably order your temporal deportation as unintegrated individuals. The sanity of Sol will be in danger otherwise.'

'Why, yuh – ' Belgotai snarled and reached for his gun. Saunders clapped a hand on the warrior's arm.

'Take it easy, you bloody fool,' he said furiously. 'We can't fight a whole planet. Why should we? There'll be other ages.'

Belgotai relaxed, but his eyes were still angry.

They stayed at the College for two days. Avard and his colleagues were courteous, hospitable, eager to hear what the travelers had to tell of their periods. They provided food and living quarters and much-needed rest. They even pleaded Belgotai's case to the Solar Council, via telescreen. But the answer was inexorable: the Galaxy already had too many barbarians. The travelers would have to go.

Their batteries were taken out of the machine for them and a small atomic engine with nearly limitless energy reserves installed in its place. Avard gave them a psychophone for communication with whomever they met in the future. Everyone was very nice and considerate. But Saunders found himself reluctantly agreeing with Belgotai. He didn't care much for these overcivilized gentlefolk. He didn't belong in this age.

Avard bade them grave good-by. 'It is strange to see you go,' he said. 'It is a strange thought that you will still be traveling long after my cremation, that you will see things I cannot dream of.' Briefly, something stirred in his face. 'In a way I envy you.' He turned away quickly, as if afraid of the thought. 'Good-by and good fortune.'

4300 A.D. The campus buildings were gone, but small, elaborate summerhouses had replaced them. Youths and girls in scanty rainbow-hued dress crowded around the machine.

'You are time travelers?' asked one of the young men, wide-eyed.

Saunders nodded, feeling too tired for speech.

'Time travelers!' A girl squealed in delight.

'I don't suppose you have any means of traveling into the past these days?' asked Saunders hopelessly.

'Not that I know of. But please come, stay for a while, tell us about your journeys. This is the biggest lark we've had since the ship came from Sirius.'

There was no denying the eager insistence. The women, in particular, crowded around, circling them in a ring of soft arms, laughing and shouting and pulling them away from the machine. Belgotai grinned. 'Le's stay de night,' he suggested.

Saunders didn't feel like arguing the point. There was time enough, he thought bitterly. All the time in the world.

It was a night of revelry. Saunders managed to get a few facts. Sol was a Galactic backwater these days, stuffed with mercantile wealth and guarded by nonhuman mercenaries against the interstellar raiders and conquerors. This region was one of many playgrounds for the children of the great merchant families, living for generations off inherited riches. They were amiable kids, but there was a mental and physical softness over them, and a deep inward weariness from a meaningless round of increasingly stale pleasure. Decadence.

Saunders finally sat alone under a moon that glittered with the diamond points of doomed cities, beside a softly lapping artificial lake, and watched the constellations wheel overhead – the far suns that man had conquered without mastering himself. He thought of Eve and wanted to cry, but the hollowness in his breast was dry and cold.

CHAPTER THREE

Trapped in the Time-Stream

Belgotai had a thumping hangover in the morning which a drink offered by one of the women removed. He argued for a while about staying in this age. Nobody would deny him passage this time; they were eager for fighting men out in the Galaxy. But the fact that Sol was rarely visited now, that he might have to wait years, finally decided him on continuing.

'Dis won' go on much longer,' he said. 'Sol is too tempting a prize, an' mercenaries aren' allays loyal. Sooner or later, dere'll be war on Eart' again.'

Saunders nodded dispiritedly. He hated to think of the blasting energies that would devour a peaceful and harmless folk, the looting and murdering and enslaving, but history was that way. It was littered with the graves of pacifists.

The bright scene swirled into grayness. They drove ahead.

4400 A.D. A villa was burning, smoke and flame reaching up into the clouded sky. Behind it stood the looming bulk of a ray-scarred spaceship, and around it boiled a vortex of men, huge bearded men in helmets and cuirasses, laughing as they bore out golden loot and struggling captives. The barbarians had come!

The two travelers leaped back into the machine. Those weapons could fuse it to a glowing mass. Saunders swung the main-drive switch far over.

'We'd better make a longer jump,' Saunders said as the needle crept past the century mark. 'Can't look for much scientific progress in a dark age. I'll try for five thousand A.D.'

His mind carried the thought on: *Will there ever be progress of the sort we must have? Eve, will I ever see you again?* As if his yearning could carry over the abyss of millennia: *Don't mourn me too long, my dearest. In all the bloody ages of human history, your happiness is all that ultimately matters.*

As the needle approached six centuries, Saunders tried to ease down the switch. Tried!

'What's the matter?' Belgotai leaned over his shoulder.

With a sudden cold sweat along his ribs, Saunders tugged harder. The switch was immobile – the projector wouldn't stop.

'Out of order?' asked Belgotai anxiously.

'No – it's the automatic mass-detector. We'd be annihilated if we emerged in the same space with solid matter. The detector prevents the projector from stopping if it senses such a structure.' Saunders grinned savagely. 'Some damned idiot must have built a house right where we are!'

The needle passed its limit, and still they droned on through a featureless grayness. Saunders reset the dial and noted the first half millennium. It was nice, though not necessary, to know what year it was when they emerged.

He wasn't worried at first. Man's works were so horribly impermanent; he thought with a sadness of the cities and civilizations he had seen rise and spend their little hour and sink back into the night and chaos of time. But after a thousand years . . .

Two thousand . . .

Three thousand . . .

Belgotai's face was white and tense in the dull glow of the instrument panel. 'How long to go?' he whispered.

'I – don't – know.'

Within the machine, the long minutes passed while the projector hummed its song of power and two men stared with hypnotized fascination at the creeping record of centuries.

For twenty thousand years that incredible thing stood. In the year 25,296 A.D., the switch suddenly went down under

174

Saunders' steady tug. The machine flashed into reality, tilted, and slid down a few feet before coming to rest. Wildly, they opened the door.

The projector lay on a stone block big as a small house, whose ultimate slipping from its place had freed them. It was halfway up a pyramid.

A monument of gray stone, a tetrahedron a mile to a side and a half a mile high. The outer casing had worn away, or been removed, so that the tremendous blocks stood naked to the weather. Soil had drifted up onto it, grass and trees grew on its titanic slopes. Their roots, the wind and rain and frost, were slowly crumbling the artificial hill to earth again, but still it dominated the landscape.

A defaced carving leered out from a tangle of brush. Saunders looked at it and looked away, shuddering. No human being had ever carved that thing.

The countryside around was altered; he couldn't see the old river and there was a lake glimmering in the distance which had not been there before. The hills seemed lower, and forest covered them. It was a wild, primeval scene, but there was a spaceship standing near the base, a monster machine with its nose rearing skyward and a sunburst blazon on its hull. And there were men working nearby.

Saunders' shout rang in the still air. He and Belgotai scrambled down the steep slope of earth, clawing past trees and vines. Men!

No – not all men. A dozen great shining engines were toiling without supervision at the foot of the pyramid – robots. And of the group which turned to stare at the travelers, two were squat, blue-furred, with snouted faces and six-fingered hands.

Saunders realized with an unexpectedly eerie shock that he was seeing extraterrestrial intelligence. But it was to the men that he faced.

They were all tall, with aristocratically refined features and a calm that seemed inbred. Their clothing was impossible to describe, it was like a rainbow shimmer around them, never the same in its play of color and shape. So, thought Saunders, so must the old gods have looked on high Olympus, beings greater and more beautiful than man.

But it was a human voice that called to them, a deep, well-modulated tone in a totally foreign language. Saunders remembered exasperatedly that he had forgotten the psychophone. But one of the blue-furred aliens was already fetching a round, knob-studded globe out of which the familiar translating voice seemed to come: '. . . time travelers.'

'From the very remote past, obviously,' said another man. Damn him, damn them all, they weren't any more excited than at the bird which rose, startled, from the long grass. You'd think time travelers would at least be worth shaking by the hand.

'Listen,' snapped Saunders, realizing in the back of his mind that his annoyance was a reaction against the awesomeness of the company, 'we're in trouble. Our machine won't carry us back, and we have to find a period of time which knows how to reverse the effect. Can you do it?'

One of the aliens shook his animal head. 'No,' he said. 'There is no way known to physics of getting farther back than about seventy years. Beyond that, the required energy approaches infinity and – '

Saunders groaned. 'We know it,' said Belgotai harshly.

'At least you must rest,' said one of the men in a more kindly tone. 'It will be interesting to hear your story.'

'I've told it to too many people in the last few millennia,' rasped Saunders. 'Let's hear yours for a change.'

Two of the strangers exchanged low-voiced words. Saunders could almost translate them himself: '*Barbarians – childish emotional pattern – well, humor them for a while.*'

'This is an archeological expedition, excavating the pyramid,' said one of the men patiently. 'We are from the Galactic Institute, Sarlan-sector branch. I am Lord Arsfel of Astracyr, and these are my subordinates. The nonhumans, as you may wish to know, are from the planet Quulhan, whose sun is not visible from Terra.'

Despite Himself, Saunders' awed gaze turned to the stupendous mass looming over them. 'Who built it?' he breathed.

'The Ixchulhi made such structures on planets they conquered, no one knows why. But then, no one knows what they were, or where they came from, or where they ultimately went. It is hoped that some of the answers may be found in their pyramids.'

The atmosphere grew more relaxed. Deftly, the men of the expedition got Saunders' and Belgotai's stories and what information about their almost prehistoric periods they cared for. In exchange, something of history was offered them.

After the Ixchulhi's ruinous wars the Galaxy had made a surprisingly rapid comeback. New techniques of mathematical psychology made it possible to unite the peoples of a billion worlds and rule them effectively. The Galactic Empire was egalitarian – it had to be, for one of its mainstays was the fantastically old and evolved race of the planet called Vro-Hi by men.

It was peaceful, prosperous, colorful with diversity of races and cultures, expanding in science and the arts. It had already endured for ten thousand years, and there seemed no doubt in Arsfel's calm mind that it could endure for ever. The barbarians along the Galactic periphery and out in the Magellanic Clouds? Nonsense! The Empire would get around to civilizing them in due course; meanwhile they were only a nuisance.

But Sol could almost be called one of the barbarian suns, though it lay within the Imperial boundaries. Civilization was concentrated near the center of the Galaxy, and Sol lay in what was actually a remote and thinly starred region of space. A few primitive landsmen still lived on its planets and had infrequent intercourse with the nearer stars, but they hardly counted. The human race had almost forgotten its ancient home.

Somehow the picture was saddening to the American. He thought of old Earth spinning on her lonely way through the emptiness of space, he thought of the great arrogant Empire and all the mighty dominions which had fallen to dust through the millennia. But when he ventured to suggest that this civilization, too, was not immortal, he was immediately snowed under with figures, facts, logic, the curious para-mathematical symbolism of modern mass psychology. It could be shown rigorously that the present setup was inherently stable – and already ten thousand years of history had given no evidence to upset that science . . .

'I give up,' said Saunders. 'I can't argue with you.'

They were shown through the spaceship's immense interior, the luxurious apartments of the expedition, the looming intricate machinery which did its own thinking. Arsfel tried to show them his art, his recorded music, his psychobooks, but it was no use, they didn't have the understanding.

Savages! Could an Australian aborigine have appreciated Rembrandt, Beethoven, Kant, or Einstein? Could he have lived happily in the sophisticated New York society?

'We'd best go,' muttered Belgotai. 'We don't belong heah.'

Saunders nodded. Civilization had gone too far for them, they could never be more than frightened pensioners in its hugeness. Best get on their way again.

'I would advise you to leap ahead for long intervals,' said Arsfel. 'Galactic civilization won't have spread out this far for many thousands of years, and certainly whatever native culture Sol develops won't be able to help you.' He smiled. 'It doesn't matter if you overshoot the time when the process you need is invented. The records won't be lost, I assure you. From here on, you are certain of encountering only peace and enlightenment . . . unless, of course, the barbarians of Terra get hostile, but then you can always leave them behind. Sooner or later, there will be true civilization here to help you.'

'Tell me honestly,' said Saunders. 'Do you think the negative time machine will ever be invented?'

One of the beings from Quulhan shook his strange head. 'I doubt it,' he said gravely. 'We would have had visitors from the future.'

'They might not have cared to see your time,' argued Saunders desperately. 'They'd have complete records of it. So they'd go back to investigate more primitive ages, where their appearance might easily pass unnoticed.'

'You may be right,' said Arsfel. His tone was disconcertingly like that with which an adult comforts a child by a white lie.

'Le's go!' snarled Belgotai.

In 26,000 the forests still stood and the pyramid had become a high hill where trees nodded and rustled in the wind.

In 27,000 a small village of wood and stone houses stood among smiling grain fields.

In 28,000 men were tearing down the pyramid, quarrying it for stone. But its huge bulk was not gone before 30,000 A.D., and a small city had been built from it.

Minutes ago, thought Saunders grayly, they had been talking to Lord Arsfel of Astracyr, and now he was five thousand years in his grave.

In 31,000 they materialized on one of the broad lawns that reached between the towers of a high and proud city. Aircraft swarmed overhead and a spaceship, small beside Arsfel's but nonetheless impressive, was standing nearby.

'Looks like de Empire's got heah,' said Belgotai.

'I don't know,' said Saunders. 'But it looks peaceful, anyway. Let's go out and talk to people.'

They were received by tall, stately women in white robes of classic lines. It seemed that the Matriarchy now ruled Sol, and

179

would they please conduct themselves as befitted the inferior sex? No, the Empire hadn't ever gotten out here; Sol paid tribute, and there was an imperial legate at Sirius, but the actual boundaries of Galactic culture hadn't changed for the past three millennia. Solar civilization was strictly home-grown and obviously superior to the alien influence of the Vro-Hi.

No, nothing was known about time theory. Their visit had been welcome and all that, but now would they please go on? They didn't fit in with the neatly regulated culture of Terra.

'I don't like it,' said Saunders as they walked back toward the machine. 'Arsfel swore the Imperium would keep expanding its actual as well as its nominal sphere of influence. But it's gone static now. Why?'

'Ih tink,' said Belgotai, 'dat spite of all his fancy mathematics, yuh were right. Nawthing lasts forever.'

'But – my God!'

CHAPTER FOUR

End of Empire

34,000 A.D. The Matriarchy was gone. The city was a tumbled heap of fire-blackened rocks. Skeletons lay in the ruins.

'The barbarians are moving again,' said Saunders bleakly. 'They weren't here so very long ago, these bones are still fresh, and they've got a long ways to go dead center. An empire like this one will be many thousands of years in dying. But it's doomed already.'

'What'll we do?' asked Belgotai.

'Go on,' said Saunders tonelessly. 'What else can we do?'

35,000 A.D. A pleasant hut stood under huge old trees. Here and there a broken column stuck out of the earth, remnant of the city. A bearded man in coarsely woven garments fled wildly with his woman and brood of children as the machine appeared.

36,000 A.D. There was a village again, with a battered old spaceship standing hard by. There were half a dozen different races, including man, moving about, working on the construction of some enigmatic machine. They were dressed in plain, shabby clothes, with guns at their sides and the hard look of warriors in their eyes. But they didn't treat the new arrivals too badly.

Their chief was a young man in the cape and helmet of an officer of the Empire. But his outfit was at least a century old, and he was simply head of a small troop which had been hired from among the barbarian hordes to protect this part of Terra. Oddly, he insisted he was a loyal vassal of the Emperor.

The Empire! It was still a remote glory, out there among the stars. Slowly it waned, slowly the barbarians encroached while corruption and civil war tore it apart from the inside, but it was still the pathetic, futile hope of intelligent beings throughout the Galaxy. Some day it would be restored. Some day civilization would return to the darkness of the outer worlds, greater and more splendid than ever. Men dared not believe otherwise.

'But we've got a right job here,' shrugged the chief. 'Tautho of Sirius will be on Sol's necks soon. I doubt if we can stand him off for long.'

'And what'll yuh do den?' challenged Belgotai.

The young-old faced twisted in a bitter smile. 'Die, of course. What else is there to do – these days?'

They stayed overnight with the troopers. Belgotai had fun swapping lies about warlike exploits, but in the morning he decided to go on with Saunders. The age was violent enough, but its hopelessness daunted even his tough soul.

Saunders looked haggardly at the control panel. 'We've got to go a long ways ahead,' he said. 'A hell of a long ways.'

50,000 A.D. They flashed out of the time drive and opened the door. A raw wind caught at them, driving thin sheets of snow before it. The sky hung low and gray over a landscape of high rocky hills where pine trees stood gloomily between naked crags. There was ice on the river that murmured darkly out of the woods.

Geology didn't work that fast, even fourteen thousand years wasn't a very long time to the slowly changing planets. It must have been the work of intelligent beings, ravaging and scoring the world with senseless wars of unbelievable forces.

A gray stone mass dominated the landscape. It stood enormous a few miles off, its black walls sprawling over incredible acres, its massive crenellated towers reaching gauntly into the sky. And it lay half in ruin, torn and tumbled stone distorted by energies that once made rock run molten, blurred by uncounted millennia of weather – old.

'Dead,' Saunders' voice was thin under the hooting wind. 'All dead.'

'No,' Belgotai's slant eyes squinted against the flying snow. 'No, Mahtin, Ih tink Ih see a banner flying.'

The wind blew bitterly around them, scaring them with its chill. 'Shall we go on?' asked Saunders dully.

'Best we go find out wha's happened,' said Belgotai. 'Dey can do no worse dan kill us, and Ih begin to tink dat's not so bad.'

Saunders put on all the clothes he could find and took the psychophone in one chilled hand. Belgotai wrapped his cloak tightly about him. They started toward the gray edifice.

The wind blew and blew. Snow hissed around them, covering the tough gray-green vegetation that hugged the stony ground. Summer on Earth, 50,000 A.D.

As they neared the structure, its monster size grew on

them. Some of the towers which still stood must be almost half a mile high, thought Saunders dizzily. But it had a grim, barbaric look; no civilized race had ever built such a fortress.

Two small, swift-shapes darted into the air from that cliff-like wall. 'Aircraft,' said Belgotai laconically. The wind ripped the word from his mouth.

They were ovoidal, without external controls or windows, apparently running on the gravitic forces which had long ago been tamed. One of them hovered overhead, covering the travelers, while the other dropped to the ground. As it landed, Saunders saw that it was old and worn and scarred. But there was a faded sunburst on its side. Some memory of the Empire must still be alive.

Two came out of the little vessel and approached the travelers with guns in their hands. One was human, a tall well-built young man with shoulder-length black hair blowing under a tarnished helmet, a patched purple coat streaming from his cuirassed shoulders, a faded leather kilt and buskins. The other . . .

He was a little shorter than the man, but immensely broad of chest and limb. Four muscled arms grew from the massive shoulders, and a tufted tail lashed against his clawed feet. His head was big, broad-skulled, with a round half-animal face and cat-like whiskers about the fanged mouth and the split-pupilled yellow eyes. He wore no clothes except a leather harness, but soft blue-gray fur covered the whole great body.

The psychophone clattered out the man's hail: 'Who comes?'

'Friends,' said Saunders. 'We wish only shelter and a little information.'

'Where are you from?' There was a harsh, peremptory note in the man's voice. His face – straight, thin-boned, the countenance of a highly bred aristocrat – was gaunt with strain. 'What do you want? What sort of spaceship is that you've got down there?'

'Easy, Vargor,' rumbled the alien's bass. 'That's no spaceship, you can see that.'

'No,' said Saunders. 'It's a time projector.'

'Time travelers!' Vargor's intense blue eyes widened. 'I heard of such things once, but – time travelers!' Suddenly: 'When are you from? Can you help us?'

'We're from very long ago,' said Saunders pityingly. 'And I'm afraid we're alone and helpless.'

Vargor's erect carriage sagged a little. He looked away. But the other being stepped forward with an eagerness in him. 'How far back?' he asked. 'Where are you going?'

'We're going to hell, most likely. But can you get us inside? We're freezing.'

'Of course. Come with us. You'll not take it amiss if I send a squad to inspect your machine? We have to be careful, you know.'

The four squeezed into the aircraft and it lifted with a groan of ancient engines. Vargor gestured at the fortress ahead and his tone was a little wild. 'Welcome to the hold of Brontothor! Welcome to the Galactic Empire!'

'The Empire?'

'Aye, this is the Empire, or what's left of it. A haunted fortress on a frozen ghost world, last fragment of the Old Imperium and still trying to pretend that the Galaxy is not dying – that it didn't die millennia ago, that there is something left besides wild beasts howling among the ruins.' Vargor's throat caught in a dry sob. 'Welcome!'

The alien laid a huge hand on the man's shoulder. 'Don't get hysterical, Vargor,' he reproved gently. 'As long as brave beings hope, the Empire is still alive – whatever they say.'

He looked over his shoulder at the others. 'You really are welcome,' he said. 'It's a hard and dreary life we lead here. Taury and the Dreamer will both welcome you gladly.' He paused. Then, unsurely, 'But best you don't say too much

184

about the ancient time, if you've really seen it. We can't bear too sharp a reminder, you know.'

The machine slipped down beyond the wall, over a gigantic flagged courtyard to the monster bulk of the – the donjon, Saunders supposed one could call it. It rose up in several tiers, with pathetic little gardens on the terraces, toward a dome of clear plastic.

The walls, he saw, were immensely thick, with weapons mounted on them which he could see clearly through the drifting snow. Behind the donjon stood several long, barracks-like buildings, and a couple of spaceships which must have been held together by pure faith rested near what looked like an arsenal. There were guards on duty, helmeted men with energy rifles, their cloaks wrapped tightly against the wind, and other folk scurried around under the monstrous walls, men and women and children.

'There's Taury,' said the alien, pointing to a small group clustered on one of the terraces. 'We may as well land right there.' His wide mouth opened in an alarming smile. 'And forgive me for not introducing myself before. I'm Hunda of Haamigur, general of the Imperial armies, and this is Vargor Alfri, prince of the Empire.'

'Yuh crazy?' blurted Belgotai. 'What Empire?'

Hunda shrugged. 'It's a harmless game, isn't it? At that, you know, we are the Empire – legally. Taury is a direct descendant of Maurco the Doomer, last Emperor to be anointed according to the proper forms. Of course, that was five thousand years ago, and Maurco had only three systems left then, but the law is clear. These hundred or more barbarian pretenders, human and otherwise, haven't the shadow of a real claim to the title.'

The vessel grounded and they stepped out. The others waited for them to come up. There were half a dozen old men, their long beards blowing wildly in the gale, there was a being with the face of a long-beaked bird and one that had the shape of a centauroid.

'The court of Empress Taury,' said Hunda.

'Welcome.' The answer was low and gracious.

Saunders and Belgotai stared dumbly at her. She was tall, tall as a man, but under her tunic of silver links and her furred cloak she was such a woman as they had dreamed of without ever knowing in life. Her proudly lifted head had something of Vargor's looks, the same clean-lined, high-cheeked face, but it was the countenance of a woman, from the broad clear brow to the wide, wondrously chiseled mouth and the strong chin. The cold had flushed the lovely pale planes of her cheeks. Her heavy bronze-red hair was braided about her helmet, with one rebellious lock tumbling softly toward the level, dark brows. Her eyes, huge and oblique and gray as northern seas, were serene on them.

Saunders found tongue. 'Thank you, your majesty,' he said in a firm voice.

'If it please you I am Martin Saunders of America, some forty-eight thousand years in the past, and my companion is Belgotai, free companion from Syrtis about a thousand years later. We are at your service for what little we may be able to do.'

She inclined her stately head, and her sudden smile was warm and human. 'It is a rare pleasure,' she said. 'Come inside, please. And forget the formality. Tonight let us simply be alive.'

They sat in what had been a small council chamber. The great hall was too huge and empty, a cavern of darkness and rustling relics of greatness, hollow with too many memories. But the lesser room had been made livable, hung with tapestries and carpeted with skins. Fluorotubes cast a white light over it, and a fire crackled cheerfully in the hearth. Had it not been for the wind against the windows, they might have forgotten where they were.

' – and you can never go back?' Taury's voice was sober. 'You can never get home again?'

'I don't think so,' said Saunders. 'From our story, it doesn't look that way, does it?'

'No,' said Hunda. 'You'd better settle down in some time and make the best of matters.'

'Why not with us?' asked Vargor eagerly.

'We'd welcome you with all our hearts,' said Taury, 'but I cannot honestly advise you to stay. These are evil times.'

It was a harsh language they spoke, a ringing metallic tongue brought in by the barbarians. But from her throat, Saunders thought, it was utter music.

'We'll at least stay a few days,' he said impulsively. 'It's barely possible we can do something.'

'I doubt that,' said Hunda practically. 'We've retrogressed, yes. For instance, the principle of the time projector was lost long ago. But still, there's a lot of technology left which was far beyond your own times.'

'I know,' said Saunders defensively. 'But – well, frankly – we haven't fitted in any other time as well.'

'Will there ever be a decent age again?' asked one of the old courtiers bitterly.

The avian from Klakahar turned his eyes on Saunders. 'It wouldn't be cowardice for you to leave a lost cause which you couldn't possibly aid,' he said in his thin, accented tones. 'When the Anvardi come, I think we will all die.'

'What is de tale of de Dreamer?' asked Belgotai. 'You've mentioned some such.'

It was like a sudden darkness in the room. There was silence, under the whistling wind, and men sat wrapped in their own cheerless thoughts. Finally Taury spoke.

'He is the last of the Vro-Hi, counselors of The Empire. That one still lives – the Dreamer. But there can never really be another Empire, at least not on the pattern of the old one. No other race is intelligent enough to coordinate it.'

Hunda shook his big head, puzzled. 'The Dreamer once told me that might be for the best,' he said. 'But he wouldn't explain.'

'How did you happen to come here – to Earth, of all planets?' Saunders asked.

Taury smiled with a certain grim humor. 'The last few generations have been one of the Imperium's less fortunate periods,' she said. 'In short, the most the Emperor ever commanded was a small fleet. My father had even that shot away from him. He fled with three ships, out toward the Periphery. It occurred to him that Sol was worth trying as a refuge.'

The Solar System had been cruelly scarred in the dark ages. The great engineering works which had made the other planets habitable were ruined, and Earth herself had been laid waste. There had been a weapon used which consumed atmospheric carbon dioxide. Saunders, remembering the explanation for the Ice Ages offered by geologists of his own time, nodded in dark understanding. Only a few starveling savages lived on the planet now, and indeed the whole Sirius Sector was so desolated that no conqueror thought it worth bothering with.

It had pleased the Emperor to make his race's ancient home the capital of the Galaxy. He had moved into the ruined fortress of Brontothor, built some seven thousand years ago by the nonhuman Grimmani and blasted out of action a millennium later. Renovation of parts of it, installation of weapons and defensive works, institution of agriculture.

... 'Why, he had suddenly acquired a whole planetary system!' said Taury with a half-sad little smile.

She took them down into the underground levels the next day to see the Dreamer. Vargor went along too, walking close beside her, but Hunda stayed topside; he was busy supervising the construction of additional energy screen generators.

They went through immense vaulted caverns hewed out of the rock, dank tunnels of silence where their footfalls echoed weirdly and shadows flitted beyond the dull glow of fluorespheres. Now and then they passed a looming monstrous bulk, the corroded hulk of some old machine. The night and loneliness weighed heavily on them, they huddled together and did not speak for fear of rousing the jeering echoes.

'There were slideways here once,' remarked Taury as they started, 'but we haven't gotten around to installing new ones. There's too much else to do.'

Too much else – a civilization to rebuild, with these few broken remnants. How can they dare even to keep trying in the face of the angry gods? What sort of courage is it they have?

Taury walked ahead with the long, swinging stride of a warrior, a red lioness of a woman in the wavering shadows. Her gray eyes caught the light with a supernatural brilliance. Vargor kept pace, but he lacked her steadiness, his gaze shifted nervously from side to side as they moved down the haunted, booming length of the tunnels. Belgotai went cat-footed, his own restless eyes had merely the habitual wariness of his hard and desperate lifetime. Again Saunders thought, what a strange company they were, four humans from the dawn and the dusk of human civilization, thrown together at the world's end and walking to greet the last of the gods. His past life, Eve, MacPherson, the world of his time, were dimming in his mind, they were too remote from his present reality. It seemed as if he had never been anything but a follower of the Galactic Empress.

They came at last to a door. Taury knocked softly and swung it open – yes, they were even back to manual doors now.

Saunders had been prepared for almost anything, but nonetheless the appearance of the Dreamer was a shock. He had imagined a grave white-bearded man, or a huge-skulled spider-thing, or a naked brain pulsing in a machine-tended case. But the last of the Vro-Hi was – a monster.

No – not exactly. Not when you discarded human

standards, then he even had a weird beauty of his own. The gross bulk of him sheened with iridescence, and his many seven-fingered hands were supple and graceful, and the eyes – the eyes were huge pools of molten gold, lambent and wise, a stare too brilliant to meet directly.

He stood up on his stumpy legs as they entered, barely four feet high though the head-body unit was broad and massive. His hooked beak did not open, and the psychophone remained silent, but as the long delicate feelers pointed toward him Saunders thought he heard words, a deep organ voice rolling soundless through the still air. 'Greeting, your majesty. Greeting, your highness. Greeting, men out of time, and welcome!'

Telepathy – direct telepathy – so that was how it felt!

'Thank you . . . sir.' Somehow, the thing rated the title, rated an awed respect to match his own grave formality. 'But I thought you were in a trance of concentration till now. How did you know – ' Saunders' voice trailed off and he flushed with sudden distaste.

'No traveler, I did not read your mind as you think. The Vro-Hi always respected privacy and did not read any thoughts save those contained in speech addressed solely to them. But my induction was obvious.'

'What were you thinking about in the last trance?' asked Vargor. His voice was sharp with strain. 'Did you reach any plan?'

'No, your highness,' vibrated the Dreamer. 'As long as the factors involved remain constant, we cannot logically do otherwise than we are doing. When new data appear, I will reconsider immediate necessities. No, I was working further on the philosophical basis which the Second Empire must have.'

'What second Empire?' sneered Vargor bitterly.

'The one which will come – some day,' answered Taury quietly.

The Dreamer's wise eyes rested on Saunders and

Belgotai. 'With your permission,' he thought, 'I would like to scan your complete memory patterns, conscious, subconscious, and cellular. We know so little of your age.' As they hesitated: 'I assure you, sirs, that a nonhuman being half a million years old can keep secrets, and certainly does not pass moral judgements. And the scanning will be necessary anyway if I am to teach you the present language.'

Saunders braced himself. 'Go ahead,' he said distastefully.

For a moment he felt dizzy, a haze passed over his eyes and there was an eerie thrill along every nerve of him. Taury laid an arm about his waist, bracing him.

It passed. Saunders shook his head, puzzled. 'Is that *all?*'

'Aye, sir. A Vro-Hi brain can scan an indefinite number of units simultaneously.' With a faint hint of a chuckle: 'But did you notice what tongue you just spoke in?'

'I – eh – huh?' Saunders looked wildly at Taury's smiling face. The hard, open-voweled syllables barked from his mouth: 'I – by the gods – I can speak Stellarian now!'

'Aye,' thought the Dreamer. 'The language centers are peculiarly receptive, it is easy to impress a pattern on them. The method of instruction will not work so well for information involving other faculties, but you must admit it is a convenient and efficient way to learn speech.'

'Blast off wit me, den,' said Belgotai cheerfully. 'Ih allays was a dumkoff at languages.'

When the Dreamer was through, he thought: 'You will not take it amiss if I tell you all that what I saw in both your minds was good – brave and honest, under the little neuroses which all beings at your level of evolution cannot help accumulating. I will be pleased to remove those for you, if you wish.'

'No, thanks,' said Belgotai. 'I like my little neuroses.'

'I see that you are debating staying here,' went on the Dreamer. 'You will be valuable, but you should be fully warned of the desperate position we actually are in. This is not a pleasant age in which to live.'

'From what I've seen,' answered Saunders slowly, 'golden

ages are only superficially better. They may be easier on the surface, but there's death in them. To travel hopefully, believe me, is better than to arrive.'

'That has been true in all past ages, aye. It was the great mistake of the Vro-Hi. We should have known better, with ten million years of civilization behind us.' There was a deep and tragic note in the rolling thought-pulse. 'But we thought that since we had achieved a static physical state in which the new frontiers and challenges lay within our own minds, all beings at all levels of evolution could and should have developed in them the same ideal.

'With our help, and with the use of scientific psychodynamics and the great cybernetic engines, the coordination of a billion planets became possible. It was perfection, in a way – but perfection is death to imperfect beings, and even the Vro-Hi had many shortcomings. I cannot explain all the philosophy to you; it involves concepts you could not fully grasp, but you have seen the workings of the great laws in the rise and fall of cultures. I have proved rigorously that permanence is a self-contradictory concept. There can be no goal to reach, not ever.'

'Then the Second Empire will have no better hope than decay and chaos again?' Saunders grinned humorlessly. 'Why the devil do you want one?'

Vargor's harsh laugh shattered the brooding silence. 'What indeed does it matter?' he cried. 'What use to plan the future of the universe, when we are outlaws on a forgotten planet? The Anvardi are coming!' He sobered, and there was a set to his jaw which Saunders liked. 'They're coming, and there's little we can do to stop it,' said Vargor. 'But we'll give them a fight. We'll give them such a fight as the poor old Galaxy never saw before!'

CHAPTER FIVE

Attack of the Anvardi

'Oh, no – oh no – oh no – '

The murmur came unnoticed from Vargor's lips, a broken cry of pain as he stared at the image which flickered and wavered on the great interstellar communiscreen. And there was horror in the eyes of Taury, grimness to the set of Hunda's mighty jaws, a sadness of many hopeless centuries in the golden gaze of the Dreamer.

After weeks of preparation and waiting, Saunders realized matters were at last coming to a head.

'Aye, your majesty,' said the man in the screen. He was haggard, exhausted, worn out by strain and struggle and defeat. 'Aye, fifty-four shiploads of us, and the Anvardian fleet in pursuit.'

'How far behind?' rapped Hunda.

'About half a light year, sir, and coming up slowly. We'll be close to Sol before they can overhaul us.'

'Can you fight them?' rapped Hunda.

'No, sir,' said the man. 'We're loaded with refugees, women and children and unarmed peasants, hardly a gun on ship – Can't you help us?' It was a cry, torn by the ripping static that filled the interstellar void. 'Can't you help us, your majesty? They'll sell us for slaves!'

'How did it happen?' asked Taury wearily.

'I don't know, your majesty. We heard you were at Sol through your agents, and secretly gathered ships. We don't want to be under the Anvardi, Empress; they tax the life from us and conscript our men and take our women and children . . . We only communicated by ultrawave; it can't be traced, and we only used the code your agents gave us. But as we passed Canopus, they called on us to surrender in the name of their king – and they have a whole war fleet after us!'

'How long before they get here?' asked Hunda.

'At this rate, sir, perhaps a week,' answered the captain of the ship. Static snarled through his words.

'Well, keep on coming this way,' said Taury wearily. 'We'll send ships against them. You may get away during the battle. Don't go to Sol, of course, we'll have to evacuate that. Our men will try to contact you later.'

'We aren't worth it, your majesty. Save your ships.'

'We're coming,' said Taury flatly, and broke the circuit.

She turned to the others, and her red head was still lifted. 'Most of our people can get away,' she said. 'They can flee into the Arlath cluster; the enemy won't be able to find them in that wilderness.' She smiled, a tired little smile that tugged at one corner of her mouth. 'We all know what to do, we've planned against this day. Munidor, Falz, Mico, start readying for evacuation. Hunda, you and I will have to plan our assault. We'll want to make it as effective as possible, but use a minimum of ships.'

'Why sacrifice fighting strength uselessly?' asked Belgotai.

'It won't be useless. We'll delay the Anvardi, and give those refugees a chance to escape.'

'If we had weapons,' rumbled Hunda. His huge fists clenched. 'By the gods, if we had decent weapons!'

The Dreamer stiffened. And before he could vibrate it, the same thought had leaped into Saunders' brain, and they stared at each other, man and Vro-Hian, with a sudden wild hope . . .

Space glittered and flared with a million stars, thronging against the tremendous dark, the Milky Way foamed around the sky in a rush of cold silver, and it was shattering to a human in its utter immensity. Saunders felt the loneliness of it as he had never felt it on the trip to Venus – for Sol was dwindling behind them, they were rushing out into the void between the stars.

There had only been time to install the new weapon on the dreadnought, time and facilities were so cruelly short, there had been no chance even to test it in maneuvers. They might, perhaps, have leaped back into time again and again, gaining weeks, but the shops of Terra could only turn out so much material in the one week they did have.

So it was necessary to risk the whole fleet of the entire fighting strength of Sol on this one desperate gamble. If the old *Vengeance* could do her part, the outnumbered Imperials would have their chance. But if they failed . . .

Saunders stood on the bridge, looking out at the stellar host, trying to discern the Anvardian fleet. The detectors were far over scale, the enemy was close, but you couldn't visually detect something that outran its own image.

Hunda was at the control central, bent over the cracked old dials and spinning the corroded signal wheels, trying to coax another centimeter per second from a ship more ancient than the Pyramids had been in Saunders' day. The Dreamer stood quietly in a corner, staring raptly out at the Galaxy. The others at the court were each in charge of a squadron, Saunders had talked to them over the inter-ship visiscreen – Vargor white-lipped and tense, Belgotai blasphemously cheerful, the rest showing only cool reserve.

'In a few minutes,' said Taury quietly. 'In just a few minutes, Martin.'

She paced back from the viewport, lithe and restless as a tigress. The cold white starlight glittered in her eyes. A red cloak swirled about the strong, deep curves of her body, a Sunburst helmet sat proudly on her bronze-bright hair. Saunders thought how beautiful she was – by all the gods, how beautiful!

She smiled at him. 'It is your doing, Martin,' she said. 'You came from the past just to bring us hope. It's enough to make one believe in destiny.' She took his hand. 'But of course it's not the hope you wanted. This won't get you back home.'

'It doesn't matter,' he said.

'It does, Martin. But – may I say it? I'm still glad of it. Not only for the sake of the Empire, but – '

A voice rattled over the bridge communicator: 'Ultrawave to bridge. The enemy is sending us a message, your majesty. Shall I send it up to you?'

'Of course.' Taury switched on the bridge screen.

A face leaped into it, strong and proud and ruthless, the Sunburst shining in the green hair. 'Greeting, Taury of Sol,' said the Anvardian. 'I am Ruulthan, Emperor of the Galaxy.'

'I know who you are,' said Taury thinly, 'but I don't recognize your assumed title.'

'Our detectors report your approach with a fleet approximately one-tenth the size of ours. You have one Supernova ship, of course, but so do we. Unless you wish to come to terms, it will mean annihilation.'

'What are your terms?'

'Surrender, execution of the criminals who led the attacks on Anvardian planets, and your own pledge of allegiance to me as Galactic Emperor.' The voice was clipped, steel-hard.

Taury turned away in disgust. Saunders told Ruulthan in explicit language what to do with his terms, and then cut off the screen.

Taury gestered to the newly installed time-drive controls. 'Take them, Martin,' she said. 'They're yours really.' She put her hands in his and looked at him with serious gray eyes. 'And if we should fail in this – good-by, Martin.'

'Good-by,' he said thickly.

He wrenched himself over to the panel and sat down before its few dials. *Here goes nothing!*

He waved one hand, and Hunda cut off the hyperdrive. At low intrinsic velocity, the *Vengeance* hung in space while the invisible ships of her fleet flashed past toward the oncoming Anvardi.

Slowly then, Saunders brought down the time-drive switch.

And the ship roared with power, atomic energy flowed into the mighty circuits which they had built to carry her huge mass through time – the lights dimmed, the giant machine throbbed and pulsed, and a featureless grayness swirled beyond the ports.

He took her back three days. They lay in empty space, the Anvardi were still fantastic distances away. His eyes strayed to the brilliant yellow spark of Sol. Right there, this minute, he was sweating his heart out installing the time projector which had just carried him back . . .

But no, that was meaningless, simultaneity was arbitrary. And there was a job to do right now.

The chief astrogator's voice came with a torrent of figures. They had to find the exact position in which the Anvardian flagship would be in precisely seventy-two hours. Hunda rang the signals to the robots in the engine room, and slowly, ponderously, the *Vengeance* slid across five million miles of space.

'All set,' said Hunda. 'Let's go!'

Saunders smiled, a mirthless skinning of teeth, and threw his main switch in reverse. Three days forward in time . . .

To lie alongside the Anvardian dreadnought!

Frantically Hunda threw the hyperdrive back in, matching translight velocities. They could see the ship now, it loomed like a metal mountain against the stars. And every gun in the *Vengeance* cut loose!

Vortex cannon – blasters – atomic shells and torpedoes – gravity snatchers – all the hell that had ever been brewed in the tortured centuries of history vomited against the screens of the Anvardian flagship.

Under that monstrous barrage, filling space with raving energy till it seemed its very structure must boil, the screens went down, a flare of light searing like another nova. And through the solid matter of her hull those weapons bored, cutting, blasting, disintegrating. Steel boiled into vapor, into atoms, into pure devouring energy that turned on the remaining solid material. Through and through the hull that fury raged, a waste of flame that left not even ash in its track.

And now the rest of the Imperial fleet drove against the Anvardi. Assaulted from outside, with a devouring monster in its very midst, the Anvardian fleet lost the offensive, recoiled and broke up into desperately fighting units. War snarled between the silent white stars.

Still the Anvardi fought, hurling themselves against the ranks of the Imperials, wrecking ships and slaughtering men even as they went down. They still had the numbers, if not the organization, and they had the same weapons and the same bitter courage as their foes.

The bridge of the *Vengeance* shook and roared with the shock of battle. The lights darkened, flickered back, dimmed again. The riven air was sharp with ozone, and the intolerable energies loosed made her interior a furnace. Reports clattered over the communicator:' – Number Three screen down – Compartment Number Five doesn't answer – Vortex turret Five Hundred Thirty Seven out of action – '

Still she fought, still she fought, hurling metal and energy in an unending storm, raging and rampaging among the ships of the Anvardi. Saunders found himself manning a gun, shooting out at vessels he couldn't see, getting his aim by sweat-blinded glances at the instruments – and the hours dragged away in flame and smoke and racking thunder . . .'

'They're fleeing!'

The exuberant shout rang through every remaining compartment of the huge old ship. *Victory, victory, victory –* She had not heard such cheering for five thousand weary years.

Saunders staggered drunkenly back onto the bridge. He could see the scattered units of the Anvardi now that he was behind them, exploding out into the Galaxy in the wild search of refuge, hounded and harried by the vengeful Imperial fleet.

And now the Dreamer stood up, and suddenly he was not

a stump-legged little monster but a living god whose awful thought leaped across space, faster than light, to bound and roar through the skulls of the barbarians. Saunders fell to the floor under the impact of that mighty shout, he lay numbly staring at the impassive stars while the great command rang in his shuddering brain:

'*Soldiers of the Anvardi, your false emperor is dead and Taury the Red, Empress of the Galaxy, has the victory. You have seen her power. Do not resist it longer, for it is unstoppable.*

'*Lay down your arms. Surrender to the mercy of the Imperium. We pledge you amnesty and safe-conduct. And bear this word back to your planets:*

'"*Taury the Red calls on all the chiefs of the Anvardian Confederacy to pledge fealty to her and aid her in restoring the Galactic Empire!*"'

CHAPTER SIX

Flight Without End

They stood on a balcony of Brontothor and looked again at old Earth for the first time in almost a year and the last time, perhaps in their lives.

It was strange to Saunders, this standing again on the planet which had borne him after those months in the many and alien worlds of a Galaxy huger than he could really imagine. There was an odd little tug at his heart, for all the bright hope of the future. He was saying good-by to Eve's world.

But Eve was gone, she was part of a past forty-eight thousand years dead, and he had *seen* those years rise and die, his one year of personal time was filled and stretched by the vision of history until Eve was a remote, lovely dream. God keep her, wherever her soul had wandered in these millennia – God grant she had had a happy life – but as for him, he had his own life to live, and a mightier task at hand than he had ever conceived.

The last months rose in his mind, a bewilderment of memory. After the surrender of the Anvardian fleet, the Imperials had gone under their escort directly to Canopus and thence through the Anvardian empire. And chief after chief, now that Ruulthan was dead and Taury had shown she could win a greater mastery than his, pledged allegiance to her.

Hunda was still out there with Belgotai, fighting a stubborn Anvardian earl. The Dreamer was in the great Polarian System, toiling at readjustment. It would be necessary, of course, for the Imperial capital to move from isolated Sol to central Polaris, and Taury did not think she would ever have time or opportunity to visit Earth again.

And so she had crossed a thousand starry light-years to the little lonely sun which had been her home. She brought ships, machines, troops. Sol would have a military base sufficient to protect it. Climate engineers would drive the glacial winter of Earth back to its poles and begin the resettlement of the other planets. There would be schools, factories, civilization, Sol would have cause to remember its Empress.

Saunders came along because he couldn't quite endure the thought of leaving Earth altogether without farewell. Vargor, grown ever more silent and moody, joined them, but otherwise the old comradeship of Brontothor was dissolving in the sudden fury of work and war and complexity which claimed them.

And so they stood again in the old ruined castle, Saunders and Taury, looking out at the night of Earth.

It was late, all others seemed to be asleep. Below the balcony, the black walls dropped dizzily to the gulf of night

200

that was the main courtyard. Beyond it, a broken section of outer wall showed snow lying white and mystic under the moon. The stars were huge and frosty, flashing and glittering with cold crystal light above the looming pines, grandeur and arrogance and remoteness wheeling enormously across the silent sky. The moon rode high, its scarred old face the only familiarity from Saunders' age, its argent radiance flooding down on the snow to shatter in a million splinters.

It was quiet, quiet, sounds seemed to have frozen to death in the bitter windless cold. Saunders had stood alone, wrapped in furs with his breath shining ghostly from his nostrils, looking out on the silent winter world and thinking his own thoughts. He had heard a soft footfall and turned to see Taury approaching.

'I couldn't sleep,' she said.

She came out onto the balcony to stand beside him. The moonlight was white on her face, shimmering faintly from her eyes and hair, she seemed a dim goddess of the night.

'What were you thinking, Martin?' she asked after a while.

'Oh – I don't know,' he said. 'Just dreaming a little, I suppose. It's a strange thought to me, to have left my own time forever and now to be leaving even my own world.'

She nodded gravely. 'I know. I feel the same way.' Her low voice dropped to a whisper. 'I didn't have to come back in person, you know. They need me more at Polaris. But I thought I deserved this last farewell to the days when we fought with our own hands, and fared between the stars, when we were a small band of sworn comrades whose dreams outstripped our strength. It was hard and bitter, yes, but I don't think we'll have time for laughter any more. When you work for a million stars, you don't have a chance to see one peasant's wrinkled face light with a deed of kindness you did, or hear him tell you what you did wrong – the world will all be strangers to us – '

For another moment, silence under the far cold stars, then, 'Martin – I am so lonely now.'

He took her in his arms. Her lips were cold against his, cold with the cruel silent chill of the night, but she answered him with a fierce yearning.

'I think I love you, Martin,' she said after a very long time. Suddenly she laughed, a clear and lovely music echoing from the frosty towers of Brontothor. 'Oh, Martin, I shouldn't have been afraid. We'll never be lonely, not ever again – '

The moon had sunk far toward the dark horizon when he took her back to her rooms. He kissed her good night and went down the booming corridor toward his own chambers.

His head was awhirl – he was drunk with the sweetness and wonder of it, he felt like singing and laughing aloud and embracing the whole starry universe. Taury, Taury, Taury!

'Martin.'

He paused. There was a figure standing before his door, a tall slender form wrapped in a dark cloak. The dull light of a fluoroglobe threw the face into sliding shadow and tormented highlights. Vargor.

'What is it?' he asked.

The prince's hand came up, and Saunders saw the blunt muzzle of a stun pistol gaping at him. Vargor smiled, lopsidedly and sorrowfully. 'I'm sorry, Martin,' he said.

Saunders stood paralyzed with unbelief. Vargor – why, Vargor had fought beside him; they'd saved each other's lives, laughed and worked and lived together – Vargor!

The gun flashed. There was a crashing in Saunders' head and he tumbled into illimitable darkness.

He awoke very slowly, every nerve tingling with the pain of returning sensation. Something was restraining him. As his vision cleared he saw that he was lying bound and gagged on the floor of his time projector.

The time machine – he'd all but forgotten it, left it

standing in a shed while he went out to the stars, he'd never thought to have another look at it. The time machine!

Vargor stood in the open door, a fluoroglobe in one hand lighting his haggard face. His hair fell in disarray past his tired, handsome features, and his eyes were wild as the low words that spilled from his mouth.

'I'm sorry, Martin, I really am. I like you, and you've done the Empire such a service as it can never forget, and this is as low a trick as one man can ever play on another. But I have to. I'll be haunted by the thought of this night all my life, but I have to.'

Saunders tried to move, snarling incoherently through his gag. Vargor shook his head. 'Oh, no, Martin, I can't risk letting you make an outcry. If I'm to do evil, I'll at least do a competent job of it.

'I love Taury, you see. I've loved her ever since I first met her, when I came from the stars with a fighting fleet to her father's court and saw her standing there with the frost crackling through her hair and those gray eyes shining at me. I love her so it's like a pain in me. I can't be away from her, I'd pull down the cosmos for her sake. And I thought she was slowly coming to love me.

'And tonight I saw you two on the balcony, and knew I'd lost. Only I can't give up! Our breed has fought the Galaxy for a dream, Martin – it's not in us ever to stop fighting while life is in us. Fighting by any means, for whatever is dear and precious – but fighting!'

Vargor made a gesture of deprecation. 'I don't want power, Martin, believe me. The consort's job will be hard and un-glamorous, galling to a man of spirit – but if that's the only way to have her, then so be it. And I do honestly believe, right or wrong, that I'm better for her and for the Empire than you. You don't really belong here, you know. You don't have the tradition, the feeling, the training – you don't even have the biological heritage of five thousand years. Taury may care for you now, but think twenty years ahead!'

Vargor smiled wryly. 'I'm taking a chance, of course. If you do find a means of negative time travel and come back here, it will be disgrace and exile for me. It would be safer to kill you. But I'm not quite that much of a scoundrel. I'm giving you your chance. At worst, you should escape into the time when the Second Empire is in its glorious bloom, a happier age than this. And if you do find a means to come back – well, remember what I said about your not belonging, and try to reason with clarity and kindness. Kindness to Taury, Martin.'

He lifted the fluoroglobe, casting its light over the dim interior of the machine. 'So it's good-by, Martin, and I hope you won't hate me too much. It should take you several thousand years to work free and stop the machine. I've equipped it with weapons, supplies, everything I think you may need for any eventuality. But I'm sure you'll emerge in a greater and more peaceful culture, and be happier there.'

His voice was strangely tender, all of a sudden. 'Good-by, Martin my comrade. And – good luck!'

He opened the main-drive switch and stepped out as the projector began to warm up. The door clanged shut behind him.

Saunders writhed on the floor, cursing with a brain that was a black cauldron of bitterness. The great drone of the projector rose, he was on his way – *Oh no – stop the machine, God, set me free before it's too late!*

The plastic cords cut his wrists. He was lashed to a stanchion, unable to reach the switch with any part of his body. His groping fingers slid across the surface of a knot, the nails clawing for a hold. The machine roared with full power, driving ahead through the vastness of time.

Vargor had bound him skillfully. It took him a long time to get free. Toward the end he went slowly, not caring, knowing with a dull knowledge that he was already more thousands of irretrievable years into the future than his dials would register.

He climbed to his feet, plucked the gag from his mouth, and looked blankly out at the faceless gray. The century needle was hard against its stop. He estimated vaguely that he was some ten thousand years into the future already.

Ten thousand years!

He yanked down the switch with a raging burst of savagery.

It was dark outside. He stood stupidly for a moment before he saw water seeping into the cabin around the door. Water – he was under water – short circuits! Frantically, he slammed the swich forward again.

He tasted the water on the floor. It was salt. Sometime in that ten thousand years, for reasons natural or artificial, the sea had come in and covered the site of Brontothor.

A thousand years later he was still below its surface. Two thousand, three thousand, ten thousand . . .

Taury, Taury! For twenty thousand years she had been dust on an alien planet. And Belgotai was gone with his wry smile, Hunda's staunchness, even the Dreamer must long ago have descended into darkness. The sea rolled over dead Brontothor, and he was alone.

He bowed his head on his arms and wept.

For three million years the ocean lay over Brontothor's land. And Saunders drove onward.

He stopped at intervals to see if the water had gone. Each time the frame of the machine groaned with pressure and the sea poured in through the crack of the door. Otherwise he sat dully in the throbbing loneliness, estimating time covered by his own watch and the known rate of the projector, not caring any more about dates or places.

Several times he considered stopping the machine, letting the sea burst in and drown him. There would be peace in its depths, sleep and forgetting. But no, it wasn't in him to quit that easily. Death was his friend, death would always be there waiting for his call.

But Taury was dead.

Time grayed to its end. In the four-millionth year, he stopped the machine and discovered that there was dry air around him.

He was in a city. But it was not such a city as he had ever seen or imagined, he couldn't follow the wild geometry of the titanic structures that loomed about him and they were never the same. The place throbbed and pulsed with incredible forces, it wavered and blurred in a strangely unreal light. Great devastating energies flashed and roared around him – lightning come to Earth. The air hissed and stung with their booming passage.

The thought was a shout filling his skull, blazing along his nerves, too mighty a thought for his stunned brain to do more than grope after meaning:

CREATURE FROM OUT OF TIME, LEAVE THIS PLACE AT ONCE OR THE FORCES WE USE WILL DESTROY YOU!

Through and through him that mental vision seared, down to the very molecules of his brain, his life lay open to Them in a white flame of incandescence.

Can you help me? he cried to the gods. *Can you send me back through time?*

MAN, THERE IS NO WAY TO TRAVEL FAR BACKWARD IN TIME, IT IS INHERENTLY IMPOSSIBLE. YOU MUST GO ON TO THE VERY END OF THE UNIVERSE, AND BEYOND THE END, BECAUSE THAT WAY LIES –

He screamed with the pain of unendurably great thought and concept filling his human brain.

GO ON, MAN, GO ON! BUT YOU CANNOT SURVIVE IN THAT MACHINE AS IT IS. I WILL CHANGE IT FOR YOU . . . GO!

The time projector started again by itself. Saunders fell forward into a darkness that roared and flashed.

*

Grimly, desperately, like a man driven by demons, Saunders hurtled into the future.

There could be no gainsaying the awful word which had been laid on him. The mere thought of the gods had engraven itself on the very tissue of his brain. Why he should go on to the end of time, he could not imagine, nor did he care. But go on he must!

The machine had been altered. It was airtight now, and the experiment showed the window to be utterly unbreakable. Something had to be done to the projector so that it hurled him forward at an incredible rate, millions of years passed while a minute or two ticked away within the droning shell.

But what had the gods been?

He would never know. Beings from beyond the Galaxy, beyond the very universe – the ultimately evolved descendants of man – something at whose nature he could not even guess – there was no way of telling. This much was plain: whether it had become extinct or had changed into something else, the human race was gone. Earth would never feel human tread again.

I wonder what became of the Second Empire? I hope it had a long and good life. Or – could that have been its unimaginable end product?

The years reeled past, millions, billions mounting on each other while Earth spun around her star and the Galaxy aged. Saunders fled onward.

He stopped now and then, unable to resist a glimpse of the world and its tremendous history.

A hundred million years in the future, he looked out on great sheets of flying snow. The gods were gone. Had they too died, or abandoned Earth – perhaps for an altogether different plane of existence? He would never know.

There was a being coming through the storm. The wind flung the snow about him in whirling, hissing clouds. Frost was in his gray fur. He moved with a lithe, unhuman grace, carrying a curved staff at whose tip was a blaze like a tiny sun.

Saunders hailed himself through the psychophone, letting his amplified voice shout through the blizzard: 'Who are you? What are you doing on Earth?'

The being carried a stone ax in one hand and wore a string of crude beads about his neck. But he stared with bold yellow eyes at the machine and the psychophone brought his harsh scream: 'You must be from the far past, one of the earlier cycles.'

'They told me to go on, back almost a hundred million years ago. They told me to go to the end of time!'

The psychophone hooted with metallic laughter. 'If *They* told you so – then go!'

The being walked on into the storm.

Saunders flung himself ahead. There was no place on Earth for him anymore, he had no choice but to go on.

A billion years in the future there was a city standing on a plain where grass grew that was blue and glassy and tinkled with a high crystalline chiming as the wind blew through it. But the city had never been built by humans, and it warned him away with a voice he could not disobey.

Then the sea came, and for a long time thereafter he was trapped within a mountain, he had to drive onward till it had eroded back to the ground.

The sun grew hotter and whiter as the hydrogen-helium cycle increased its intensity. Earth spiraled closer to it, the friction of gas and dust clouds in space taking their infinitesimal toll of its energy over billions of years.

How many intelligent races had risen on Earth and had their day, and died, since the age when man first came out of the jungle? *At least*, he thought tiredly, *we were the first*.

A hundred billion years in the future, the sun had used up its last reserves of nuclear reactions. Saunders looked out on a bare mountain scene, grim as the Moon – but the Moon had long ago fallen back toward its parent world and exploded into a meteoric rain. Earth faced its primary now; its day was as long as its year. Saunders saw part of the sun's huge blood-red disc shining wanly.

So good-by, Sol, he thought. *Good-by, and thank you for many million years of warmth and light. Sleep well, old friend.*

Some billions of years beyond, there was nothing but the elemental dark. Entropy had reached a maximum, the energy sources were used up, the universe was dead.

The universe was dead!

He screamed with the graveyard terror of it and flung the machine onward. Had it not been for the gods' command, he might have let it hang there, might have opened the door to airlessness and absolute zero to die. But he had to go on. He had reached the end of all things, but he had to go on.

Beyond the end of time –

Billions upon billions of years fled. Saunders lay in his machine, sunk into an apathetic coma. Once he roused himself to eat, feeling the sardonic humor of the situation – the last living creature, the last free energy in all the cindered cosmos, fixing a sandwich.

Many billions of years in the future, Saunders paused again. He looked out into blackness. But with a sudden shock he discerned a far faint glow, the vaguest imaginable blur of light out in the heavens.

Trembling, he jumped forward another billion years. The light was stronger now, a great sprawling radiance swirling inchoately in the sky.

The universe was reforming.

It made sense, thought Saunders, fighting for self-control. Space had expanded to some kind of limit, now it was collapsing in on itself to start the cycle anew – the cycle that had been repeated none knew how many times in the past. The universe was mortal, but it was a phoenix which would never really die.

But he was disturbingly mortal, and suddenly he was free of his death wish. At the very least he wanted to see what the next time around looked like. But the universe would, according to the best theories of twentieth-century cosmology, collapse to what was virtually a point-source, a featureless blaze of pure energy out of which the primal atoms would be reformed. If he wasn't to be devoured in that raging furnace, he'd better leap a long ways ahead. A hell of a long ways!

He grinned with sudden reckless determination and plunged the switch forward.

Worry came back. How did he know that a planet would be formed under him? He might come out in open space, or in the heart of a sun . . . Well, he'd have to risk that. The gods must have forseen and allowed for it.

He came out briefly – and flashed back into time-drive. The planet was still molten!

Some geological ages later, he looked out at a spuming gray rain, washing with senseless power from a hidden sky, covering naked rocks with a raging swirl of white water. He didn't go out; the atmosphere would be unbreathable until plants had liberated enough oxygen.

On and on! Sometimes he was under seas, sometimes on land. He saw strange jungles like overgrown ferns and mosses rise and wither in the cold of a glacial age and rise again in altered life-form.

A thought nagged at him, tugging at the back of his mind as he rode onward. It didn't hit him for several million years, then: *The moon! Oh, my God, the moon!*

His hands trembled too violently for him to stop the machine. Finally, with an effort, he controlled himself enough to pull the switch. He skipped on, looking for a night of full moon.

Luna. The same old face – *Luna!*

The shock was too great to register. Numbly, he resumed his journey. And the world began to look familiar, there were low forested hills and a river shining in the distance . . .

He didn't really believe it till he saw the village. It was the same – Hudson, New York.

He sat for a moment, letting his physicist's brain consider the tremendous fact. In Newtonian terms, it meant that every particle newly formed in the Beginning had exactly the same position and velocity as every corresponding particle formed in the previous cycle. In more acceptable Einsteinian language, the continuum was spherical in all four dimensions. In any case – if you traveled long enough, through space or time, you got back to your starting point.

He could go home!

He ran down the sunlit hill, heedless of his foreign garments, ran till the breath sobbed in raw lungs and his heart seemed about to burst from the ribs. Gasping, he entered the village, went into a bank, and looked at the tear-off calendar and the wall clock.

June 17, 1936, 1:30 P.M. From that, he could figure his time of arrival in 1973 to the minute.

He walked slowly back, his legs trembling under him, and started the time machine again. Grayness was outside – for the last time.

1973.

Martin Saunders stepped out of the machine. Its moving in space, at Brontothor, had brought it outside MacPherson's house; it lay halfway up the hill at the top of which the rambling old building stood.

There came a flare of soundless energy. Saunders sprang back in alarm and saw the machine dissolve into molten metal – into gas – into a nothingness that shone briefly and was gone.

The gods must have put some annihilating device into it. They didn't want its devices from the future loose in the twentieth century.

But there was no danger of that, thought Saunders as he walked slowly up the hill through the rain-wet grass. He had seen too much of war and horror ever to give men knowledge they weren't ready for. He and Eve and MacPherson would have to suppress the story of his return

211

around time – for that would offer a means of travel into the past, remove the barrier which would keep man from too much use of the machine for murder and oppression. The Second Empire and the Dreamer's philosophy lay a long time in the future.

He went on. The hill seemed strangely unreal, after all that he had seen from it, the whole enormous tomorrow of the cosmos. He would never quite fit into the little round of days that lay ahead.

Taury – her bright lovely face floated before him, he thought he heard her whisper in the cool wet wind that stroked his hair like her strong, gentle hands.

'Good-by,' he whispered into the reaching immensity of time. 'Good-by, my dearest.'

He went slowly up the steps and in the front door. There would be Sam to mourn. And then there would be the carefully censored thesis to write, and a life spent in satisfying work with a girl who was sweet and kind and beautiful even if she wasn't Taury. It was enough for a mortal man.

He walked into the living room and smiled at Eve and MacPherson. 'Hello,' he said. 'I guess I must be a little early.'

FOOTFALL

NIVEN & POURNELLE

It was big all right, far bigger than any craft any
human had seen. Now it was heading for Earth.

The best brains in the business reckoned that any
spacecraft nearing the end of its journey would just
have to be friendly.

But they were wrong! Catastrophically wrong!

The most successful collaborative team in the history
of science fiction has combined again to produce a
devastating and totally convincing novel of alien
invasion.

FOOTFALL – the ultimate disaster

GENERAL FICTION   0 7221 6339 8   £3.95

From the Hugo and Nebula award-winning author

TIME
PATROLMAN
by POUL ANDERSON

DEFENDER OF THE PAST . . .

The creaking Phoenician ship slowly approached its destination. Everard gazed out over the sparkling water at the ancient port of Tyre. "A grand sight indeed," he murmured to the captain, glad of the easy electrocram method of learning the language. His gaze went forward again; the city reminded him not a little of New York.

Time patrolmen like Everard guard the past. No matter how good or evil an event, it must be held inviolate. The slightest slip, and Time would become Chaos, and all that has ever been or will ever be will tumble into darkness. When the Birth of Civilization is endangered by the malign counter-emperor Varagan, the patrol must be on its mettle . . .

SCIENCE FICTION   0 7221 1290 4   £2.50

A SUMPTUOUS NEW NOVEL
FROM A BESTSELLING AUTHOR

SECRETS
Danielle Steel

When *Manhattan* was conceived as a new TV-series it offered more than just the chance for a network to make the ratings. For the stars involved it meant the chance of a lifetime – if they were prepared to pay the price.

Sabina Quarles saw a second chance to love when it had seemed her life was over. For Bill Warwick it meant salvation from a tangled web of unhappiness he'd been powerless to escape. And as the viewers watched the drama unfold the actors shared their passions and pain in the performance of their lives . . .

0 7221 8306 2   GENERAL FICTION   £2.95

A selection of bestsellers from SPHERE

FICTION

NIGHT WARRIORS	Graham Masterton	£2.95 ☐
THE DAMNATION GAME	Clive Barker	£3.50 ☐
SECRETS	Danielle Steel	£2.95 ☐
KING OF THE GOLDEN VALLEY	Alan Scholefield	£2.95 ☐
TODAY AND TOMORROW	Mandy Rice Davies	£2.95 ☐

FILM AND TV TIE-IN

SHORT CIRCUIT	Colin Wedgelock	£2.50 ☐
MONA LISA	John Luther Novak	£2.50 ☐
9$\frac{1}{2}$ WEEKS	Elizabeth McNeil	£1.95 ☐
BOON	Anthony Masters	£2.50 ☐
AUF WIEDERSEHEN PET 2	Fred Taylor	£2.75 ☐

NON-FICTION

DUKE: THE LIFE AND TIMES OF JOHN WAYNE	Donald Shepherd & Robert Slatzer	£3.95 ☐
WHITEHALL: TRAGEDY & FARCE	Clive Ponting	£4.95 ☐
GODDESS: THE SECRET LIVES OF MARILYN MONROE	Anthony Summers	£3.95 ☐
1945: THE WORLD WE FOUGHT FOR	Robert Kee	£4.95 ☐
MY MOTHER'S KEEPER	B. D. Hyman	£3.50 ☐

All Sphere books are available at your local bookshop or newsagent, or can be ordered direct from the publisher. Just tick the titles you want and fill in the form below.

Name _____

Address _____

_____

Write to Sphere Books, Cash Sales Department, P.O. Box 11, Falmouth, Cornwall TR10 9EN.

Please enclose cheque or postal order to the value of the cover price plus:

UK: 55p for the first book, 22p for the second and 14p per copy for each additional book ordered to a maximum charge of £1.75.

OVERSEAS: £1.00 for the first book and 25p for each additional book.

BFPO & EIRE: 55p for the first book, 22p for the second book plus 14p per copy for the next 7 books, thereafter 8p per book.

Sphere Books reserve the right to show new retail prices on covers which may differ from those previously advertised in the text or elsewhere, and to increase postal rates in accordance with the PO.